ALSO BY KATHERINE SUTCLIFFE

Fever

Published by POCKET BOOKS

KATHERINE SUTCLIFFE

OBSESSION

POCKET BOOKS

NEW YORK LONDON TORONTO SYDNEY

This book is a work of fiction. Names, characters, places and incidents are products of the author's imagination or are used fictitiously. Any resemblance to actual events or locales or persons, living or dead, is entirely coincidental.

An *Original* Publication of POCKET BOOKS

POCKET BOOKS, a division of Simon & Schuster, Inc.
1230 Avenue of the Americas, New York, NY 10020

ISBN: 0-7434-1198-6

First Pocket Books printing January 2004

10 9 8 7 6 5 4 3 2 1

POCKET and colophon are registered trademarks of Simon & Schuster, Inc.

Cover art by Greg Gulbronson

Manufactured in the United States of America

For information regarding special discounts for bulk purchases, please contact Simon & Schuster Special Sales at 1-800-456-6798 or business@simonandschuster.com

OBSESSION

✑ 1 ✑

Haworth
Yorkshire, England

THE DOWAGER DUCHESS OF SALTERDON perched like a crow on the church pew, her stubborn old chin outthrust, her liver-spotted brow creased, and her shoulders slightly humped within the black garment she wore—she was not, after all, here to celebrate the most gossiped about marriage since my brother Clayton had wed some red-haired waif who haunted a crumbling old lighthouse and stole the King's horses.

The dowager's gnarled, bejeweled fingers curled around the crook of the cane she used to hobble around, and she impatiently bumped the cane upon the chapel floor, looking neither right nor left, seemingly oblivious to the whispers and occasional giggles of the guests who had packed the church, more for entertainment and perverse curiosity than to honor the bride and groom.

She wasn't oblivious, of course. I, Trey Hawthorne, the dishonorable, infamous, and disgraceful Duke of Salterdon—the bane of the dowager's existence—suspected my grandmother's hearing was still as sharp as the diamond facets on the ridiculously ostentatious ring she wore on her left hand. If someone within a country mile so much as murmured the Salterdon name in anything other than worship, she knew about it—and God help the "hateful befouler."

"Hateful old bitch," I murmured as I gazed beyond the ajar rectory door, straight into my grandmother's eyes—gray as my own—and watched her thin, silver eyebrow lift, knowing full well she could read my lips.

I returned her look with a cold curl of my mouth, a lift of my port glass in toast, and a slight bow that was more mocking than courteous.

"There's still time to back out," came my brother's voice near my ear.

I turned my head a little too fast. The liquor in my veins slammed me hard enough to totter me backward.

My twin brother's face swam before me,

my mirror image—dark hair, slightly curly, stone gray eyes, chiseled features, and a mouth that reflected both concern and be-musement over my situation.

But that's where the similarities ended.

While Clayton Hawthorne had the heart and soul of a flipping saint, and the luck of the blessed, I was one thin hair from burning in hellfire for eternity.

My peers didn't refer to me as "Old Scratch" for nothing.

Clayton frowned and put out one hand to catch my arm, offering support. He sighed and shook his head.

"For the last three years, your objective in life has been to make Grandmother suffer—and suffer she has. You've burned through your inheritance, you consistently find ways to get your name blasted throughout the London news, and finally scandalize with the ultimate revenge—to marry not one of the acceptable young ladies of Grandmother's choosing, but a notorious, thrice-divorced, twice-widowed older woman, whose penchant for cheating on her husbands and ruining them financially exceeds even your reputation. Edwina Narwhal Frydenthrope Thromonde Wohlstetter Rhodes is a . . . a . . ."

"Hussy." I quaffed the last of the port and plunked the empty glass aside. "Whore. Doxy.

Slut. Slattern. Bawd. Harlot." I grinned and blinked sleepily at Clayton. "Shall I continue?"

"And you're marrying her."

I shrugged and adjusted my silk cravat. "So I am."

"It won't last."

"Of course it won't. But she's entertaining in bed. And she has money. In case you haven't noticed sufficiently, I need money."

Clayton's eyes narrowed. "How could I not notice? Thorn Rose Manor has gone to rack and ruin the last year. You're down to one scullery maid with a habit of pinching the family silver—or what's left of it that you haven't sold to appease your gambling debts, a butler who is too frequently prostrated by the grape, and a groom too lazy to swat flies, much less muck the stalls. Trey, if you need money—"

"I won't take it from you."

Frustration darkened Clay's face. "Damn you, brother, don't do this. I know you're still hurting—"

"I don't want to hear it."

I shoved my brother aside and walked unsteadily to the mullioned window overlooking the grounds. For as far as I could see were the fancy coaches of every high-stocking, blue-blooded family in England.

"If you bring up Maria again, I'm going to punch you. Hard."

"Admit it. You're still in love with her."

"The hell you say."

Clayton moved up behind me, placed a compassionate hand on my shoulder.

I shrugged it away and laughed, a brittle, angry sound, as heat rushed to my face.

"Obviously, the young woman wasn't nearly so serious in her supposed affection for me as I was for her, or she wouldn't have vanished. She simply didn't care to be found. At least not by me."

Looking at Clayton, I added, "Had Grandmother not sent her from the house—"

"What difference would it have made, if Maria didn't love you?"

My eyes briefly closed. The heat in the small room made me sweat. The tailored wool suit I wore clung to my skin and I began to feel nauseous.

Maria Ashton's image rose before my mind's eye—a pretty face with big blue eyes, tumbling silken flaxen hair, and a gentleness of spirit that had rescued me from hell's torment. I might have died, had she not responded to my grandmother's call for a nurse to minister me in my illness and the injury to my head inflicted by highwaymen who had left me for dead.

Maria not love me? Ah, but there was the problem in a nutshell. She had trembled with passion beneath my body, sacrificing her cherished innocence. She had vowed her love for me in a thousand ways.

The entire world had turned its back on me. Maria, daughter of a vicar, had appeared like some earth-bound angel to save me.

For the first time in my miserable life, I had actually fallen in love. Deeply. And it wouldn't leave me. Despite the betrayal of her disappearance. Despite my immense anger. Though I was about to wed another, my heart thumped like a hot lead weight in my chest when I recalled the months I had searched for her, and the letter that had eventually arrived six months to the day after she had ridden away from Thorn Rose in my grandmother's coach.

"Your Grace, what transpired between us was a mistake. I have wed another. I wish you happiness. Maria."

Maria. God, how I had adored her. In my fogged lunacy I had poured out my heart and soul to her in music—my only way, during that dreadful time, that I could confess my feelings.

Maria's Song.

Even now, three years later, the strands haunted me, playing over and over in my mind until I felt insane again.

Music from the chapel drifted to me, as did the murmuring of the collected guests. No friends there. I had no friends. Not any longer.

Dressed in their splendid clothes, arriving in their fine coaches, their wealth and titles dripping from their aristocratic pores like chips of ice—they were here for one reason. To watch a man step from the precipice of his crumbling dignity and spiral into the abyss of total ruin.

And when I plummeted into that perdition, I would drag my dowager duchess grandmother along with me.

THE PORT BEAT AT MY HEAD LIKE A CUDGEL AS the vicar spoke solemnly, first to the breath-holding onlookers, then to me, then to Edwina, who peered up at me with a knowing smirk. Her fiery red hair was covered in a lace cap and her plunging décolletage revealed the most voluptuous breasts outside of Paris.

With any luck I would get through the ceremony before I passed out completely. God forbid the vultures collected in the cushioned pews would come all this way only to have their entertainment spoiled by the groom passing out before he committed his life to total perdition.

The vicar's words floated to me, scattering like leaves in a wind—something about if anyone knew of any reason these two should not be wed, speak now. . . .

Oh, there were many, many reasons. The least of which—we didn't love one another.

But she had money. I needed money.

She needed a compliant lover to satisfy her bent for erotic escapades, and since she had burned through five husbands—the last two dying in the throes of her orgasms—there wasn't an available man on two continents who would come within a wink of her eyes.

Besides, if there was any woman on England's beloved soil my grandmother despised, it was Edwina—the duchess's deceased husband's paramour.

"I do," came a voice from the congregation.

The words were followed by a gasp and a sudden silence that rang through the room as resoundly as a church bell. The vicar, his expression frozen in shock, his face pale as flour, stared over my shoulder while the hands gripping the book went slack.

Clayton, standing at my side, let out a soft "Thank God."

Edwina spat out a curse as she slowly turned.

I shook free of my inebriation and confusion as I swayed around to focus on a drab little creature, round as she was tall, wearing a dingy cap of sorts and a gray, shapeless frock covered by an equally dingy pinafore, standing center aisle, her body shaking as if with ague.

The duchess struggled to her feet, her face gray as her hair, her eyes too big for their sockets—eyes that locked with those of the intruder, who stepped back as if she anticipated an asp strike.

Lifting one shaking hand, the rotund little woman pointed at the dowager duchess and declared in a squeak, "She done it. All of it. May me sorry soul burn in hell for keepin' shut 'bout it. But I cum soon as I heard 'bout yer weddin', Yer Grace. I cudn't keep me mouth closed a minute longer."

Clayton stepped around me. "What the devil is this about?" he demanded.

I caught his arm, stopping him in his tracks.

Focusing on the terrified woman's face, I spoke with no hint of the inebriation that had sullied my blood and brains seconds before.

"Let her speak."

The woman sidestepped past the dowager, who clutched at her cane and opened and closed her mouth, saying nothing.

" 'Tis the lass, Yer Grace. Maria? I know where she is. Where she's been since the night she done rode off in yer grandmother's coach. 'Twasn't Huddersfield where yer grandmother had her took. 'Twas Menson, Yer Grace."

Another burst of gasps, twitters of shock mingled with nervous speculation.

"Menson." I stepped from the dais, the port's

sluggishness replaced by a heat that began in my belly and sluiced through my body. "Surely you're mistaken. Menson is an asylum for the criminally insane."

The woman gulped and nodded, wrung her hands and began to cry. "Aye. Y'll find 'er there, Yer Grace. Or what be left of 'er, God bless 'er tormented young soul."

❧ 2 ❧

Menson
Asylum for the Criminally Insane

*T*HE MAN'S BREATH SMELLED OF ROTTING
teeth and kippers. His right ear, or what I
could see of it beneath his fringe of long,
greasy gray hair, had been mauled to a nub.
Human teeth marks scarred the remaining
flap of skin.

I twisted my fists in the man's filthy shirt,
and for the third time slammed him hard
against the stone wall.

"Answer me, you idiot. Where is she? Maria
Ashton. Where have you buried her? If you
don't answer me, I'll snap your sorry neck so
fast you'll be eating kippers in hell by nightfall."

"What is the meaning of this?"

I looked around.

An obese man of some fifty years stood in the doorway. His head appeared much too small for his immense girth. Large, protuberant eyes, bulging with shrewdness and feverish with ambition, marked him as one who would sell his own mother's soul if it would enrich his coffers.

There wasn't an iota of doubt in my mind that my grandmother had enriched him a great amount.

Behind him crowded several behemoth-sized assistants prepared to initiate an attack, should the order be given. Judging by the authoritarian's expression, however, there would be no such order. Realization glazed his eyes. He knew exactly who I was and why I was there.

"Who the devil are you?" I demanded.

"Ruskin. Rupert Ruskin." He cleared his throat. "Might you release Mr. Swift? He really has no authority to help you, Your Grace. Killing him will accomplish little, and besides, he's stupid as a rock, as I'm certain you've already gathered."

I released my grip and the man shuffled out the door.

Ruskin forced a thin smile. "You've come for the girl, I assume."

"Obviously."

Ruskin gave a sharp nod, dismissed his guards with a flip of his hand, and stepped from the room, pausing to allow me to join him in the dark corridor.

As we moved down the dank stone tunnel, Ruskin rummaged through a ring of keys that jangled and clanked in his hands, his only show of nervousness.

No doubt Ruskin had already contemplated the ramifications of this despicable circumstance—suffer under the lash of my grandmother's tantrums if he divulged the truth of Maria's confinement at Menson, or die a quick and painful death at my hands as I choked the truth out of him.

I was capable of killing him with my bare hands. I wanted to do it in that moment. He recognized it in my eyes and clenched fists, my burning face and locked jaw. Had anyone attempted to thwart me I would have lost what little thread of self-control I had and become as criminally insane as the lunatics howling from their cages.

Yet I contained my hunger for murder by naively, perhaps obstinately, telling myself that this was all falsity—perhaps another of my grandmother's schemes to manipulate my life and keep me from marrying a woman who would bring further scandal to the Salterdon reputation.

I wanted to believe that with such desperation that my entire body shook. Surely whatever creature resided behind one of these locked doors could not be the angel who had saved my life and soul from hell's fiery abyss.

Coming to an iron door, Ruskin slid the key into the lock, gritted his teeth as he struggled to turn it, grunted as it gave with a rusty scratch of metal upon metal, then shouldered the door open with a heave of his immense weight.

Stench washed over me in a stomach-turning wave.

The howls of the insane battered my ears, nonsensical babbles of madness. Insanity peered out at me from slits in the doors.

With each step deeper into the gloom, the hatred for my grandmother mounted. Fury expanded in my chest so that each putrid breath of air became a combustible sear of heat. I shook, not just with fury, but also with fear. It turned my every raw nerve into excruciating pain.

I was not a particularly religious man; I had given up God when forced to watch my father being devoured by sharks after the ship in which we were sailing caught fire—setting dozens of passengers adrift at sea, clinging to fragments of the ship; entire families dying from the heat, starvation, drowning; the devils who silently slinked up from the depths to feed. . . .

But in that moment, walking through the halls of this certain hell, I prayed, actually prayed with every fiber of my less-than-spiritual soul, that this was simply another of my drunken dreams.

Oh, there had been plenty of them over the last years—at first, romantic visions of finding Maria, of our rushing into one another's arms and covering each other in frantic, impassioned kisses. Then the letter had come—declaring that our *affaire de coeur* had been a mistake and she had married another. Then my romantic fantasies had turned to hideous nightmares of such hate that I oft dreamed of killing her.

But this was no dream.

No dream could assault my senses to such a degree!

Dare I pray, then, that this path on which I was being led would reveal some macabre mistake—that the weeping little nurse had been wrong; that the sweating, smelly man with a dough face and compassionless eyes shambling at my side was wrong, as well?

It staggered me that my grandmother would bow to such extreme cruelty and criminality. Disbelief hammered at my brain as the maddened howls reverberated along the damp stone walls. Bile crawled up my throat, acid and bitter.

As we rounded into a dim-as-twilight corridor, we happened upon a pitiful creature being dragged by attendants to his cell as he wept and babbled incoherently. I stopped, incapable of moving, watching as through a spinning tunnel as Ruskin moved ahead, halting at a narrow door.

Ruskin's fat hands fumbled with keys—I was certain their jingling would become a scar on my memory, as would every crevice of the stone walls and floors, every hateful nuance of Ruskin's colorless face as it turned slowly toward me, as he shoved open the door and waited.

"Your Grace," he said with a simple lift of one eyebrow.

I moved. Slowly. One foot carefully placed before the other, like one balancing upon a high beam, the cold of my shock giving way to an internal heat that made sweat run down my back and sides.

Dark loomed inside the cell. The stench burned my eyes and nostrils, forcing me to remove a kerchief from my suit coat and cover my nose.

Slowly, my gaze moved along the straw-littered floor until—

Dear Merciful God.

Rocked back by the sight, I closed my eyes. Ruskin's voice came to me, sounding garbled, and an assistant moved around me with a lamp that cast dingy light upon the creature cowering in one corner of the cell.

No. No. This was not Maria! My Maria. With gentle blue eyes and an angel's face. Whose soft, pale hair had brushed my cheeks with scented sweetness.

"She's naked."

'Twas all I could mutter in that moment.

"Of course she is," Ruskin replied. "She might have hanged herself otherwise. It happens frequently."

The kerchief floated from my hand, dropping softly as a feather at my feet. I stared down at it momentarily, thinking how odd it looked—such absurd foppishness juxtaposed against the fouled straw.

I blinked sweat from my burning eyes, then yanked at the buttons on my coat—tore them away in my fumbling haste to remove the garment as I staggered toward her—whoever she was—not Maria—surely *not* Maria. But whoever she was, she deserved to be shielded from the men who stood looking at her as if she were a slab of butchered meat.

"No." Ruskin's hand clamped upon my shoulder, halting me. "She may appear docile, Your Grace, but I assure you, she isn't."

"Get your hand off me," I said through clenched teeth. "*Now.*"

Closer, he said, barely above a whisper, "Your Grace, Miss Ashton is insane."

I turned on Ruskin and drove him back against the wall, my hands twisting his collar, knuckles buried into the flabby flesh of his throat.

"That's not Maria. Now tell me what you've done with her. My Maria. Maria Ashton of Huddersfield." My voice broke. "That . . . animal is not Maria."

He said nothing, just blinked with rummy eyes, bulging as a toad's.

Then I heard it—the dreaded sound.

Humming.

Recognition sluiced through my heart and mind.

Humming.

Maria's Song.

The love melody I had once composed for her lifted sweetly as birdsong along her cage walls.

As Ruskin tremblingly peeled my fingers from his coat, I stumbled back, my gaze drawn again to the frail woman crouched in the dim corner. Her blank gaze stared off into nothingness as she rocked, her knees drawn up to her breasts, her shorn hair a tangled filthy mass around her gaunt face.

I covered my eyes with my hands, then my ears, attempting to block out the soft sound of the song—certain that I was teetering on the brink of insanity myself.

No, this reality was not the insanity.

The insanity must surely lurk in my grandmother's mind. Who in their right mind, with a grain of goodness in their heart, would dispose of another human being in such a way all for the sake of lineage? Just so the long line of blue blood running through the Hawthorne veins wouldn't be tainted by a commoner, so the Salterdon title would not become a laughing-stock to be tittered about, so the doors of aristocracy would not be slammed in their faces?

The dowager duchess would pay for this. Sorely.

Unbreathing, I removed my coat and forced myself to approach, her name tripping upon my lips.

"Ma—ria?"

Her eyes shifted. Her lids narrowed.

There was no recognition in the blank orbs that had once embraced me with their compassion and love.

She sprang with no warning, feral as a wild cat, the impact of her body driving me backward and down into the morass on the floor.

Her ragged nails tore at my cheeks; her hands pummeled me. Her legs kicked, knee driving into my ribs with such force the air expelled from my lungs and I suddenly felt as if I were a child again, driven deep into sea water by fragments of an exploding ship— bludgeoned and drowning.

The assistants fell upon her, lifting her off me as she thrashed like an animal in a trap, horrible, inhuman sounds boiling from the mouth that had once lavished me with kindness.

At last, dragging in a fragment of breath, I managed only, "Don't hurt her."

"For the love of God."

Clayton pushed his way through the gaping onlookers crowding the doorway, disheveled from his frantic ride on horseback to Menson. He took my arm and hauled me to my feet, his expression one of shock and repulsion as we watched the attendants struggle to restrain her.

As swiftly as she had roused to strike me, she collapsed into the arms of a hulk of a man who dropped her in a pile of straw as if she were nothing more than a lot of rags.

I turned on Ruskin, who had retreated, his face slack with dread.

Clayton stepped between us and threw his shoulder into me, his every muscle straining to restrain me, knowing that should I get my hands on Ruskin, I would most likely kill him for what he had allowed to transpire here.

"You'll do Maria no good if you get yourself imprisoned for murder," Clayton said as matter-of-factly as possible.

I flashed him a hot look. "I'm a duke. Those wigged bastards wouldn't dare imprison me."

"Your Grace, you're the scourge of aristocracy. The King himself would sink you into the deepest, darkest hole of perdition if he wasn't so fond of our grandmother."

"I fully intend to kill her, too."

"Promises, promises." Clayton's lips curved, and I felt myself relax.

Clayton removed a kerchief from his vest pocket and shoved it into my hand, then touched one finger to his cheek, reminding me of the scratches that only then began to pulsate with sharp pain.

I pressed the linen to my face, and the cloth was quickly tainted with blood. As I stared down at it, the absolute reality of this place and its people, of the cowering, once-beautiful lunatic huddled in the corner, bore down on me, a behemoth weight that made me feel as breakable as thin glass.

Clayton ushered me from the cell.

I collapsed against the corridor wall, head down, remotely watching drops of blood from my cheek spot my shoes like dark teardrops.

"What do you propose to do now?" Clayton leaned back against the wall and crossed his arms over his chest. "Need I remind you that you left a church full of guests and an abandoned fiancée at the altar?"

"The wedding is off, of course."

He looked back at Maria's cell. "That goes without saying. I was referring to . . . this. *Her*. Brother, I sense you're much too late to do her any good. She's quite gone, I'm afraid."

"I'll take her home, where she belongs."

"Huddersfield?"

"Thorn Rose."

Clay's gray eyes regarded me solemnly. "She'll need a staff of nurses and servants. I'll see to it immediately."

"Unnecessary." I straightened and stared at the wall. "She's my burden to bear. If it weren't for me—"

"Trey." Clay moved closer, his voice softening. "This isn't your doing."

I looked at my brother. "Aye, it is. I loved her. That was enough."

ॐ 3 ॐ

Thorn Rose Manor

I SAT IN A CHAIR IN THE SECOND-FLOOR gallery, in a pool of sunlight fractured through mullioned glass, the heat making the back of my neck damp with warmth. My cheek throbbed from the scratches Maria had inflicted the day before, ragged trenches that would undoubtedly scar.

Portraits of Salterdon ancestors lined the walls, all of whom stared down at me with such righteousness, my face burned.

I might have been twelve again, ordered to my grandmother's apartment to be disciplined for some infraction unworthy of a future duke. The wait had been a punishment in itself— giving me and, less frequently, Clayton, ample time to ponder the consequences she would lay upon our backsides.

Occasionally, if Grandfather were in the house, he would attempt to dissuade her from inflicting her sort of justice.

"Boys will be boys," he would guffaw, and she would crow, "And dukes will be dukes."

I had spent my entire life trying to prove her wrong.

As I stared at the locked door of Maria's room, the large ornate silver key resting on my thigh, I listened for any sound to alert me that she had arisen from the drugged state in which she had traveled from Menson to Thorn Rose. It had been a hellish journey, with Maria bound and occasionally rousing from her opiate stupor to howl in horror from the rich squabs of my coach while I rode up with Maynord, who drove the conveyance as if all the hounds of Hades were in pursuit.

Herbert, my man, butler, cook, and swigger of my finest port stood near, having delivered hot water and the scented soap that I had recently purchased in Paris for my affianced—lovely, taloned, and fanged Edwina, who even now must be planning my demise over this turn of events.

Not that she would have been at all humiliated over having been left at the altar. Nor would she have been heartbroken. She didn't love me any more than I loved her. I needed her money, and she needed a husband . . . and

a father for the babe flourishing in her womb—
sire unknown.

Not mine, for certain. She was too far gone
when I first had her.

With my desertion, however, she would be
forced to deal with her situation on her own.
She was no more prepared for motherhood
than I was for fatherhood; we were much too
self-absorbed. Children were for men like my
brother, who found baby babble and drool
somehow endearing, who enjoyed romping
like wild puppies in the gardens, spending
dreary winter nights sharing fairy tales before
roaring fires, and reading Bible scriptures.

Together, however, we might have made a
go of it. She had the money to supply the child
enough nurses to keep it dry, fed, and pacified
while Edwina and I went about our business,
entertaining ourselves with lovers, Faro, and
the occasional foray into London's dark East
Side, where bounders like myself indulged in
unmentionable but pleasurable sins.

There was a sound, at long last, from behind the locked door.

I took the key in my suddenly sweating
hand and slowly stood, my gaze locked upon
the door as if it were a causeway to hell.

How could I possibly fear her?

She, whose hands had once soothed my
fevered brow, and stroked my phallus with

such incredible gentleness that the very act of orgasmic climax into her warm, yielding body seemed a sacrilege.

Sick bastard.

Even as I stood outside her door, the memories of our lovemaking slugged me with a desire for her that made my lower body rouse with a heat and firmness that made me clench my teeth.

I had ached for Maria Ashton from the first moment I looked into her eyes those years ago. She had become, in a curve of her full, crimson mouth, my sole cause for survival.

My . . . exquisite obsession.

I slid the key into the lock slowly as I pressed my ear hard to the door, listening for another hint of her revival, turning the key until it clicked, so loud in the tense moment that I flinched.

Placing my fingertips lightly upon the door, I shoved it open.

Sunlight spilled through the open window where Maria crouched on the broad sill. Having shed the soft, thin cotton sleeping gown in which I had dressed her, her naked skin, pale as milk and marred by deep bruises, glowed with an iridescence that made her appear some ethereal spirit prepared to take flight.

She was poised, face turned up into the

late afternoon sun, faded blue eyes glistening, the tufts of her once-beautiful hair stirring with the breeze that billowed the curtains on either side of her.

Her head turned, and those wide, as-yet innocent irises regarded me—first with the look of a deer staring into its stalker's hungry eyes, then confusion, then—

She was gone.

Before my fear-frozen limbs could spring toward the window to stop her, she was gone, arms outstretched like a soaring bird.

A sound rose in my throat as I stumbled to the open window and looked down to where she lay on her back upon the thick, dark green grass with its sprinkling of wild anemones. One arm was crooked over her head, one leg straight, the other bent at the knee, giving her the appearance of a marionette.

Her eyes were open, staring up into mine, her red lips curved as they had always been in my dreams.

"HER CONDITION IS DEPLORABLE, OF COURSE. Extreme malnourishment. While her leap from the window appears to have done little harm, there is evidence of formerly broken bones. You see here, along the femur—how it crooks slightly there. It was broken and poorly set, if set at all. And the fingers here, and here just below the knuckle. The open sores on her feet and legs are no doubt due to the unsanitary conditions in which she was forced to live. Also, Your Grace, she appears to be in a disassociated state."

"Meaning?"

I glared at the old physician, Jules Goodbody. Herbert had located him in Haworth, just exiting the Black Bull, cheeks flushed by ale. He boasted a baritone bark, abrupt in utterance—little to assure the dying of much more than the inevitability of their demise.

"She's quite mad," he explained, then flipped open the face of his watch and regarded the time with a down quirking of his lips. "Yes, yes, quite mad. I should return her to Menson posthaste if you know what's good for you."

"I expect you to cure her."

He closed the watch with a click and tucked all but the ornate silver fob back into his vest pocket. Pondering, he gazed out the window to the distant winding lane and pennines, and the sunken stone wall where legions of rooks lined the lichen-covered stones.

"Curing such injuries isn't so simple as lancing poison from a boil or splinting a broken bone. We cannot open the skull, prod about it with an instrument, and pluck out the malady."

"There has to be something—some way to help her."

"Only time, Your Grace. Kindness. Gentleness. Above all, patience." He punctuated "patience" with a sharp jab of one finger toward the ceiling.

"Ah, patience." I laughed dryly into the man's face. "Am I not renowned for my *impatience, unkindness,* and *deviltry,* sir?"

"You might try repenting, Your Grace."

"In hopes that God will be so very pleased over the conquest of yet another sinner, He'll suddenly shower me in the attributes I am so sorely lacking?"

"I shouldn't attempt such a wholesale redemption too quickly. 'Twould seem a bit hypocritical, I think."

I picked up my glass of port and regarded it. "God hasn't done me any favors."

"On the contrary. You were born into position and prosperity, to loving parents—"

"Who were taken from me and my brother when we were only ten, depositing us into the care of a manipulating, heartless old crone who would sacrifice the body and soul of the angel in that bed, in order to keep me a prisoner of her control.

"Oh, and let's not forget that He allowed

highwaymen to bash my head so I was little more than one of those dribbling idiots at Menson. What was that for? God's way of reminding me I should be thankful my skull is hard as a coconut?"

"Had your coconut not been knocked, you wouldn't have met her, would you?"

"Touché. However, had she not met me, she would no doubt be happily married to that limpish little vicar—John Rees or something—from Huddersfield, who was so madly in love with her. He showed up on my doorstep once with his heart on his sleeve, wishing to whisk Maria away before I could sully her innocence."

"Occasionally, God's road to happiness comes with pits and valleys. Such is life, Your Grace. Sublimity is made all the more divine if one must suffer to attain it."

"The road to heaven being paved with flagellation seems a touch hypocritical of a God who is supposed to epitomize kindness. Doesn't it?"

"If life was meant to be bliss, Your Grace, there would be no rational reason to look forward to heaven. Would there?"

"You sound like a bloody vicar. I thought physicians were prone to atheism, along with science scholars, philosophers, and mathematicians."

Goodbody looked down at Maria, and his

brow furrowed. "I should hate to think this life is all we have to look forward to, else what a damnable waste of time it all is."

He sighed. "Take care in the way you handle her. I sense she could be dangerous."

MARIA DANGEROUS? NOT POSSIBLE. NOT THE angel who had delivered me from my own hell.

Maria Ashton epitomized kindness. She had been the first true goodness to influence my life since the death of my parents. How confident she had been in God's charity. To this very moment, her words of God's benevolence tapped upon my memory.

"I believe Him to be patient and kind and all-forgiving—no matter what the sin, or sins. His hand is always outstretched. All one needs, Your Grace, is faith and courage, and a repentant heart."

Such damned, naive conviction, and this is how He repaid her faith in Him?

"Your Grace."

Herbert entered the room carrying a tray of food, which he placed on a table near the bed. Stiffly, he then turned to face me. A thin strand of gray hair spilled over one bloodshot eye. He didn't bother to push it back.

"Will there be anything else, Your Grace?"

I regarded his rumpled white shirt. "You've forgotten your coat again, Herbert."

He looked down, looked up, and sniffed. "So I have, Your Grace. My apologies."

"What is that?" I pointed to several dark stains on the shirt front, below his chin.

"The young lady's dinner, Your Grace." He flopped a hand in the general direction of the tray. "Stew."

"Good God. Not the lamb stew you tried to feed me three days ago."

"Pigeon, Your Grace."

We looked in unison toward the now closed and locked window, where a trio of pigeons perched on the windowsill peered in at us.

I slowly turned my gaze back on Herbert. "You didn't—"

"Not personally, Your Grace. 'Twas the stableman Maynord. He was most happy to do it. Said they were—I beg your pardon, Your Grace—'shattin' on his bleedin' harness and buggy.'"

"How very . . . appetizing."

"Aye." Herbert blinked sleepily. "Will there be anything else, Sir?"

I shook my head and watched him move toward the door.

"Herbert."

He turned and looked at me.

I tossed him the key. "Lock the door from the outside."

"Lock it . . . Your Grace?" His brow creased.

"Aye."

His pink, big-knuckled fingers curled around it and he gave a reluctant bob of his head.

I watched the door slowly close, heard it click shut, and waited a long moment before I heard the scrape of the key in the lock and the shift of the bolt into place.

I listened to myself breathe.

I was not, nor ever had been, a particularly brave man. Not like my brother. Twice—only twice—had I ever rallied a stiff enough backbone to do something remotely courageous: once when I saved Clayton from drowning, the other when I told my grandmother to go to hell and rode off into the dark to find Maria.

With my shirtsleeves rolled partially to my elbows, I moved a basin of hot water to the bed, along with the ball of soap with its faint scent of peach blossom, and a cloth.

I recalled her bathing me once, sinking her body onto mine as water and bubbles surged over her pretty breasts. By the time we had finished, we had rocked most of the water from the tub. She had stood mid-room with great fluffs of bubbles on the smooth slopes of her buttocks, froth pearls beaded upon the tips of her pink nipples, and her skin rosy from the water's heat and the flush of surcease.

I had fallen in love with her in that moment.

Unequivocally.

Squeezing water from the cloth, I eased down on the bed beside her, took up her hand and lay it, palm down, upon my own. She didn't notice. She was apparently still . . . disassociated?

Her face was turned toward the window; she stared into the sunlight unblinking, as if she were asleep with her eyes open.

With one fingertip I traced the curve of her cheekbone, down into the gaunt hollow of her cheek, to the tip of her lips, along the line of her jaw to her earlobe. I smiled; she had incredible ears—delicate and shapely as shells. I once traced the little folds in her ear with my tongue, making her shiver. And giggle. And groan.

Down, lightly, barely touching, along the length of her neck—transparent as china— tracing the dark blue veins I could see beneath her thin skin, to the fluttering pulse, where I hesitated.

Each distinct throb of her heart beat inside my head.

Maria.

In that moment I felt as voiceless as I had been when she first came to Thorn Rose. As desperate, with fear, with anger. I closed my eyes and fought against the collision of emotions . . . and memories.

She had appeared to me draped in soft, flowing white cotton, a guttering candle held aloft in one pale hand. She'd floated toward me like a vision, moonlit hair shimmering in the candlelight. I had felt dizzy and desperate, but when the fierce anger roused inside me, something about her child-like look had captured me, and I had lain still, barely breathing, like one in the company of a fawn. If I had so much as blinked, she might have flown.

Ah, Maria. Sweet Maria. Could I but turn back the hours, the days, the years, I would happily trade my own sanity—aye, my own life—for the restoration of her dear soul.

As my shock and numbness began to melt away beneath the sunbeams stroking our flesh, my hand still wrapped possessively around hers, my anger mounted. I looked down on her profile, her cheek nestled into the down-stuffed pillow, and felt a fresh sense of desperation.

I had once hunted her like one possessed of the madness that gripped her now. Later, I had hated her with the viciousness of a mad dog.

Covering my eyes with my soap-slick fingers, I felt sickened with guilt. For all that my grandmother had done to her—to us—and for all that I had cursed upon her undeserving soul when hearing she had married another.

What little trust and faith I had harbored in my heart. Falling in love with her had become a raging wound that festered until disillusionment and hate had devoured me.

She could be dangerous.

There was nothing dangerous about her arms as I drew the damp, warm cloth down the soft, pale skin from her elbow to her wrist.

Nothing dangerous about her shoulders, thin and slightly sloping, white as the sheets upon which she rested, her gaze still locked upon the window and her face gilded by sunlight.

Nor about her breasts. Soft globes that had once tasted as sweet as marzipan—I ached to touch them even now, to cup them into my palms and lift each delicate dusty-rose tip to my waiting lips.

There came a light tapping at the door.

I slid the sheet up over Maria's breasts, then moved to the door as it opened.

Herbert stood there, still coatless and droopy-eyed, his expression rattled.

" 'Tis the woman," he declared in the monotone he used to announce Edwina.

I briefly closed my eyes. "I suppose it was inevitable."

"Would you like me to fetch you a drink,

Your Grace? You're going to need it. She's in a right mood, I assure you."

"How bad is it?"

He scratched his tuft of gray hair. "The claws are sharpened and I detected a gnashing of teeth."

"Ah, so she's in a relatively *good* mood, then."

We exchanged dry smiles.

❧ 4 ❧

"**B**ASTARD! THERE HAS NEVER BEEN A CHARI-table, kind, or concerned bone in your body. Your reputation and name personify hedonism. Yet you walk away from your commitment to me for some mousey little nurse—"

"There was nothing remotely mousey about Maria. She's the most beautiful woman I've ever known."

With a flurry of her skirts, Edwina marched to the door of the drawing room and glared up the stairs toward the second floor.

"You assured me that you were over what feelings you once felt for her."

She turned and focused her blue eyes hard on mine. "Now what am I supposed to do? I blame you for my predicament."

I drank deeply of my port and set aside the empty glass, preparing myself for the inevitable tantrum. I was beginning to feel numb—not just from inebriation, but from a weariness that made my bones ache.

Had it only been three days since I had stood on an altar prepared to marry the little she-bitch? Only days since the course of my very existence had shifted, since long-dead hope had ignited to fan dreams I had once imagined were only for men like my brother?

"I had nothing to do with your predicament, Edwina. Had you practiced abstinence occasionally—"

"Had you not volunteered marriage, I might have flushed this unfortunate situation from my life. Now it's too late. Dear God, what am I supposed to do with a child on my own?"

"You have money. Buy it a nanny and chuck it under the chin occasionally. Send him off to school as soon as possible, and you needn't worry about him but for the occasional holiday."

"My God, can you imagine what it all will do to my breasts? The idea of something tugging my nipple makes my blood run cold."

"Since when?" I smirked.

She narrowed her eyes. "Tell me, darling. Is this rush to rescue your little nurse simply a way to once again spit in your grandmother's eye?"

"What do you think, Edwina?"

"Hmm. By the looks of you, I could almost believe you're sincere."

"I was very forthright regarding my feelings for Maria."

"Yes, I do seem to recall your moping over her . . . when you weren't ranting about killing her. I think I'm jealous."

"I think not."

"How much will it take to change your mind?"

"Are you attempting to bribe me?"

"It worked before."

She approached me where I sat, sprawled in a deeply cushioned high-back chair near a window. She had the look of a feline in heat, and I knew what was coming.

Edwina used sex to manipulate those whose minds functioned on one level—between their legs. She had the ability to sniff out such weaknesses as adeptly as a hound on a wounded fox. Hounds, however, went for the quick kill, a gnashing of their teeth in the terrified animal's throat. Edwina, on the other hand, enjoyed the game—toying with the emotionally sick and enfeebled, driving them to madness.

I understood that, and for that she both respected and feared me. I was a challenge, and she had been more than willing to pay for it. Dearly.

As she eased to her knees between my legs, the skirt of her pale green gown rose up like sea froth beneath her magnificent breasts, revealed by the low-cut décolleté frock fitting snugly beneath her bosom.

Her breasts were like soft white pillows into which I enjoyed burying my face. She always smelled like rose petals—drenched in dizzying fragrance. Even now her aroused nipples thrust through the thin material—twin peaks of deliciousness that, despite my inebriation—because of it—made me grow hard.

I *was* a man, after all.

Once, I would have taken the filmy material covering those breasts and roughly torn it asunder. Roughness excited her, made her pant and squirm and beg for more. The rougher the better.

Once.

A month ago. A week ago. Hours ago.

Once.

Her hands slid up my inner thighs, and she shoved my legs wider, until the rapidly growing bulge in my trousers ached with the bite of the material cupping me.

Her fingers lightly traced the ridge as her eyes regarded me from behind her drowsy lashes, her cherry-red mouth curving, her face shimmering with moist heat as her excitement mounted.

Her long, slender fingers manipulated my trouser closing, opening it little by little as she lowered her head to my crotch and breathed against it—moist heat that made a groan crawl inside my throat.

I swallowed it, allowed her a faint smile as she raised her head and looked at me, lips parted, her breath coming in short, audible little pants. Her tongue flitted over her lower lip, then her upper lip, moistening them so they glistened slightly in the failing sunlight spilling through the window.

Then she went down.

I closed my eyes. And reached for her. Buried both hands in her luxurious red hair like silk entwined around my fingers.

And drew back her head. Too roughly.

Her small chin thrust upward and her eyes, wide and shocked and confused, focused on mine.

"No," I said.

Surprise froze her features.

"No," I repeated.

"You don't want me." It wasn't a question.

"I'm sorry."

"Liar." She struggled, growing frantic. "Liar. You bastard liar."

My hands gripped her tighter.

"You need me."

"I needed your money. Not you, Edwina. You know that."

She struggled again, her small hands in fists that buried into my thighs. Her eyes filled with tears and an unfamiliar desperation carved deep grooves in her brow and around her mouth.

For a moment—as asinine as it was—I almost believed that the emotion contorting her face into distress might have been love. But I didn't care to consider such a possibility. It would only complicate matters even more.

Besides, Edwina was incapable of truly loving anyone. She'd said so herself.

"What do you hope to accomplish by this idiocy?" she demanded. "Do you imagine somehow salvaging your ragamuffin's sanity?"

"Yes. I do. I hope to."

"And for what? So you can spend the rest of your life as a pauper? Need I remind you that you've squandered your inheritance, not to mention the Salterdon name, in your attempts to humiliate your grandmother? Do you intend to get by on the charity of your brother?"

I shoved her away angrily and adjusted my trousers. "Careful, Edwina. My tolerance has its limits." Struggling to her feet, her anger mounting, her hair a wild blazing flood of color spilling over her breasts, she faced me like a snorting, bloodied bull as I rose from the chair, anticipating the fight.

She swept like a cyclone round the room, her gaze flying from breakable object to breakable object. "You pay what little help you have with silver candlesticks. The clubs in London have cut you off. It's only a matter of time before they come after Thorn Rose— or what's left of it, that isn't falling in with neglect.

"You're a laughingstock, Salterdon. Your friends—what's left of them—wager when you and this place will crumble to dust in complete disgrace. What will this heroism for a lunatic get you? Will you content yourself with spending the remainder of your miserably failed life peddling pigs and potatoes at market in order to feed yourself?"

"Preferable to submitting myself to a whoring shrew, certainly."

A china figurine sailed toward my head. I ducked and it shattered against the wall. She followed with a decanter of port. I attempted to catch it mid-air, but too late. To my despair I watched as it careened through the open window and crashed on the cobblestone path, drenching a clump of peonies.

"Damn," I said through my teeth. "You've

gone too far, Edwina. That was my finest port."

Suddenly the fury left her. Silence—like that after a storm has passed—filled up the room.

She took a ragged breath, and it occurred to me with a jolting intensity that I had never seen her cry. Rant, yes. Shrill, definitely. Our emotional and physical parries had been as turbulent as war. But the tears streaming down her face were new and disconcerting.

"I'll buy you more port, Trey. A lifetime's worth. The finest. Just . . . marry me."

"Edwina—"

"I'll employ nurses for her. Physicians. She'll want for nothing."

"Don't do this."

I looked out the window, discomfited by the raw desperation I saw on her face. Not *just* desperation, but also that other emotion I had, moments ago, toyed upon. Not possible. She did not love me. She could not.

"I love you, Salterdon," came her voice, and I stiffened as if from a blow.

I focused hard on the darkening panorama— trees becoming silhouettes against the horizon, the clumps of peonies dissolving beneath the lengthening night shadows. The thousands of tiny roses growing wildly upon the stone fence walls stared back at me like ghostly white faces.

She came beside me, and together we watched the first sprinkling of stars emerge. Her scent of roses teased me—once, it would have been enough to rouse me. I would have eased up her skirts with little pretense and thrust my body hard into hers. We would have rutted like dogs and I would have reveled in the momentary oblivion—it had been my only escape from the memories of Maria.

"She has nothing to offer you," Edwina said.

"Perhaps."

"She's not the same woman. She never will be."

"That's not certain."

"What if she never heals? Will you content yourself with living like a monk for the rest of your life?"

I watched a shooting star flash across the deep purple sky. Then it was gone.

"A woman's body has been your curse since you were old enough to take your first whore. You simply can't help yourself. You have needs, like any other man, but more than most men. Even if she were to awaken from her idiocy and become the woman you once loved—would she, could she satisfy you to the end of your days?

"You said once her purity cleansed the wretched sin from your soul. 'An angel,' you called her. Your . . . salvation.

"Will she be able to satisfy your base hungers? What will you do when your sins corrupt her innocence, when she is no longer the angel? Or worse, will you ultimately grow weary of her naivete and hunger for the whore?

"I'm sure of it. We're much alike, you and I. We're . . . empty, and starving to be filled. It's what bonded us, I think. Our neediness."

"You could be right," I said wearily. "But I don't love you. I'm sorry."

"I know. I've always known. You're honest, if nothing else. But you do care for me; I know that. As much as you are capable of caring for anyone but yourself and your own needs. This desire you have for the woman—I'm sure it stems now from guilt. You think you owe her something."

"I destroyed her."

"Your grandmother destroyed her." Edwina sighed. "I won't give up. You'll eventually grow tired of this encumbrance. Your hunger for flesh will erode this momentary obsession for self-sacrifice, and you'll need me again. I'll make it so.

"When you rest in your bed at night, alone, you'll think of me—of what we shared. I'll return again and again. I'll break you down. I'll erode your willpower. Maria Ashton may claim your heart—for the moment—but I'll claim your soul. I vow it."

DARKNESS. COMFORTING. SHIELDING. A VEIL OF oblivion. Oh, how she loved it. Craved it. Worshipped it, the oblivion.

"Paul?" she whispered. "Paul, are you there?"

She waited, barely breathing in anticipation.

A new fear taunted her, an uneasiness that threatened her fragile stability. It had begun with the light.

"Are you there?" she cried.

Aye, sweetheart. I'm always here. You know that.

"Am I dead at last?"

Dead? No, not at all. What makes you think that?

"The light, of course. I thought I saw it."

I've told you, I shan't let you die.

"But I'm certain I saw the light. It was so bright, and beckoned me."

Silence.

"Paul?" Panic mounting. "You haven't left me?"

Not yet.

"You must never leave me. Not again."

I'll stay for a while longer. For as long as you need me.

"I can't see you. Come closer so I might see you. Why are you remaining in the dark?"

There. Is that better?

She relaxed. "Yes. Come and sit beside me. Here. Near me. Have you spoken to Mama?"

Mother sends her love.

"Is she truly happy?"

Happy and relieved, now that the pain is behind her.

"I miss her terribly."

I know.

"Perhaps I'll see her soon. And the three of us will never say goodbye again."

It isn't your time, Maria. You mustn't give up. Not now. You must continue to fight. Now, more than ever.

"Why are you smiling in such a way? You look so very . . . sad."

I am. And glad, too. Do you know why?

"Tell me."

The light you saw. It wasn't heaven, Maria. It was the sun.

"Don't be daft. There is no sun in this horrible place."

Look around you.

"Nay. I won't look! 'Tis dreadful. And they will soon come. Why do you suggest such a thing? This place is painful and frightening—"

Give me your hand.

"Why?"

I have something to show you. Come along. Carefully. Stand here. Look yonder. What do you see?

"Darkness."

Try harder.

"I don't want to. Why are you doing this?"

I see vast green meadows. And a beautiful

stone wall whereon lovely white roses are growing wildly and lavishly. Dusk is kissing the horizon— pink here and golden there. The sun hovers upon the darkening treetops like a giant fiery melon. Do you feel it? The warmth on your face?

"No."

Try harder.

"No. No. I shan't! I want to go back to sleep."

Beyond the wall is a winding lane. It travels for miles. I see a shepherd with his sheep and a dog— black and white, dashing here and there, herding them into a cluster.

"Like the lane near our house?"

A little. Only prettier.

"Remember how, as children, we ran down the lane to the pond beyond the church? We ate apples beneath the rowan until our bellies ached. Mama would scold us and put us to bed. We would lie beneath the covers and giggle and recount Father's sermons word for word, then you would tell me stories—I was always a princess, and my love, a knight in shining armor who saved me from dragons."

I remember.

"You broke my heart when you left."

I'm sorry. It couldn't be helped.

"I so wanted to go with you. Paul? Paul, where are you? Don't go."

Shhhh, Maria. They'll think you mad.

✺ 5 ✺

*I*RIS, THE SCULLERY MAID, BEDECKED IN HER rumpled black dress and pigeon-stained pinafore, a pale gray feather thrusting out of her haphazardly upswept silvering hair, stood with her ear pressed against the bedroom door. Her brown eyes were wide as coins and her mouth formed a tight pucker of distress.

She had obviously been lighting the girandoles along the gallery when her curiosity had inspired her to linger a moment outside Maria's room. As she watched me approach, she straightened and pressed one plump finger to her lips, to shush any tart comment I was prepared to make regarding her skulkery.

"Shay's babblin' to 'erself, Yer Grace. Full-on conversation with someone called Paul."

Paul. The name tapped upon some familiarity in my memory.

As I approached the door, the key in my hand, Iris stepped back and shook her head. "She's crazy as a loon, I vow. 'Erbert tells me she tried to fly like a bleedin' pigeon out the window."

I plucked the feather from her hair and regarded it.

"Ya ain't payin' me enuff to work 'round no loon, Sir. I've got me poor husband to think about. If ought happened to me wot would become of him?"

I sighed and allowed the feather to float to the floor. "She isn't dangerous."

Her eyes widened and focused on the scratches on my cheek. "That ain't wot I hear . . . Sir. 'Erbert tells me she's wot done that to yer face. Tried to rip out yer throat, he says, and woulda done had she not been yanked from ya in the nicka time."

"Herbert talks too much, I think."

I pressed my ear to the door, hearing nothing.

Paul. Ah, yes. Her brother. Died young, as I recalled. They had been close—very close. His death had affected her greatly. She had never fully gotten over it. She had admitted as much once, when we lay in one another's arms, learning each other as only lovers in love would do.

I handed Iris the key.

"Lock the door behind me and unlock it for no reason, no matter what you might hear. Don't disturb us until morning. For breakfast, I'll expect porridge with honey. And *fresh* bread. Not that stale rubbish you tried to feed me before because you were too damn lazy to rise out of your bed.

"Edwina is staying the night. Prepare her a room—the red room in the east wing. She desires a bath. See that her water is warmed sufficiently or suffer the consequences. You know what she's like."

Iris rolled her eyes.

As I slid the key into the lock, the servant moved away, prepared to flee at the first sign of trouble.

I hesitated. Listened again, then reached for the lit candle sitting on a table near the door.

I tossed Iris the key, then entered the room, dark but for the starlight filtering through the closed window.

I moved around the room, lighting each lamp, my gaze fixed on the bed in an attempt to see Maria, becoming at last aware that she wasn't there. Frantic, I looked around, closer at the window for fear she had attempted to fly away again. It was closed and locked, just as I had left it.

My gaze flashed around the shadowed room,

and found her just as she had been in her cell, curled up in a corner, her knees drawn up to her breasts and her arms crossed over her tucked head.

"Maria," I called softly.

She didn't respond.

I set the candle aside, near her, so the glow illuminated her form, then crouched at arm's length, uncertain if I should touch her.

"I won't hurt you. Maria, look at me. Please. It's Trey. Remember? No one is ever going to hurt you again. You needn't be frightened ever again. Dear heart . . . look at me."

She coiled more tightly and began to tremble. In the frail light of the candle, her gauntness became disturbingly more evident, the bruises deepened by shadows.

Fresh anger roused inside me—hot and cutting, drawing my hands into fists, my lungs into tight knots that made breathing painfully labored.

"Let me help you," I said, my voice rough with emotion. I held my hand out toward her—a mistake.

She exploded from the corner like a startled hare from its discovered hiding place, forcing me to fling myself aside or risk being trampled. Like a wild thing blinded by fear, she crashed into the walls, the chairs, then turned for the window.

I lunged and grabbed her as her feet left the floor, my arms wrapped around her waist. We hit the floor, rolled in a tangle of her kicking legs and flailing fists.

I caught her wrists and pinned her to the floor beneath me. My heart pounded as I stared down into her face, tear-streaked and anguished, her wide eyes looking through me as if witnessing something too wretched to bear. A sound escaped her—pitiful it was, heart-rending, like the weeping of a dying doe.

"Hush. Hush. I won't hurt you. How could I hurt you. Maria! Stop fighting. You'll harm yourself. Stop. *Stop!*"

"Trey!" Edwina cried outside the door, then she banged on it with her fist. "Are you all right?"

"Go away. Leave us alone."

"Stop this madness before you're killed. Come out of there. Now."

"Get the hell away from here. Go to bed."

The door flung open and Edwina entered, nightgown flowing from her shoulders in folds of gossamer silk. She froze at the sight of me, straddling Maria, my chest heaving from exertion, the scratches on my face broken open by a jab she had landed against my cheek.

Edwina gasped and covered her mouth with one hand.

"Dear God. She's an animal."

Lifting my head, I stared into her horrified eyes. "And you're a heartless bitch. Get out before I throw you out. Not just out of this room, but out of Thorn Rose; before I make you regret you were ever born. I'm capable of it, Edwina. More than you know."

"You're as mad as she is to put yourself through this . . . hell," she declared breathlessly.

"Aye, and growing madder by the moment. Now get *out!*"

"Fine. I'll get out. You deserve one another."

She stormed from the room, slamming the door behind her and relocking it. I heard her bark orders at Iris and Herbert before something broke. A vase? I hoped to Hades it wasn't the Chinese dragon figurine I had planned on selling to the magistrate's wife for enough to pay Herbert's wage come Sunday.

The fight having left her, Maria seemed to melt in my grasp—lifeless, to my despair. What little rationality had gripped her in those moments vanished as if she had, once again, retreated into that strange void where I could no longer reach her.

Lifting her in my arms, I gently placed her on the bed, propped her on the pillows, and draped her in the sheet.

She looked little more than a frail child as

the sheet molded to her thin curves. The image made my chest grow tight. So little of the woman I had known remained—her breasts once full, her hips once shapely, comforting me as I lay on her, inside her, feeling her heart beat against mine.

I briefly closed my eyes and listened to the rapid thump of my heart in my ears until my breathing became steady once again and the anger had settled somewhere deep in the black pit of me.

Then I looked at her again.

Her face was turned away from me—her long lashes shadows upon her milky cheek. How the vision of her in that moment roused the images of another time—when we had lain upon the meadow grass, her naked body sprinkled by anemones as pure white upon the upper surface of the petals as her skin, and beneath, pale rose to match her lips. I had nestled my naked body close to hers, and whispered:

"Coy anemone that ne'er uncloses
Her lips until they're blown on by the wind."

Aye, my precious, fragile anemone had been battered. I would crush the guilty culprits with my own hands, if I could. My need for retribution shook me.

I moved to the window and thrust it open—then drank in the air in hopes it would assuage the heat of rage building, building in my every fiber. The wind arose, as if somehow disturbed by the turbulence of my emotions, tossing the dark firs, filling the night with the sounds of whispers. A sharp coolness brushed my face, a hint of changing weather, sending a shiver down my spine.

Upon the horizon rose the eerily gyrating light of the distant coal mines. Soon I would smell the acrid stench of the burn, and the deep black smoke boiling into the sky would obliterate the stars.

As a boy cursed by a vivid and wild imagination, I had oft believed the fires to be belching dragons and I a knight in Arthur's court sent to slay them. My brother and I, caught up in such inventions, would parry with invisible swords while bouncing on our beds, until Grandmother would sweep in and staunch our fantasy with reminders that dukes had men slay dragons for them.

Ah, Grandmother, the hateful and hated dowager duchess.

She would come to Thorn Rose, of course, and I would be forced to face her. She was not, nor ever had been, a woman to back down in the face of adversity. Clayton had once sworn that she would stand toe to toe

with the devil himself if it meant protecting
the Salterdon lineage. I had no doubts.

Yet, in that moment, I felt more evil than
the devil.

I SLEPT OFF AND ON THROUGHOUT THE NIGHT IN
a chair by Maria's bed, and awoke, neck and
back stiff, to find a gray morning outside the
window, tumbling clouds above the treetops
and the first spitting of rain against the mullioned panes.

Edwina stood over me with a breakfast
tray, her gaze fixed on my hand that was
wrapped around Maria's.

There was little of the previous evening's
emotionalism on Edwina's face. She wore an
emerald green dressing gown and had
brushed her flowing hair until it shone like
silken fire. As usual, she smelled of roses.

"I wonder which of you is more insane,"
she said. "I've brought her porridge and you
look like hell."

Groggy and aching, I took the tray. "She's
not insane."

"No? Then what is she?"

"Frightened."

She floated to a nearby chair into which
she gracefully dropped, watching as I moved
with the bowl of porridge to the bed.

"I thought you were leaving," I said as I regarded Maria's face. She was staring again at the window.

"In time."

"The weather's turning sour. Best leave before the roads become impassable."

"You know I can't tolerate travel in this sort of climate. Besides . . ." She lay her hand on her belly. "I don't feel well. And something else."

Sitting on the bed, I looked toward Edwina, waiting.

"I felt the child move."

Wind rattled the window.

I stirred the porridge, watching the thin golden streams of honey dissolve. "In most cases, I would say that congratulations are in order."

"What an annoyance." Her voice quavered. "I was certain I awoke with a raging case of dyspepsia."

Her blue eyes widened and her face flushed. "There it is again. For God's sake, Trey, do something. Make it stop. I can't bear it. Any of it. This . . . dreadful illness . . ."

She jumped up and ran for the chamber pot.

I looked away while she retched as ladylike as possible. When she finished, she leaned against the wall and turned her sweating face toward mine.

"I could kill you for this."

"You'll survive. Stop sniveling and come help me."

"I'm not sniveling. For God's sake, I expect a modicum of compassion from you."

"Seems I recall more than a few times when you've reminded me that I'm compassion*less*, Edwina."

"Obviously, I was right."

"Obviously. Now come here."

She made a face and reluctantly stood at my side, refusing to fully approach the bed, as if Maria's malady would somehow infect her. Her carriage remained rigid, her expression one of repulsion.

"Lift her slightly," I ordered, dipping the spoon into the cooling porridge.

"I won't. She's . . . filthy." She glared at Maria, whose soft features were as smooth and pale as the cold melted taper wax on the table.

Although I had never struck a woman, in that moment I wanted to slap the haughtiness from Edwina's face.

Something in my mien must have warned her that my patience had grown much too thin to tolerate her behavior. Still, she made no attempt to hide her disgust as she slid one arm under Maria's shoulders and barely lifted her from the pillow.

Maria's head rested upon Edwina's shoulder like a sleeping child's, causing Edwina to gasp and tense up.

Looking into Maria's face, I smiled.

"Why are you smiling?" Edwina asked, frowning.

"Her eyes." I stirred the porridge again. "She has beautiful eyes. I've never known a woman who could so love with her eyes." I smiled again. "She could undo a man's soul with her eyes."

Edwina looked away. "Get on with it, will you? I'm feeling desperately ill again."

I lifted the spoon of porridge to Maria's mouth. "Eat," I said gently.

Nothing.

I wedged the tip of the spoon slightly between her lips. "Please."

Nothing.

I allowed the porridge to slide from the spoon, onto her tongue.

It ran, unswallowed, down her chin.

Again.

Nothing.

Again, my frustration mounting. My hand shook. My brow sweat.

"She doesn't want it," Edwina said.

Again.

"You must eat, Maria. Please. Listen to me."

"She doesn't hear you."

"It's Trey, dear heart. Please. For me."

"She *can't* hear you."

"*Please.*"

"For the love of God, darling, she's dying. Accept it and let her go."

"Damn you!" I exploded into Edwina's shocked face, then hurled the bowl of porridge as hard as I could against the wall and stormed from the room.

IN THE LIBRARY, I POURED A GENEROUS GLASS OF Scotch and paced as I drank it too fast. It burned my throat and hit my gut like a firepunch. Then I poured another, drank it as swiftly, then another, pacing, doing my best to dilute the impact of Edwina's words. I wanted to return to Maria's room and force the sustenance down her throat, wanted like hell to obliterate Edwina's words, which boiled like something toxic in my brain.

A fire burned in the hearth. Dropping into a chair before it, I stared into the little crackling flames, hearing the patter of light rain against the windows.

I suddenly felt crushed by the weight of my despair and helplessness.

"Trey," came Edwina's gentle voice.

"Get the hell away from me, why don't you? Leave me the hell alone. For the love of God, Edwina . . . just go home."

She moved to the chair and dropped to her

knees, one hand lightly resting upon my thigh. Her pale face reflected the glow of the fire as she watched me.

"I'm sorry," she offered.

Sinking back into the chair, I turned my face away, unwilling to let her see the raw emotion I was feeling at that moment.

"You would have to have known her, Edwina. She was so damn pure. Too good for me. So full of trust and kindness. To think that I, in some way, have brought this upon her . . ."

I swallowed, the Scotch dragging me down. The room swam and I felt like a man drowning, going under for the final time and too damn weary to struggle.

"I can't lose her again."

Edwina removed the empty glass from my hand and set it aside. "You're inebriated, darling. And exhausted. You can't help her if you're like this. You need rest."

"You're right. She's dying; she's given up. If I could only reach her—but I don't know how."

Edwina left momentarily and returned with several tasseled pillows, which she placed on the floor in front of the fire.

"Come here." She extended her hand. "Come to Edwina. Poor darling. That's right. Lay your head here on my lap, as you did last month in Paris. Remember how we made love all night? You lay naked with your head in my lap as we watched the sun rise. There, there. Let me stroke your brow. Close your eyes. Do you remember, darling?"

"Maria," I whispered, drifting into the dark.

YOU HAVE TO WAKE UP NOW. MARIA?

"I don't want to. I'm so cold. Please, just let me sleep. I'm so very tired."

I said to wake up.

"You're angry. Why are you so angry with me, Paul?"

You have to eat.

"No. I don't want it. It's . . . vile."

We have to talk.

"Not now. Later. I'm so very tired."

I'll leave and I won't come back.

"No! No, please. Don't say that. Don't ever, ever say that!"

You can't continue like this, Maria. You can't will yourself to die. You have to fight.

"I'm too bloody tired to fight. Besides, it's so much gentler here, in the dark. It's too frightening there. Too . . . horrible."

I can't help you if you won't help yourself.

"Why won't you let me die? Then we can be together forever; you, Mama, and I. Like it used to be, before you went away."

We're not children any longer.

"I wish we were."

Maria, you must stop being afraid to come out of the dark.

"Never. I'll never come out, ever again."

Things have changed.

"Never. Not for you. Not for anyone. I'm lost, I tell you. I'm lost."

❦ 6 ❧

"SHE'S GONE, YER GRACE. THE LASS IS gone! Fled like a chick from a coop, she has. Vanished!"

The cry wedged through my murky confusion and thrust me into a frail reality where pain drove a sledge against my temple.

Iris stood upon the library threshold flapping her arms in excited agitation, her face a mask of fear and despair. As I roused, I blearily wondered if I was still mentally tangled in some dreadful nightmare.

"She's gone," Iris repeated in a horrified whisper.

I shoved Edwina's hands from me and jumped to my feet. "What the hell are you saying, she's gone?"

"The door was unlocked. 'Twas open. 'Erbert and me has looked all over. She ain't in the house, Yer Grace."

As I stumbled from the room, numb and sluggish from inebriated sleep, I came face to face with Herbert wearing a long dressing gown and night cap. He smelled heavily of my Scotch, and his eyes were rimmed red as a summer sunset.

"Who left the damnable door unlocked?" I demanded through my teeth.

"She did, Your Grace." Herbert pointed at Edwina. "She were the last one out of the gel's room."

Her eyes wide, Edwina took a cautious step back, her mouth opening and closing, saying nothing.

"I'll deal with you later," I threatened, trembling with a fury that made me feel too dangerous to linger in Edwina's presence a moment longer. I bolted from the room, slamming the door behind me with a fierceness that rattled the windows and caused Iris to jump like one scalded and Herbert to turn tail and flee down the gallery, his hairy, banty legs flashing with each extended stride.

I stormed from the house, into the inclement midnight—to what intent or purpose,

I could scarcely tell. Where would I go? Where would I search?

The night was black as pitch and wet, bitterly cold, and the prospect of finding Maria seemed vastly unlikely. A chaos of heart-pounding emotions swept upon me like an avalanche, rendering me paralyzed and drowning in a whirlpool of helplessness.

I had never loathed Thorn Rose more than I did in that moment. I despised every wild privet hedge that might hide her from my sight, every wall that barricaded me from a glimpse of her body.

I half rushed, half staggered like a blind man along the cobbled paths, my stocking feet splashing in the puddles, the wind-whipped drizzle clawing at my face and making me struggle for each breath.

I trampled through plots of wild anemones and crushed the pummeled peonies and raked my shins through rose briars that tore at my breeches and scored my flesh like razors, crying her name again and again.

"Maria!"

It pounded inside my head and my heart, louder with each beat of mounting fear and self-recrimination.

"Maria!"

The horror of her vulnerability drove me

on, a wild search of every privet and recessed nook within the manor's towering stone walls.

Where?

"*Maria!*"

God, where had she gone?

Think. Think.

Stopping, I gasped for air that bit sharply at my aching lungs, as my frantic gaze rushed from one hedge to another. Then I lifted my sight toward the long tongue of lapping fire illuminating the sky in the distance.

The light! Merciful God. Would she search out the light?

I leaped or tumbled over the rose-strewn walls. The lea stretched out before me and behind me, black as perdition—my soul in a paroxysm of anger and despair.

I earnestly prayed for death in those moments—an end to the guilt that razed my conscience. No crime of the heart I had ever committed, no iniquity I had perpetrated upon some innocent soul, no gambled and lost farthing had left me so teeming with torment and misery.

What if I were to find her lying on the damp earth, dying, or already dead—God forbid?

The appalling possibility drove me onward until I reached the wide river-bed that curved like a serpent's back through the dales, its water shallow but cold—so very cold as I plunged into it that its icy grip climbed up my ankles and calves and sent dull blades of ache up my legs.

There was no sound but the chuckling of the water and the splash of my feet as I slipped on the round stones that made my path as treacherous as ice.

On the opposite bank, I slipped in the mud and tripped over the stunted, gnarled thorn brush clinging with exposed roots to the steepening hillside. Farther I ran, breathing labored, muscles burning in my calves and thighs, up the hill toward the hellish orange light of the smelt fires.

The stinking, gritty ash fell in damp raindrops on my face, burning my eyes and suffocating my lungs. The fires growled, low and ominous. I could feel the workings of the mine beneath my feet, tremors as if the earth would open and spiral me straight to hell.

What if she had fallen in one of their pits? The old shafts were long forgotten, their barricades rotten—she could have tumbled to her death some four hundred feet below.

What if what if what if . . .

I finally reached the craggy summit, pulled myself upright, and stared upon the belching inferno of the working mines and the men who moved like sooted wraiths in and out of the shaft openings.

As a lad, I had oft sneaked away from my grandmother's protective eye and wandered up the deep grooves in the hillsides. Rushes, they were called, once produced by the damming of streams in order to reveal the dark gray veins of lead. I had sat with legs crossed, hidden within the wild gorse, and watched the troops of stoop-shouldered men move in and out of the shafts like armies of ants.

Oh, how I had envied them. Yes, envied. They were men of sweat and brawn—of immense courage. They were the true dragon slayers.

That was, of course, before my parents had died. Before the full weight of my lot in life had been scored into my mind—aye, and my heart. Before my soul had become as black as the horrid spume of poison smoke belching into the sky.

From the haze and light of the fire-cast smelter, I saw the silhouette of a man move toward me, his booted feet crashing upon the fractured sleeves of lead on the ground.

He carried Maria in his arms.

Frozen, speechless, I fixed my gaze on the man's grooved and sooty face, which revealed no hint of her well-being. Wrapped in a tattered wool blanket, she was draped as lifeless as death itself across his massive arms, her weight of no more consequence than a wilted flower.

I slid and stumbled down the hill until I was forced to grab a thorny gorse for fear of tumbling heels over head.

He approached me, silent and grim, and upon reaching me, said, "Seems y've lost somaught, eh?"

"Is she dead?" I asked, still watching his eyes.

"Nay."

"Where did you find her?"

"Yonder." He motioned in no particular direction with a nod of his head. "Starin' up at the light and callin' out fer Paul. Are ya Paul?"

I shook my head.

"Who's Paul?"

"Her brother."

"Then best I give 'er over to 'er brother."

"Her brother is dead."

"Is she daft, then?"

"She's . . . ill."

"Who are ya, then?"

"Salterdon."

He looked me up and down, at my muddy stockinged feet and grime-covered clothes, my hair rain-plastered to my head. "Right,

then," he said. "I reckon one nut deserves another."

With that, he handed her over to me. "Best
ya cum out t'rain for a bit. Yonder." He pointed
one big scarred finger toward a small cottage
in the distance. "The woman'll see to 'er, if
she can."

❧ 7 ❧

I HOISTED MARIA THE BEST I COULD CLOSER against my body, feeling that I would never make it to the cottage. My legs felt as wobbly with relief as they did with fatigue. My feet had gone numb.

As if sensing my dilemma, the man gave a grunt and reached for Maria again, cradled her as gently as a babe, and covered her face with a corner of the blanket. Then he turned and made his way along the path as I followed.

The towering smelt chimney belched long tongues of fire and billows of black smoke. The cranking and rolling of the barrows in and out of the black shafts, pulled by laboring Shetlands along the iron tracks, made me cover my ears. Even as I watched, a small pony, weakened by its load, fell wheezing onto its front knees, its quivering nostrils causing ground soot to rise in horrible little black puffs into its eyes.

The cottage was a hut of dark stone with light beaming from a solitary window. The miner gave a shout and the door immediately opened, revealing a round woman with ruddy cheeks and sparkling green eyes.

"Lud," she declared upon seeing Maria. "Wot 'ave ya dug up in t'bloody mine now, Thomas?"

"Quiet, woman, and set 'bout t'fire. Lass be half dead, I vow. Now scuddle yer skirts and see that the coffee be hot and stout. And free up a bit o'that bread puddin' ya fed me fer supper. Thin as she be, I 'spect she'll appreciate a mouthful or two. The lass be light as a canary."

She looked past her husband and her eyes widened even more, regarding me up and down, focusing on my feet that were now blocks of mud. Then she gave a sharp nod.

"Right. Ye'll be needin' a fix for them as well," she said, pointing to my feet. "Sit."

She whipped a blanket up from the cot against the wall of the room, roughly shoved me toward the hearth, and shoved me even harder into a stiff, cane-seated ladder-back chair. She had obviously been knitting by the firelight; a great spool of red woolen yarn and a pair of needles lay on the floor, as well as what appeared to be a partially knitted sweater.

"Put the lass on me cot," she ordered sharply, "and bring the cot closer. She needs her warmth, fer sure. T'coffee be hot. Pour a cup and be quick 'bout it. And while yer 'bout it, a drab for this un as well. He looks like a whipped cat. Lud, a man of yer age should know better than to go traipsin' about in this weather in aught but his stockin's. Are ya daft?"

"Watch yer bleedin' tongue, woman," Thomas scolded. "Yer speakin' to a damn blue blood."

She plunked her hands on her wide hips. "Ya don't say. And who might he be? The bloody King of England?"

"Salterdon."

She didn't so much as blink. "Give over. Wot would that demned divil be doin' scuttin' 'bout the night in his skivvies?"

"Wife! Watch yer mouth or I'll be smackin' it proper."

She gave a humph of dismissal. "If he be Salterdon, I'm the bleedin' Queen."

Having poured a generous mug of the thick black coffee, he shoved it into his wife's hand. "There ya be, yer saucy Highness. Now shut yer trap and see to His Grace before he be seein' our sorry carcasses hangin' from a demned gibbet."

The woman continued to regard me with a gleam of contempt in her squinted eye. " 'Fess up," she said. "Be ya the divil Salterdon or no?"

I glanced at her husband, who was tucking the warmed blanket around Maria. "What have you got against Salterdon?" I asked, caution tapping as I accepted the thick-as-pitch coffee. The heat of it rose in an aromatic mist into my face.

"Ever'thin', that's wot. The demned lot of 'em been tryin' to shut down these mines since t'old man kicked up his boots and was buried in hell proper. 'Twas t'old lady who brung the trouble 'pon us, harpin' on that the smelt putrified 'er fine air. Demned lot of 'em would put us all out of work and homeless, and fer wot? So's they kin lounge in their pretty gardens and have their bleedin' soirees without the stink of the smelt assaultin' their cockleheaded sensibilities?"

"Enough." Thomas pointed a rough finger at her. "I've got t'be back in the mine and I'll not have ya distraughtin' a guest in our house. See they're taken care of properly, or I'll lay ya over me lap and swat yer perty arse good and proper."

Tugging his hat down over his ears, Thomas gave me a glance and a grunt and left the house.

Her keen eye still upon me, the woman grabbed up a long-bladed knife and snatched up a loaf of bread. "Well?" she said. "Are ya Salterdon or not?"

"No," I replied, staring at the knife. "I . . . work for Salterdon."

"Ah." She nodded. "Thought so. All's the pity fer it. Didn't think ya looked the sort. Wot do ya do for the lot of divils?"

The blade sliced through the bread as if through warm butter. I swallowed. "This and that."

She nodded toward Maria. "Wife?"

"Yes," I lied. How else could I explain her?

"Tiched, is she?"

I looked at Maria, bundled in the blanket. She stared toward the hearth fire, unblinking.

Sinking back against the chair, I closed my eyes. "Yes. I suppose she is."

"Bless 'er." Her broad backside swaying from side to side, she moved to the cot with a bowl of warmed, sweetened milk bread studded with plump, dark currants.

"Hand me yonder gown and be quick 'bout it. She's shiverin' cold. And them stockin's as well. Legs are as thin as willow whips."

Upon fetching the flannel gown and leggings, I sat on the cot and watched the woman tend to Maria with a gentleness that seemed odd for a woman of her gruffness.

She poured warm water from a ewer into a bowl and with a soft cloth cleansed the dried mud from Maria's feet and legs, her brow growing creased and the hard glint returning to her eyes.

" 'Ave ya beaten her?" she asked. "Is that why she's tiched? That why she's yonder, wanderin' 'bout in the rain and dark—to escape yer demned cruelty? Because if it is, I'll run me knife up yer arse s'far I'll skewer yer foul heart."

"No. I would never hit her."

"I s'pose she got them bruises from fallin' out a tree."

I turned away, and with elbows on my knees, stared at the floor between my feet. "I would never hit her," I repeated wearily.

"Ach. I've seen the likes of a' before. Thinkin' a woman is aught more than a beast of burden. Half starved, she is."

"She won't eat."

"We'll see 'bout that. Aye, Bertha'll have 'er right as spring rain in no time."

I opened my mouth to argue, but all spirit had fled me. My bones ached. Chill had gnawed into my muscles so they burned as if a fiery pike had been thrust through them. And hunger. My belly fisted, and the nausea of complete emptiness rose bitterly up my throat. I looked toward the kettle of boiled meat and potatoes and felt my gut clench.

"If yer hungry, eat," Bertha declared. "Y've the look of a starvin' calf about ya."

I stood unsteadily, my gaze still locked on the bubbling mélange, helped myself to a heaping bowl of it, and tore a portion of warm bread off in my hands.

Bertha continued to gently bathe the muck from Maria's arms and legs. "Are ya homeless?" she asked.

"Homeless?" I tore a piece of bread off with my teeth.

"Are ya deaf as well as daft? Are ya homeless? Ya said ya toiled fer Salterdon. Did the divil cast ya and the gel out?"

"What makes you think that?"

"Word gits round, aye. T'old place has gone to rack and ruin since t'old man died. Heard the demned duke has gone poor as a beggar. Serves him right, I says, though me hoosband says we aught to pity the bugger. Him who got no conscience or common sense don't know when they is well off. Man who ain't forced to work for his meat and tators can't appreciate the fine rewards of his labor—of knowin' he's earned his bread and butter."

She stood erect and made a noise that caused me to turn.

"Where are yer children?" she asked.

"There are no children."

"No?" She shook her head, bent, and examined the pale skin of Maria's lower belly more closely. Her expression softened. "Poor lass. Right bonnie little thing, ain't she? Reminds me of me own. . . ."

She straightened suddenly and looked away, her eyes pooling. She dabbed the corner of her apron to them and took a quivering breath.

I was not one for conjecturing on the thoughts or feelings of a human, man or woman. In truth, I had rarely cared—too wrapped up in my own life to give a damn about others. Aye, I had been a bastard about it. But something in the woman's faraway look evoked a sting of piteous curiosity in me.

"Have you children of your own?" I asked gently.

"Aye, we did." She drew back her shoulders and stared into the fire. "Three of 'em. Two lads. One lass. Strappin' boys, they was. The sort to make any ma and da proud. They was killed not long since. In the mine. Buried 'em side by side just yonder."

She motioned toward the little window partially curtained by thin, colorless muslin.

"The lass, we called her Kate. Died two year ago this winter. Frail she was, from the day she was born right there on that very cot. 'Twas the smelt that killed her at last. Strangled 'er pitiful lungs."

I stared at her profile. "I'm sorry."

"Such is life. We live and we die. We learn to make do with what God grants us, and be thankful for wot we got. There are plenty t'others wot be worse off. I got a fine hoosband and a fair roof over me head. If he be taken from me tomorrow . . . well . . . I'll make do. We take care of our own here, ya see."

She looked again at Maria, then at me. "Y've a place to stay here if ya need it. I'll do what I can to help yer lass. I'm thinkin' she needs a woman's touch, frail as she is. And if it's a job ya be needin', there's plenty of 'em, if ya ain't afraid of hard labor."

My gaze fixed on her stoic countenance, which, only briefly, had succumbed to the grief she must have felt in her heart. Whatever tragedy had been so unjustly inflicted upon her family, it had left no bitterness upon her soul.

'Twas just after sunrise when I awoke to the sounds of laughing men outside the house. As I moved from the bedroom, I discovered the door open and sunlight spilling through the room, turning the interior stone to a dull golden glow. The air felt brisk but clean.

I looked toward the cot where I had left Maria in Bertha's care hours before. She was gone. Beside the cot was what appeared to be an emptied bowl of porridge and a last rasher of pork.

A gang of men collected outside the house—just off their shift in the mines, faces black, so the whites of their eyes were a startling contrast. They drank pints of amber ale as they sat on crude stools, their clothes as filthy as their faces and hands.

The wives of the men collected beneath a nearby tree, chatting among themselves, directing their fond gazes toward their husbands. It took me a moment to recognize Maria.

Gone was the pitiful wraith I had taken from Menson. Beneath Bertha's gentle ministerings over the last hours, she had become once again the pale angel of my dreams.

In some distant place in my mind, I noted the sudden silence of laughter and chatter, of all heads turning at once to fix me with looks of curiosity. My gaze still locked on Maria—who sat on a quilt, dressed in a simple blue cotton dress and resting back against the tree. I moved through the grouped men like one in a trance.

How clearly blue were her eyes—not gleaming, but bright and steady. They were fixed upon the rising sun with a sort of wonder-look, as if they could see what no one else surrounding her could see—something profoundly splendid. Such vast depths of emotion showed in them that it seemed her very spirit was shimmering from within her.

Upon her normally colorless complexion, the brisk air had kissed a blush of color upon her cheeks. Her lips looked tinted as if she had been eating berries straight from the briar. Full they were, and deliciously red, the corners tipped up slightly as if she were reminiscing upon some fond image.

The women remained silent as I walked to the edge of the patch-work quilt and stood staring down into Maria's face. Her hair—clean and shining—fluffed softly around her magnificently shaped head, a soft, curling bang drifting over her forehead, nearly to her eyes.

My throat tight, I eased to one knee and whispered, "She's so beautiful again."

Bertha beamed, and the women all smiled and nodded among themselves.

In a quiet voice, Bertha said, "She's been havin' a right nice talk with Paul this mornin'."

My face froze and my cheeks flushed with discomposure. "Christ."

"Right spirited conversation," a diminutive woman with gray-streaked brown hair and dark, twinkling eyes declared, then giggled. "I vow they was givin' each other a right go over. Back and forth and back and forth—"

"And she ain't 'bout to have any of it," a younger woman said. They all broke out in a pleasant tittering, making me wonder if they were all as tiched as Maria.

I looked from face to face—ruddy-cheeked, with sparkling eyes despite the hardship of their lives. Their expressions appeared . . . discomfitingly knowing, as if they could easily read my thoughts, and pitied me for them. I suddenly felt as if I were the only lunatic among them.

"She ate a right goodly amount of porridge," Bertha informed me. "Pleasant as a babe, she were, though I got the impression it were more to please 'er brother than to pacify 'er own hunger. They was quite close, I take it."

I nodded, my attention focused on Maria's face. In that moment, her lunacy seemed little more than a trick of my imagination. She looked as sane as the women around her.

Yet as I moved closer, she appeared to draw away, her features to dull, the light in her eyes to diminish, until her mien became numb once again, blank and immovable, as if the sun had suddenly been absorbed by storm clouds, leaving the world—her world— gray as fog.

Bertha leaned forward and placed her hand on my shoulder. Her eyes looked deeply into mine.

" 'Tis a woman's touch she needs now. Give 'er time, luv. She'll cum round when she's good'n ready."

As I stood, my frustration mounting, Bertha stood with me, caught my arm with a surprising fierceness, and pulled me aside. A sternness drew her face into hard planes and deep creases.

"Mind yer temper, sir," she declared. "I can see yer a man of little patience and even less understandin' of a woman's sensibilities."

She lowered her voice. "I know where she's been, sir. Aye. 'Tis there on the inside of her arm, the asylum's mark. They brand 'em like sheep, they do, in case they escape. Now, I ain't gonna ask ya right off wot she were there for, but I got me own ideas. I ain't fallen off a turnip wagon on me head lately.

"The two of ya . . . ya ain't hoosband and wife, I sense that much—aye. She's runnin' from sumaught, and I ain't decided yet if it's from you or sumaught else. And I got me own ideas of why she's gone palsied of the mind. I've been that close to the edge meself more than I care to remember. Leave 'er t'me, sir. For a while."

"If anyone can bring 'er round, me own Bertha can," came her husband's voice, and I turned to find him smiling fondly into his wife's eyes. His night's labor showed in weary creases in his face; his big hands were scratched and scabbed by new blood.

He thrust a frothing pint into my hands. "The name is Thomas, by the way. Thomas Whitefield. Now cum 'long and I'll interduce ya to the lads. They'll be eager to make yer acquaintance."

I SAT AMONG THE TWO DOZEN MINERS, DRINKING ale, my attention drifting between their boisterous conversation and Maria, who continued to sit with her beautiful face tipped up toward the sky, her expression one of sublimity. I hardly noticed when the talk and laughter fell to a heavy hush.

A frail woman draped in a shawl moved through the streaks of morning light to join them. One by one, the men all stood. The women's smiles became grim, their gazes watchful and worried.

Once, she had clearly been a comely lass, with thick dark hair that had become faded by years and stress, as had her green eyes. She carried a paper fisted in her hand. She focused on Thomas, who stepped forward to meet her.

"Is it Richard, Lou?" he asked, as she stopped and raised her chin, her bottom lip quivering.

"If yer askin' if me husband is dead yet, then I can say that he's alive still, bless his

tormented spirit, though the blood is comin'
frequent now and the pain grows more unbearable by the day. God forgive me, but I
wish He would take him and be done with his
sufferin'."

She glanced at each of the men's faces as
if daring them to judge her. When her gaze
found me, she looked me up and down
slowly, eyes narrowing before turning away
and drawing back her shoulders, raising her
fisted hand into the air.

"It's come. The demned company is tossin'
me and me near-dead husband out of the
house. We're to be gone by week's end. The
bastards say that if he's too sick to work to
pay for his rent, then best get out so they can
put a healthy man in his place.

"He's devoted fifteen years of his life to the
company, and this is all the thanks he gets.
They won't even let him die in peace, when
it's the poison from their own mine that has
killed him."

"I'll have a word with them," Thomas said
gently.

"I'll not have ya riskin' yer jobs any longer
for me. And I'll not take another pence from
any of ya. Y've got yer own lives and families'
welfare to think about."

Bertha moved up beside the woman and
put her arm around her. "We'll not have one

of our own lost to the company, lass. Now, come sit with us a while."

"I've got to be back to my husband, Bertha—"

"Just for a minute. I've someone here I'd like ya to meet. Her name is Maria."

As the woman reluctantly joined the others, Thomas turned back to the silent men. "Well, there ya have it. The demned mine has leeched the life from another of us, and what thanks does Richard get for it? A grave yonder and a widow unable to care for herself."

"I say we strike," one declared, punctuating the comment with a thrust of his pint, causing the brew to slosh over the cup lip and spatter on his dusty boots.

Thomas shook his head. "There ain't a one of us who can go without our salary, not with families to feed and shelter. Besides . . ."

He drank deeply from his cup, then wiped his mouth with his sleeve. "We c'not risk pissin' too loudly 'bout our sorry lot, can we? Not with the demmed Warwick Minin' Company threatenin' t' shut us down."

I watched the woman sit next to Maria, the anger on her face melting into one of friendly compassion. She glanced my way and nodded, her lashes lowering slightly before she turned away.

"What will happen to them?" I asked,

causing Thomas to look toward the troubled woman and frown.

"What usually happens, once we're of no consequence to the company. They care aught about us other than what we dig out of the demned pits."

Thomas looked back at his friends, their faces black with soot and carved by hardship. Fear shone in their eyes, each man knowing that he faced a similar fate.

❦ 8 ❧

"*I*'M SORRY," EDWINA CRIED AS SHE WRUNG her hands. "I didn't mean to leave the door unlocked. I forgot—"

"You forgot," I sneered. "At least be honest about your motives. You want Maria dead; admit it. You'd like nothing more than to see her pitiful little body a worm's feast in yonder crypt."

I stalked her as she backed away, her face colorless and her throat constricting. "You've become a maniac again. As senseless as she."

"I should send you to hell, Edwina, where you might at long last find the company of one who can appreciate your bent for cruelty."

"You sanctimonious hypocrite. You have the heart of a devil."

"Aye."

I wrapped one hand around her throat and pushed her against the wall, pressed her there like a butterfly pinned beneath glass.

"If I thought for a moment you had intentionally left that door unlocked, I would snap your neck in two and toss your voluptuous little corpse to my starving swine."

Her eyes widened and her mouth curved. "Wonderful! There's hope yet. You're sounding more like yourself every minute."

Eyes narrowing, I turned away, walked to the liquor cabinet, and poured myself a drink.

Edwina moved up behind me. "So what have you done with her?"

I tossed back the Scotch and poured another. "What do you care?"

"I suppose any hope that you returned her to Menson would be—"

"Idiotic."

She ran her hand up my arm. "You're filthy, darling. Why don't I have Iris draw us up a warm bath—"

"Why don't you have Iris draw *me* up a warm bath?" I smiled at her dryly. "I do believe you were just leaving."

Taking the glass from my hand, she eased up against me. "Really, darling, can't we at least be civil to one another?"

"My dear Edwina, there hasn't been anything remotely civil about you since you were old enough to spit out your first insult."

"Your Grace," came Herbert's slurred voice from the doorway. "You have visitors."

"Christ," I said, "not my grandmother." I was too bloody bone-weary to take her on right now and hope to survive.

"Grandmother, indeed," declared the jovial voice that I immediately recognized as Lord Darian Parkhurst.

As he stepped into the room, he bowed slightly and gestured at his legs wrapped in rough leather riding chaps. "Your Grace, am I not walking on these appendages? Had I been your dowager duchess grandmother I would have *slithered* in on my belly."

"Smashing!" cried Oscar Whitting from the atrium. "Quite a good one, old man. The Salterdon hydra strikes again."

Whitting entered the room with a flourish of his coattails and tossed his hat on the nearest table. His wild hair blazed orange as a pumpkin, as did the freckles on his face.

"Ah, the blushing couple. I expected to find you both absorbed in your disappointment over having the nuptials spoiled at the last moment. Yet here you are, looking at one another as scornfully as ever. Are we too late for the fits of tantrum, heaving bosoms, and tearing of hair?"

Edwina gave a huff, spewed several vulgarities, and flounced from the room.

"Imagine it," Oscar said as he watched her go. "I finally succeeded in insulting her. Declare, Salterdon: has the wench an actual fiber of feeling about her?"

Having poured another Scotch, I moved to the window. "Who can tell?" I felt suddenly drained of energy. "With Edwina, 'tis all or nothing, isn't it?"

Parkhurst joined me at the window as Whitting poured them generous servings of brandy. Leaning one shoulder against the windowsill, he crossed his arms over his chest and fixed me with his green eyes.

"I've seen sick swine look better than you, Trey. Had a rough go of it, have you?"

"How did you find the gel?" Whitting asked as he joined us, handing Parkhurst his drink.

I stared out the window toward the thin stream of black smoke rising over the moor. I touched the claw marks on my cheek—as yet slightly tender—and tried to force away the image of her in Menson.

"She's quite mad," I said softly, the admission a tear in my throat.

They stared at me a long moment, their mouths open.

Finally, Parkhurst cleared his throat. "Too bad, old man. What do you intend to do about it?"

"I . . . don't know."

"Where is she?"

"Do tell," Whitting cried. "What have you done with her?"

I sipped the drink, my gaze shifting from one bounder to the other. Suspicion crawled up my spine. I knew them only too well; knew the lengths they would go to for a farthing or two. I was, or had been, one of their own not so long ago.

"Did my grandmother send you here to ferret out information about me?" I asked in a soft, threatening tone.

They looked at one another and burst out laughing.

"Imagine it." Whitting choked and gasped for air. "The old crow daring to ask *us* for a favor. She would gnaw her own heart out before acknowledging our existences."

"Come, come, Trey." Parkhurst gave a toss of his head, causing a wave of dark brown hair to spill over his brow. "You know us better than that."

"I know for a fact that you've blown through your monthly stipend and your father refuses you another farthing for the moment. I also know that you're in debt to your ass to the Groom Porter—just as I am. If they're threatening you with collection as doggedly as they're threatening me, you would do just about anything to get your hands on money."

Whitting declared, "This from the old dog

who would have sold his soul to Edwina to settle his financial woes. Talk about the pot calling the kettle black."

"At least I wouldn't have been stabbing my best friend in the back . . . would I, Whitting?"

Whitting snorted and turned away.

Parkhurst gave me a sardonic smile. "Seriously, my Duke. You look like hell. Is it really that bad?"

"Worse than you could ever imagine."

The humor disappearing from his face, Parkhurst followed my gaze to the moor. "Sorry to hear it. I suppose there's nothing we can do to help?"

"No."

"What do you intend to do now? About your grandmother, I mean. I vow the whole of England is holding its breath waiting for your next move."

"I'm not sure. But I'll tell you this: she'd better stay away. From Maria. And from me." I cut my gaze to his. "You might pass on the word should you happen to bump into her along the way."

I AWOKE SUDDENLY, SHIVERING. I HAD BEEN dreaming again of Maria, of falling to my knees beside an abandoned mine shaft, calling her name, and looking down into the dark where flames writhed like serpents.

Only it wasn't her face that looked back at me from the inferno, but my own, mouth open in a silent scream of horror.

Naked between my sheets, I rolled my head and did my best to focus my blurred vision on the open window. Night shadows were fast creeping over the landscape, and I found myself watching, breathless, for the first flicker of light from the smelts. The breeze rolling in felt bracing, and I shivered again as the memory of Maria in a blue cotton dress sparkled in my mind, obliterating the nightmare.

My need to see her in that moment, to assure myself that my removing her from the asylum had not been a dream, filled me with a desperation that made my chest ache. Yet Bertha had told me to stay away—just for a while—as if my presence agitated Maria's sensibilities.

Daft bastard, of course my presence would agitate her sensibilities, I reminded myself. If there was a solitary ember of sanity left in her, she would—should—hate me with every fiber of her being.

"You missed dinner," Edwina whispered into my ear.

I turned my head and stared into her drowsy eyes. Her naked breasts were nestled against me, one thigh resting over my loins.

Her hair formed a copper blaze upon the pillow.

"God," I said hoarsely. "I didn't get *that* drunk, did I?"

"What do you think?" She gave me a languid smile.

"I seem to recall telling you to get the hell out of my bath—that was just before Parkhurst and Whitting burst in with some wild rambling about Herbert falling headfirst into the rain barrel."

She slid her hand down my belly. I caught her wrist, stopping her.

"Then I recall sending you to see about the poor bastard. I'm quite certain I was fully embraced by oblivion by the time you returned. Besides, I sense no fresh claw marks on my ass."

With a huff of exasperation, she rolled to her back.

"Have Parkhurst and Whitting gone?" I asked, glancing again toward the window, where the first tinge of firelight had begun to glimmer on the distant craggy summit.

Soon Thomas would be trooping with others into the mine, and I found my mind drifting to that deep, dark place where men toiled to survive. Normal men. Those who had not been born in a privileged family. To . . . aristocracy.

And what of Maria?

Christ. I had waited three long years to embrace her again, and yonder, beyond my ability to see her, to touch her, she remained with a total stranger.

"Quite the contrary. They've ensconced themselves very comfortably downstairs. I'm sure they've slugged back your last precious bottle of port by now—along with sending Iris into the vapors by demanding smoked pheasant for their meal. When she told them you were fresh out of smoked pheasant—in fact, smoked *anything*—they very seriously told her to go out and shoot something."

"What *did* she feed them?"

"Pigeon."

I winced.

Sighing, Edwina stretched, causing the sheet to slide off her breasts and rest across the small mound on her lower belly.

"It moves constantly now," she informed me. "The child, I mean. Flutters around inside me like a bat in a cave. There! It's doing it again."

She took my hand and slid it beneath the sheet, cupped it around the swelling, and held it there. We both stared at the ceiling; then—

The being moved against my hand.

I might have jerked my hand away, but she

held it there, and again it skittered along my palm as ticklishly as a feather.

We turned our heads at once and stared into one another's eyes. A grin touched my lips. Hers quivered. Suddenly, her enormous eyes filled with tears that streamed down her cheeks.

"What shall I do, Trey? I'm . . . terrified."

She rolled her body into mine again and clung like a frightened child, her face buried in the crook of my neck. Her tears fell hot and wet upon my skin as her body shook. Oh, that the body in my arms, so willing and heated, was Maria's. The ache for her settled like a hot stone between my legs.

"Damn it all," Edwina wept. "It seems all I do is cry anymore. And eat. Then vomit it up. Then cry some more. And my breasts hurt, among other things."

Lifting her wet face, she looked into my eyes. "Don't you feel a little sorry for me?"

I forced another grin. My skin felt hot and clammy. "A touch."

"I'll stand no chance of landing another husband now."

"What makes you think so?"

"All those rutting animals care about is my body."

"Don't forget your money."

"Really, Salterdon, you're not *that* daft.

There are plenty of wealthy women around just begging to take on a husband. The only difference between us is that at least while they lay me, they needn't cover my face with a pillow."

"Oh, I don't know." Rolling, I grabbed my pillow and covered her face with it.

Letting out a scream, her tears turning to giggles, she kicked and beat at my shoulders. We wrestled until I fell beside her, laughing and breathing hard. Spreading her body over mine, she gazed down into my face, her own pale in the deepening darkness.

"We were so good together," she said softly. "Admit it."

"We had our moments," I admitted, nudging a coiling tendril from her brow.

"Many of them."

"You're not going to get weepy again?"

"Only if you promise me that I'll remain as desirable after I've given birth."

"Why wouldn't you?"

"How could we? Our bodies distend to the bursting point, breasts and belly ravaged by scars—I understand men never enjoy us as much, if you know what I mean."

"If that were the case, Edwina, there would be very few siblings running about."

She pressed her lips lightly against mine, and for an instant—just for an instant—I responded, the surge of lust for Maria still full and hot inside me. I buried one hand in her hair and drew her closer, opened my mouth over hers, and thrust my tongue inside her.

She made a sound in her throat—more like a laugh than a groan of desire—a growl of conquest that slammed me back to reality, and made the rancid bite of acknowledgment roll over in my gut.

A woman's body has been your curse since you were old enough to take your first whore. You simply can't help yourself. . . . Will you ultimately grow weary of her naivete and hunger for the whore? I'm sure of it. We're much alike—you and I. We're . . . empty, and starving to be filled. It's what bonded us, I think. Our neediness.

I thrust her away and rolled from the bed.

❦ 9 ❧

I MANAGED TO SURVIVE THE NEXT TWO DAYS OF frustration by occupying myself with Park-hurst and Whitting as they hunted grouse and pheasant, joined them in depleting my dwindling stock of liquor, played cards until I grew too stupid with boredom to hold open my eyes—while Edwina lounged in my bed, vowing herself too ill to travel. I didn't doubt it; how could I, when I was forced to witness her heaving into a chamber pot whenever I entered the room?

It was Parkhurst and Whitting I didn't fully trust. They weren't the sort to waste their time whiling away their days and precious nights rambling around the cold and drafty halls of a country estate without a good reason.

They weren't fooling me. Not for a mo-

ment. My grandmother had got to them . . .
bribed them, bought them off. Somewhere
close by, she was waiting like some wily fox
for them to return with whatever information
she needed to initiate her next plan to further
ruin my life.

What surprised me was Parkhurst's duplic-
ity. I could only surmise that his debts were
so vast and urgent that he must bow to my
grandmother's scheme or suffer dire consequences.

For that, I was forced to forgive him. Such
extreme desperation had been my constant
companion for most of my adult life, and was
still. It lurked more apparent every day—as
bleak as the gathering winter clouds on the
horizon.

In truth, their reasons for coming here and
remaining bothered me very little, compared
to my mounting hunger to be with Maria
again. The growing need boiled my blood. It
drove me from my bed to wander the hall-
ways all night, surely crazed as any Menson
lunatic.

I would return to the music room again
and again, sit in a chair and stare as if in a
trance at the dust-covered pianoforte, the dia-
pasons of *Maria's Song* swirling between my
temples, memories of my own mental confusion making my heart beat rapidly.

My mental confusion had been caused by an injury to the head.

Maria's, however, had been caused by an injury to her heart.

More and more, my patience grew thin. *Give her time,* Bertha had suggested.

How much?

A week? A month? A bloody year?

Was it not enough that I had spent three long years suffering over her disappearance? Imagining her in the arms of another man, loving him as I loved her?

What hateful realization, to acknowledge my own culpability for her madness—that she languished in that dreadful place while I hated her, believing she had married another.

What irony that we had both wasted our minds and hearts, not to mention our lives the last years.

Damnable waste.

Damnable evil!

VIOLENT THUNDERED THE WIND FROM THE NORTH, cold and roaring like lions amid the crags of the house's dark stones.

As I stepped from the house into the midnight tumult, I paused and glanced around, my eyes narrowed against the gale, my ears deafened by the howl of the wind in the trees.

No light shone from the windows of the

rooms where Parkhurst and Whitting slept. I knew what I was risking, even though they had fallen drunk into their beds. Should they discover me gone, they would search. They might even find me.

I was willing to risk it. I had no choice. The need to see Maria had become unbearable. I had to assure myself that she was all right. I had to touch her, and smell her, look into her eyes and embrace her soul.

Yet the wind beat me back, piercing me with cold, robbing me of breath as if all the demons of hell were intent on keeping me from her. I fought my way along the gill, caught my breath as I splashed through the stream, shivering as it clawed its way up my legs, colder and deeper now due to the rains further north.

At long last topping the wind-swept summit, I paused and looked back. Low black clouds skittered along the desolate fields and bent fir tops, revealing the hulk of the manor house briefly before it vanished from my eyes. But not before I noted a light in a window—where before there had only been darkness.

"Parkhurst, you bastard," I said between my teeth.

I had no choice. I had come too far already.

The very thought of seeing Maria again

had infused me with an energy that propelled me onward.

Fixing my sight on Whitefield's house, its window shining with light, I trudged down the footpath, half running and stumbling as the wind careened around my legs. Finally arriving at the house, breathing hard from my exertion, I cautiously moved to the window and looked in.

She was there! Before the fire. Sitting in the little ladder-back chair, wearing the blue dress, gazing serenely into the flames.

Dear God, how angelic was her profile. How pale and perfect! There was no lunacy in that mien now. No hysterics; no fear. She looked as normal as any young woman lost in her thoughts.

"She ain't ready," came Bertha's voice, and I spun round to look down into her stern eyes, illuminated by the light through the window. The wind whipped at her skirt as she moved around me for the door, a basket in one hand, the other raised to shield the sting of the wind from her face.

"She looks fine," I countered.

"Well, she ain't. Not yet. Y'll do 'er no favors by confrontin' her now."

"When?" I demanded.

"Patience."

I slammed my fist against the stone wall. "Madam, I am *not* a patient man."

"Aye, I know that. Ya needn't state the obvious."

"I've waited too *bloody* long—"

"Y'll wait longer. A day, perhaps. A week. A month. Until she's ready."

I stood stubborn and rigid, my hands fisted and trembling from an anger so fierce, I felt frightened for Bertha in that instant.

"The hell, you say," I sneered. "A month? I'll take her this very minute—"

"Go on, then. Take 'er." Bertha reached for the door as she glared at me. "I've got no right to 'er. 'Twon't be me own conscience that'll be screamin' if she passes."

Looking back through the window, I focused on Maria again, her slightly bowed head and her pale profile as she gazed into the flames in a sort of strange anticipation.

What a damned twisted strait. What *should* have been my life's joy was, instead, an agony so dreadful it coiled in my chest like something evil.

Guilt!

Bitter consequence!

Their venom burned in me, retribution for all the sins I had perpetrated in my life. What better reprisal for my iniquities than to rob me of what I most coveted and craved?

"Tell me the truth," I choked. "Is she lost to me?"

Bertha placed her hand on my arm. "Not so much as I first believed when me hoosband carried her through this door and put 'er on the cot. Not even so much as the mornin' ya went away. 'Tis a tenuous thread on which she totters, sir. She cums and goes. Sometimes to the very brink of a sort of breakthrough, then she fades again. But yer not wrong. It's yer right to take 'er, if ya want. She's yer lady love. No other's."

My lady love. Aye. She was that.

"Go, then," I told her, my gaze still fixed on Maria. "Before I change my mind."

With a quick nod, Bertha shouldered open the door, paused for a moment in the threshold as she gazed back at me, then closed the door in my face.

Again, I moved to the window, the wind and cold making my eyes tear, burning my cheeks. The powerful gusts rocked my body. I watched Bertha drape a shawl around Maria's shoulders, then prod the fire so the flames leapt high and cast bright gold light within the cozy room.

Resting my forehead against the windowpane, I exhaled wearily and watched her image grow dim behind the condensation of my breath upon the glass.

"Goodnight," I whispered.

———·∞·———

YET I REMAINED, REFUSING TO RETURN TO THORN Rose, unable to remove myself from Maria's proximity.

As the wind whipped wildly through the scattering of trees and the occasional spear of rain drove into the ground, the cold cut me to the marrow as I huddled with my back against a rowan trunk and gazed from a distance through the window, occasionally catching a glimpse of Bertha, and less frequently, Maria, until the lights in the window were extinguished and all that was left for me was the fiery glow of the burning smelt stack.

"Y'll catch yer death, man," came a feminine voice behind me, and I turned to discover Louise.

Strong and horizontal thundered the current of wind from the north; it whipped the woman's long, loose hair and molded her skirt against her slender legs as her eyes, shadowed by night, regarded me fixedly.

"Come into the house until the rain passes."

I followed her, my body numb from the cold.

The small house was identical to the Whitefields'. A cot close to the fireplace revealed her invalid husband, his face blue-tinged, his chest heaving with every labored breath.

Waiting with my back to the closed door, I watched her tug the shawl from her shoulders and point at the chair before the hearth.

"Sit," she commanded.

I sat, my focus still on her pitiful husband.

As Louise prepared tea, she glanced at me occasionally, then at her husband, her countenance weary, and I noted that she had a good face, too marked, perhaps, by life's hardships, but of fine character.

" 'Tis a horrible thing to watch a loved one die, sir."

"Aye," I said, forcing my gaze back to the flames, thinking of the pain I felt over Maria and my fear of losing her—that I might have already lost her.

"Lou," her husband called faintly.

She hurried to his side and took his hand, smiling bravely. "Aye, my love?"

"Who's come, lass?"

"An acquaintance of Thomas and Bertha."

"Let me see him."

She looked at me, and, reluctantly, I joined her at the bed.

His dark dull eyes fixed me, and he smiled weakly. "Welcome, sir."

I tried to smile.

"Have you brewed him a pot?" Richard asked.

"Aye, love."

"Good wife." He struggled for a breath. "You look cold, sir. Fetch him a blanket, Lou."

As I continued to look into his eyes, I felt a chill more biting than the cold of the climate. Death loomed around us like a shroud. It crawled over my damp skin and pressed upon my heart like a heavy stone.

"What are you called, sir?"

"Trey."

"Are you from these parts?"

"He works for Thorn Rose," Louise said, as she tossed a blanket around my shoulders.

"Ah. More's the pity to ya, sir."

His eyes drifted closed and he groaned.

"Hush now," Louise whispered. "Save yer strength, husband."

" 'Tis little strength to save, love." He managed a weak smile and lifted his hand to her. She clasped it to her bosom, against her heart. "Ah, lass," he whispered. "I've failed ya and I'm sorry."

"Nonsense." Her eyes flashed.

"No children to take care of ya once I'm gone. What will ya do, love?"

"I'll manage."

His chin quivered and I moved away, back to the fire where I sat staring into the flames, the sound of his soft sobs making my face burn that I should witness this sadness.

When he at last rested, Louise prepared the tea and placed the steaming cup into my hands. She took a chair next to mine and pulled her shawl tightly around her thin shoulders. Her face looked haggard with grief.

"What will you do?" I asked softly.

"I don't know," she whispered.

"No family at all?"

"None."

She withdrew the letter from her skirt pocket, opened it with her trembling hands, and read it again by firelight before turning her face to look at me.

"He doesn't know it's come. I don't dare tell him. He'll give up. Let go."

I took the letter from her and read it—the demand that since her husband was no longer employable, they should vacate the company's house within a fortnight as they would replace Richard with a new man to work the mine.

"I assume if he were to get better and return to work, there would be no issue of your vacating the house."

"Aye." She shook her head. "But we're beyond miracles, sir. My husband is dyin'."

Her stoic bravery crumbled and she covered her face with her hands, tears falling and her slender shoulders shaking.

Leaving the chair, I gently lifted her up and

held her against me, feeling her body shake and her warm tears soak through my shirt. There was nothing I could say, no comfort to impart.

I simply held her.

⨳ 10 ⨳

A T LAST, WITH GREAT RELIEF, I BID PARKHURST and Whitting goodbye. Still, I kept my distance from Maria, occupied the long hours by holding Edwina's hand as she continued to heave into the chamber pot at every opportunity. I had given up on the idea that she would leave Thorn Rose, and no longer cared. She was company, if nothing else. She tolerated my ever worsening mood and mounting impatience.

We played an occasional hand of cards, read to one another, and debated names for the child that grew more active in her belly every day. I would lie in bed at night, staring out the window at the fiery halo of the smelt mill, Edwina's belly pressed up against my back, and feel the movement of the babe against my spine.

Always I imagined the arms around me were Maria's, and my fear mounted that they never would be.

I had heard nothing from my grandmother so far, and although I wanted desperately to believe she had washed her hands of me, and Maria, I knew at the bottom of my own black heart that she would eventually come scratching at my door.

No, it was best that Maria remain exactly where she was for now, whether I liked it or not.

Still, I had stood it as long as I could, and if I were going to survive this torture I would have to see her again—if only from a distance.

Would she look as beautiful as she had the last time I'd seen her, dressed in the pale blue dress, her hair shining like spring sunlight?

I imagined walking up to her, her raising her remarkable eyes up to mine, her face brightening with recognition and love. She would scream in pleasure and fling her warm, embracing arms around me. Then we could forget the last years had ever happened, and get on with our happily ever after.

So I trudged through the chilly dawn mist and arranged my seat next to the gnarled old tree with a perfect view of the Whitefields' little house, knowing that as soon as the night shift ended, the miners would march out into the awakening daylight to be greeted by their wives. Not for the first time, I thought about Louise and Richard, of the man's intense struggle to survive and the woman's predicament.

No miracles.

It was then, the spark of an idea began to flicker.

Idiotic, surely. *Insanity!* I had never had an inkling of philanthropy in my self-absorbed body. Not like my brother, who epitomized goodwill toward all men.

Saint Clayton.

Often I had scorned him for it, angered that his generosity to his fellow man caused me to acknowledge just how deeply my own selfishness ran. Clayton had been a reminder of all the potential I had failed to attain, and I had come to believe myself incapable of achievement.

Yet, as I sat there with the first rays of sunlight filtering through the mist, I felt a surge of awakening—nay, hope—spring to life inside me. The heat of it made me sweat, my body vibrate, my mind whirl until the world tipped and swayed.

I hurried down the hill path, through the heather and gorse that slapped against my legs, dodging the birds who lifted from their disturbed thorny lairs to beat the air with madly flapping wings, along the wagon-rutted course, passing the Whitefields' abode, by-passing the few women who were preparing to meet their husbands as they left their shift in the mine. Their heads turned to watch me, no doubt wondering what I was about as I marched up to Richard's door and banged on it.

It opened slightly, and Louise peered up at me. I pushed by her, entering the room that smelled of fresh coffee and baked bread, relieved to find Richard alive still. His head rolled on the pillow and his weak eyes looked into mine with an intensity that made my heart slam . . . as if he knew why I was there.

"I'll take your place in the mine," I said, breathless.

"What are ya sayin'?" Louise moved across the room and stood by the bed, her eyes sharp and cautious, as if she doubted what she'd heard.

I continued to look into Richard's eyes. "The company needn't know. We'll write them and tell them you've recovered, that there's no reason to send a replacement."

I turned to Louise, whose face was flushed, her body tense as she held her breath. "At the least, it will buy us enough time to determine a way to remedy your situation after he . . ."

"You know nothing about mining," Louise declared with a trembling voice.

"I'll learn."

She laughed sharply. "Yer too demn soft."

I glared at her. "Madam, you needn't be insulting."

She lowered her eyes. "I meant no insult, sir. The pit is cruel even to those who have been honed by years of digging. Ya aren't a young man."

I said through my teeth, "Young or not, I *am* a man. I'm capable, regardless of how you or the rest of the world view me."

She moved toward me, her step slow, her gaze steady. "Who are ya, sir, that ya should care about us? That ya would put yer own life in jeopardy for two strangers?"

I walked to the window and looked out toward the Whitefields', and imagined Maria rising from her sleep, recalled the flush of her face when she laughed, the sparkle in her eyes, now gone because of me.

"What difference does it make? I'm simply a man with regrets."

I WAS SOFT. HUMILIATINGLY SOFT. BY THE END OF my first day in the pit, my hands were bloody and my knees barely capable of holding me up without buckling. The muscles in my shoulders screamed with every movement, as if a knife were being thrust into them and ripping.

When I fell into bed, covered by dust, my body racked with coughing, Edwina stared at me, horrified.

"What in God's name are you doing? Working! You're a bloody duke, for God's sake, and you're toiling alongside a lot of— of—"

I rolled and vomited filth into the chamber pot.

"You've lost your mind, Trey. Completely. What are you hoping to accomplish?"

I sucked in air, or tried to. My lungs rebelled. My body rebelled, my stomach cramping as if I'd taken a hard punch in my gut.

As Edwina ran to the bed to comfort me, I shook my head and wheezed through my teeth, "If you touch me, I'll kill you."

"You're bleeding. Oh God, your hands, your beautiful hands—"

"Get away from me."

She dropped into a chair, her face pale. "I told you, Your Grace, I'll give you money—"

"I don't want your goddamn money."

Rolling to my back, I stared at the ceiling, eyes stinging with grit. "Christ, it's like hell down there. Black hell. I expected Satan himself to rise up any moment and cut out my heart."

"You're doing this to spite your grandmother, aren't you?"

"No." I tried to move my arms, but they wouldn't budge.

"Killing yourself in that perdition to help a total stranger is absurd." Leaving the chair, she moved closer, wringing her hands. "You're a duke," she whispered. "You weren't put on this earth to wield picks and sweat alongside commoners."

"I'm a man, first. If it wasn't for me, Maria wouldn't be wounded now."

"So this is penance."

"I suppose it is, in a manner of speaking." I closed my burning eyes.

She gently brushed the hair back from my forehead. Her fingers felt cool upon my hot skin.

"You needn't prove your manhood to anyone, Trey."

"I've come to realize, Edwina, that manhood has nothing to do with the organ between my legs." I looked at her. "It's counting for something. Contributing something. I've contributed not a bloody thing my entire life."

"I'm sure there are ways to contribute without killing yourself."

I reached for her hand, curled my dirty, ravaged fingers around hers, and watched her look at my hand as if it were a vector of some infectious disease. I gripped her tighter as she attempted to pull away.

"What's wrong, love? Now that I have dirt on my hands, I'm not fit to touch you?"

"I'm appalled by your abusing your station in life."

My eyebrows lifted. "Ah. It's all right that I sully my family's name and the peerage by gambling, whoring, and general debauchery, but laboring shoulder-to-shoulder with commoners threatens to destroy the sanctity of my heritage. Christ, you're a snob."

She yanked her hand away. "Aren't we self-righteous now, Your Grace? You, who would once step over a child beggar and not look at him twice. Do you think that if you brutalize your body, God will forgive your past transgressions and miraculously reward you by healing your little nurse?"

"I don't need you to remind me that I was once a son of a bitch, Edwina. The memories of it crawl in my conscience like maggots."

With a rustle of her skirts, she moved to the door, then paused. She tipped her haughty little chin and smiled.

"I'll have Herbert warm you a bath. You smell disgusting, you know. Oh, and one more thing. If you think this dreadful sham will uplift you in some way to the status of your philanthropic brother, you're sadly mistaken. You'll never be Clayton. You'll only be a laughingstock . . . more than you already are, of course."

———～～———

THE NEXT THREE MORNINGS HERBERT WAS forced to help me out of bed, to dress me and undress me when I returned home, too exhausted and sore to do it myself. Yet as I labored in the pit, questioning my sanity, fighting the screaming voice to give up, it was Edwina's words that inspired me to drive the pick harder, to only stumble when I might have fallen.

And always, there was Maria.

I counted the hours until my shift was over—when I could sit among the relaxing men and watch her, waiting for the moment when Bertha would give me a sign that Maria was ready to receive me.

The impatience I expected to feel over the wait was sweated out of me, replaced with an equanimity that was as foreign to me as the strength that infused my body. I would wait forever for Maria, if I had to.

By the end of the second week, my ravaged hands were becoming hard with calluses. My shirts fit snugly across my chest and arms, the muscles tight and bulging.

Yet none of these personal accomplishments pleased me more than placing my wages into Louise's hands. She wept and gripped my hand to her cheek, the appreciation in her eyes making a knot form in my belly.

When had anyone ever looked at me with anything other than disappointment or mockery?

Aye, and there was more. Much more. I had made friends among the men. Those who had first regarded my efforts with amusement had come to respect me for my tenacity. I had come to know each man by his name, and I knew each family. I came to learn, with some concern, that the company's future was in question, and therefore also the livelihoods of the miners.

As we sat one eve after our shift, I listened to their concerned conversation.

"Production is down from last month," Thomas said, staring into his ale. "The company ain't pleased."

"They ain't ever pleased," Myron Heppleborn said.

Thomas stared through the dark toward the mine. "Down from last month; down every month—down, down, down."

Craig Gosworth tossed his empty pint cup to the ground. "We're done, ya know. The demned pit is 'bout to give out. They'll shut us down, just like they've done the others last year, and then wot's to be of us?"

"I'll speak to Warwick," Thomas said. "Convince 'im to give us more time."

Myron Heppleborn shook his head, his

shoulders stooped and weary. "Why bother, Thomas? We've seen it comin' for months. We've tried to deny it to ourselves, but there ain't no denyin' it any longer. I give us another two, maybe three months, and that's that."

With a low curse, Thomas stood and walked away into the dark. I waited a moment before following to where he leaned against a tree and gazed up at the fire-belching stack.

"What will you do?" I asked.

"I'll speak with Warwick, aye. I'll convince him that she ain't done yet. Not yet."

He shifted his gaze to mine, his eyes bright with the flames burning overhead. "There's ore there yet, sir. I can smell it. Taste it. I feel it here." He punched his belly. "I vow to ya, Trey, the vein is there. A big one. Enough to keep these men set and secure for the rest of our miserable lives."

ᏕᎧ 11 ᏕᎧ

I AWOKE SUDDENLY, FROM A STRANGE AND disturbing dream—the pit again, bottomless and fiery, my face looking up at me, twisted in torment. But there was something else—something more disquieting.

Someone had shouted my name.

The clock chimed in the distance, echoing through the house. Hours yet until I was to rise and traipse over the lea and fell to the mine.

Rising from the bed, I moved to the window. The smelt fire lit the gloomy night, a pale gold veil shimmering above the horizon.

Hurry!

The voice again. I spun and searched the room, dark but for the remaining glimmer of embers in the hearth. Cold touched my face, as if from a wind. It crept up my legs and spine, a whisper brushing against my ear.

Maria! Hurry!

I dressed quickly, led by some instinct of dread that sluiced through me. Something was wrong. Something had happened. I felt it in the pit of my stomach, unnerving, rattling. It made my heart run with the sudden need to see her, to convince myself that she was all right.

By the time I topped the swell I was breathing hard, gasping in the frigid air that made my lungs burn. The cluster of houses below were dark, only an occasional glimmer of light from a distant window. There was no lamp burning in the Whitefields' cottage.

I sat against a tree and closed my eyes, took deep breaths, and imagined myself foolish to have been rattled so by a dream.

At first, the vibrations were subtle—a tremor so faint, I thought it only my own body shivering with cold.

Then again, stronger, running through the tree at my back.

I looked up to see the dying leaves shimmy and rustle as if fingered by wind. Only there was no wind, just a low growl of what sounded like thunder beneath me.

Christ, what was happening?

Stumbling to my feet, my gaze swept the landscape. Before me the distant fell began to buckle, to open, and suddenly it seemed the world began to disintegrate.

The growl became a roar and an explosion that sent a rush of foul smoke and stench rushing from the mine shaft, as if all the demons of hell had been loosed, and with it, a plume of fire suddenly erupted from the crumbling smelt chimney.

As if time were horribly grinding to a stop, the stones of the chimney began to disintegrate one by one, flying into the sky in fiery streamers to drift back through the cloud of gray smoke and falling debris and settle upon the thatched roofs of the houses that, suddenly, looked pitifully tiny beneath the monstrous enveloping black smoke clouds.

The mine. Dear God, the mine!

I ran, slid, stumbled down the fell, eyes burning, nostrils singed by the hot air and the rank odor, the earth still trembling under me. From the corner of my eyes I could see the hills undulating like a living thing, then disappear in on themselves as if some giant maw was opening and devouring creation itself.

By instinct I ran into the road, unable to see anything but the bright flare of fire rising out of the ground, the streaks of light that looked like shooting stars through the smoke.

Then the screams—women, around me, but I couldn't see them—wails of horror and grief. The rooftops aflame added to the bilge of smoke, the thatch snapping and crackling like tinder.

I came face to face with Bertha, her flesh gray with shock and fear, and the soot of lead dust and smoke. Her glassy eyes stared at me as she clutched her throat with her hand and made a horrible sound—her husband's name.

"Thomas, Thomas! Someone help me hoos-band!"

Beyond her, the roof of the Whitefields' house roared with fire.

"Maria!" I shouted in Bertha's face. "Where is Maria?"

She stumbled away. I tried to grab her, to pull her back from the oncoming billows of choking smoke. Driven by fear, she flung me aside and dissolved into the haze.

Maria squatted in the corner of the small room, much as she had the day I had found her at Menson. Fragments of burning thatch rained down around her, and the hem of the dress smoldered.

I fought my way through the smoke and flames, swept her up and out of the house, clutching her in my arms, curling her into my chest to protect her from the sparks and spewing smoke.

Running blindly through the blackness, I labored up the fell and along the footpath, lungs burning, legs cramping. I paused upon reaching the summit and looked back, down into the fiery hollow. The rumbling and roars had stopped, all but the snapping of burning thatch.

Gently, I lay Maria on the ground, took her face in my hands, and searched her for injury. Her frightened eyes looked up at me, and her hands clutched at my shirt. For an instant . . .

Turning, I ran back down the hill into the melee of screaming men and women. The cottages blazed, and I fought my way through the press of bodies who were frantic to reach the decimated mine. At last, I reached Richard's cottage.

Flames rose from the roof in snapping, lapping tongues, and even as I watched, it began to disintegrate.

Shielding my face with one arm, I kicked open the door but was driven back by the wall of fire that appeared to have consumed the tiny house.

"Lou!" I shouted, desperate to find some way in.

She was curled up on the bed, holding her

husband. Her head turned and she fixed me
with stoic eyes, her face without fear, but
with a calmness that lent a beauty to her features and hinted of the woman she had been
in her youth. A smile touched her lips, then
she was gone, beneath the hail of flaming
timbers and thatch.

"THEY'RE ALL DEAD. ALL OF THEM. NO HOPE OF
recovering them."

I stared out my bedroom window, at the
pitch-black horizon that brightened occasionally with threatening weather. I thought
of my grandmother and how pleased she
would be about the mine. No more stench in
the air.

My body covered in soot, my hands singed
by hot ash, I turned back and looked down at
Maria.

I had done everything humanly possible
to help the buried miners and the men who
had arrived for work shortly after the explosion. Alas, there had been nothing humanly
possible that could be done to help. Thanks to
a spark and a pocket of gas, the world one
hundred feet below ground had ignited to
turn the miles of shafts into oblivion.

"I did what I could," I said in a hoarse
whisper.

"Of course you did, darling." Edwina took up a wet cloth and began to scrub my black hands. She looked as pale as I had ever seen her.

"I don't think you comprehend, Edwina. They're dead."

"I understand."

"Thomas. Myron Heppleborn—he has four children and a little farm near Haworth. Craig Gosworth just got married. And John Milford's wife is expecting their first child in another few weeks. Lou and Richard. All gone."

"Thank God you weren't among them. You might have been, do you realize that? Had that explosion happened a few hours later . . . dear God, I shudder to think about it."

She tossed the filthy washcloths aside. "I'll have Herbert bring you up a hot bath."

"I don't want a bath. I want . . ." I shook my head and blinked.

My eyes burned. The women's faces had been seared into my grainy lids and their screams rang in my ears. The sense of help-lessness continued to curdle in my stomach. But more than that—fear that I had almost lost Maria again. I shook with it.

Not for the first time I thought of the dream, the voice that had roused me from bed and driven me to the mine. Coincidence, certainly.

"Christ," I whispered. "If I hadn't been there, Maria would be dead as well."

Edwina sighed. "That, of course, would have been a shame."

I cut my eyes to hers in a murderous look.

She backed away, her eyes wide and as blue as the dressing gown she wore. "Get some rest. You're exhausted. I'll have Herbert bring up some tea with your bath."

As she left the room, I walked to the bed and stared down into Maria's eyes. Disappointment weighed on me. Frustration closed off my throat.

"I thought . . . Out there on the fell, I thought for a moment that you recognized me. I suppose not."

I raked my hands through my hair, feeling as if I were going to explode as violently as the gas that had sent sixty men to their deaths. For a moment—a very brief one, I envied Thomas, Myron Heppleborn, and Craig Gosworth—no longer burdened with life's cruel twists and heart-rending disappointments.

Thunder crashed in that instant, followed by an explosion of bright light in the sky that wrung from the clouds yet another catastrophic crack, rattling the windows and shaking the floor.

Maria shifted, and her blank, emotionless expression became one of fear and confusion.

"Paul?" she whispered. "Are you there?"

I moved closer. "Maria?"

"What happened? That sound—"

I followed the direction of her gaze to the shadows just beyond the lamplight. Nothing, of course. What had I expected to find there? Paul? Christ, I was becoming as mad as she.

"Maria, please."

She sat up partially, her brow furrowing and her lower lip quivering. "What do you mean, Bertha is gone?"

"Listen to me."

"Where am I?"

Again, I glanced toward the shadows, staring as the play of lightning reflected in a shimmering glow off the wall. I thought of the voice again and a shiver ran up my back.

"I won't remain calm!" Maria cried, returning my focus back to her. She glared at the wall as her face blotched with angry color.

"Stop this," I declared with all the authority I could muster despite my rising sense of frustration. "Do you hear me? Stop it."

"Paul? Don't leave me—"

Taking her slender shoulders in my hands,

I gently shook her. "Goddamnit, you're going to listen to me."

"Bertha!" she wept. "Bertha, please—"

"She's gone, dammit. I'm afraid you're stuck with me—"

Her hands beat at my face.

"No! Don't touch me!"

She shoved me aside and rolled from the bed. Her arms flailed out in front of her, as if she were stumbling in the dark.

"You're going to stop this," I shouted, my frustration mounting, as was my fear that she was lost to me. Lost! I knew not how to reach her, and for a moment I felt as mad as Maria. "You're going to listen to me—"

"Help me! Someone help me!"

She backed into a corner and slid down the wall, her legs drawn up to her breasts, her hands buried in her hair. Her eyes closed. And she began rocking, humming *Maria's Song*.

AS I POURED HALF A BOTTLE OF EDWINA'S ROSE-scented toilet water into the steaming bath, she looked on, horrified.

"You bought me that in Paris," she cried.

"I'll buy you another."

"With what? A candlestick?"

I glared at her. "I'm in no mood to tolerate bitchiness at this moment. I suggest you make yourself useful. Help me undress her."

"You're not serious. She's . . . dangerous."

"So am I."

Her eyes widened and she swallowed. "You're going to owe me for this, Salterdon."

"Get in line, Edwina. I owe just about everyone else in this country, in one way or another."

Maria lay curled up in the bed, staring at the window. I motioned Edwina to the opposite side of the bed in case Maria attempted to run again.

She didn't, thank God, just lay as limply as a rag doll as I peeled the singed, soot-stained nightdress from her. Gently, I lifted her; she didn't struggle.

I eased her into the water, cradling her shoulders against my arm. Steam settled on my face in drops that leaked off my brow and spattered on her breasts. Her pale skin flushed with heat. Her eyes widened.

I looked quickly at Edwina and mouthed silently, "Calm her."

"Me?" she mouthed back.

"Do it," I mouthed again.

With a sigh of resignation, she eased closer to the tub. "Be at peace, Maria. Everything is going to be fine."

Maria turned her head toward the voice and stared hard, as if through the dark.

"We're not going to hurt you."

"Bertha?" she whispered. "Bertha, is that you?"

I glared at Edwina and nodded.

"Yes, dear." Edwina wrung her hand and rolled her eyes. "It's . . . Bertha."

Maria relaxed a little and I reached for the soap, skimmed it along her shoulders and down her submerged arms. Soot from my hands formed dark swirls on her skin and in the water.

"Where is Sarah?" she asked.

Edwina looked at me; I shrugged.

"Sarah? What do you want with Sarah?" Edwina asked.

"I want her. I want Sarah."

"She's . . . not here."

"I want her." Maria struggled, and I was forced to steady her. Her trepidation was returning; her body began to tremble. "Sarah!" she cried.

"Do something," I said through my teeth.

"Tell me where she is," Edwina said, trying to keep her panic under control.

"Give her to me!"

Before I could react, Maria rose partially out of the water, her beautiful face contorted in a rage that set me back on my heels. She looked directly into my eyes, her own like twin fires burning, as hot as the flames that had razed the mine and village hours before.

Suddenly her hands were in my hair, fingers twisting and nails burying into my scalp, dragging me into the tub with her, sprawling, facedown in the water, where I inhaled instinctively, sucking in rose-scented liquid that exploded in my brain.

Edwina screamed.

I heaved upward and tore myself away, choking, then retching up water that scorched my throat.

Edwina screamed again.

Through a burning blur I looked around to find Maria climbing out of the tub, her attention fixed on Edwina, who backed toward the door.

"Give her to me, you bitch," Maria growled.

"I don't have her!" Edwina cried. "Trey! Do something. She's going to—"

Maria leapt as gracefully as a cat onto Edwina, sending her flying backward to land in a jarring thump on the floor. Maria took handfuls of her hair and began to slam her head against the carpet.

Scrambling to my feet, I leapt over the tub and grabbed Maria around the waist, hauling her back, causing Edwina to howl in pain as Maria, with the tenaciousness of a snapping turtle, continued to grip Edwina's hair and shake her side to side like a dog with a bone.

"Let her go!" I shouted and tried to peel Maria's fingers from Edwina's hair.

With a snarl, she sank her little teeth into my shoulder. I felt them tear into my muscle like pointed knives.

I drove my elbow into her ribs; heard the rush of air leave her lungs as she released me. She stumbled back, no longer interested in me or Edwina as she turned round and round, her arms outstretched as she wailed, "Sarah!"

WHO THE DEVIL WAS SARAH?

As the rain pounded against the roof, I saw Maria's face over and over again as she screamed the name. There'd been no fear there, only despair so intense my heart ached to recall it.

Sarah.

I searched my mind, recalling the miners' wives—no Sarah there that I could remember. Perhaps one of the lasses I had not met? Someone who, with Bertha, had made a sort of breakthrough with Maria? Whoever it was, she had made an impact of utmost power.

As the sun rose behind the low dark

clouds of threatening rain, I took off down the muddy path once again, my progress slowed by mire and the brutal cold that had settled over the landscape in thick patches of ice-kissed mist. I didn't feel the cold—only the gnawing hope that I would locate Sarah, and she would help me.

The village sprawled like some lifeless cadaver in the hollow, the roofless stone houses like bones jutting out of the earth. Scattered among the fallen debris, men sat like stone relics of another time, picks lying on the ground, forgotten, shovels tossed away, useless.

The wraith-like figures of the dead miners' wives moved silently among the scorched houses, dragging out their pitiful furnishings and piling them high onto the backs of wagons. As I passed, a few turned their hollow-eyed looks toward me, their expressions lifting in momentary hope before realization slammed the door of reality again in their faces.

The stones of the Whitefields' house stood in stark contrast to the black hills beyond it. Carefully, I entered, paused at the burned threshold, and stared in on the charred remnants of the ladder-back chair and cot, the blackened metal cooking pots inside the hearth.

The world smelled of smoldering, wet ashes.

Bertha exited the bedroom, her arms full of bundled bedding that had, miraculously, escaped the inferno that had gutted the main room. Upon seeing me, she stopped. She had aged a decade in the last twenty-four hours. Grief had etched deep grooves in her face.

"Bertha," I said, my voice tight. "I'm sorry."

She gave me a quick nod and clamped the bundles to her chest. "Aye. So am I."

"Can I help you with that?"

"No." She shook her head.

"What will you do now?"

"I'll be movin' on."

"Where will you go?"

"Down the road. I've got me brother in Bradford. His wife passed on last year. He could use me help, I think, what with his passel of children."

She plunked the bundle on the floor and returned to the bedroom. I moved to the bedding and picked it up, waited until she returned with another arm full of what appeared to be Thomas's clothes.

"Who is Sarah?" I asked.

She stared at me a long moment as if she were lost in deep thought.

"Sarah," I repeated. "Where can I find her?"

Bertha swallowed and glanced around the room. She looked, for an instant, as if she would shatter.

"Maria is calling for her."

"Ah." She took an uneven breath. "How is the lass?"

"Violent."

" 'Tis a shame." She blinked and looked at me again. "Like I said, she needs a woman's touch."

"Perhaps this Sarah person can help. Maria seems bonded to her, somehow."

Her eyes pooling with tears, Bertha chewed her lower lip, then trudged back through the ashes into the bedroom. Exiting again, she held a baby doll in one hand. She stared at it with such pain I feared she would erupt in a torrent of tears.

She tossed it to me. "Take it. It's all I've got left of me darlin' daughter, but Maria needs it more than me. Only serves to remind me of what I've lost."

I stared down on the cracked face of the doll with big painted blue eyes and fading cupid lips. The fringe of hair spraying from its head looked like dry matted straw.

Confused, I looked again at Bertha.

"Me daughter called 'er Matilda. Thomas bought it for her once when he went to London." Her smile quivered. "Me precious girl slept with it ever' night till she died."

A doll. I stared down into its cherubic face, my confusion growing. "The doll—"

" 'Tis Sarah." She swallowed. "Maria called her Sarah."

≪ 12 ≫

REALITY—INDEED, LIFE—CAME RUSHING UPON her like a sea of fire—blinding in its brilliance and horrifying in its cacophony. It seemed to boil up from her very essence—what remained of her, at least, that had not moved into the realm of the netherworld. For as long as she could remember—which wasn't long, because nothing existed before she had, at Paul's insistence, allowed herself to slide like one drowning into the blackness—there had been silence and numbness. No fear. No happiness. No pain. Or sorrow. Only . . . numbness.

Maria wondered if she, in some miraculous twist of irony, had been hurled back into her dear mother's womb, where existence swarmed as red and hot as blood. She heard the loud beating of a heart—her *own* heart, she realized—felt each surge of her own blood rush into her chest, expanding—*beat*—withdrawing—*beat beat*—sending tingles down her arms and fingers that felt as if they were being pricked by a thousand fiery needles.

No, no! She didn't like it, this . . . awakening. 'Twas the black that sustained her, saved her from complete insanity. Beyond the blackness was evil and pain. And fear. Oh, God, the fear . . .

It had begun with a roar that had rushed through her darkness with Herculean force, and she had watched her black cocoon of comfort fracture around her like glass, allowing fragments of light and noise to stream in upon her.

She had screamed for Paul, and he had come, swiftly as always, yet . . . in the briefest of seconds he had been pulled away, sucked into a spiraling vortex of light. His face, his glorious face, always awash in such calm blissfulness, had appeared disturbed.

Then Bertha's voice, usually soothing and oh, so kind (she had been convinced that Bertha was an angel, though Paul had adamantly denied it), had risen in a horrifying wail—certainly no sound belonging to angels. Far from it. Angels didn't experience pain or horror. That's what heaven was for: to provide a haven from human misery.

With every fiber of her strength, Maria had fought to hide, to sink back into the void and pull the darkness in over her.

Yet it was crumbling. Little by little. Fractures appearing in the black walls surrounding her, allowing in the light and sound.

Hateful consciousness crashed over her now, awakened by an awareness that stole through her. Soon the screams would begin—the horrible wails of maniacs. Then they would return to poke and prod her with their feet, to laugh at her and sneer and cause her pain.

And with those monsters would come the memories. It was those that hurt her more, even more than the pain and humiliation inflicted on her by the monsters.

Cracking open one eye the tiniest bit, she peered through her lashes. She wasn't alone. Every instinct roused inside her. She always knew, no matter how hidden she was in her mind, when she wasn't alone. They were playing with her again, waiting to scare her. Waiting to remind her that she would rot in this horrible cell forever, because . . .

Because she had committed the vilest sort of crime. Worse even than murder, according to Ruskin.

She had dared to seduce a blue blood—skewed his priorities, not to mention his familial loyalties. His marriage to her would have meant the extermination of a blood line that had undoubtedly begun with Adam and Eve.

She mustn't think about it!

To allow those memories to intrude would invite the insanity—the black hate that hovered around her like death itself, waiting to invade if she let down her guard for an instant.

Once, before Paul had introduced her to the darkness, she had been consumed by hate. She had howled out her fury like the lunatics in the surrounding cells. She had obsessed herself with plotting murder—she, the daughter of a vicar, had sunk as low as Lucifer himself. Revenge had coiled and twisted through her mind like some poisonous vine.

She focused on her surroundings, confusion mounting. She heard the beating rain on the casements, the wuther of wind among trees.

The dank walls of her cell weren't dank at all.

The only light in her cell had been a thin beam that oozed through the slot in the door through which *they* had peered in on her. Yet the assault of light on her eyes now did not appear to materialize through the portal. It washed over her so blindingly bright it felt hot on her eyes, making them tear.

Where was she?

Obviously she was dreaming again—imagining that she had been removed from the horrible little cell with its fetid floors and rats as companions.

Cautiously, she lifted her head and was besieged by dizziness that settled in her empty stomach like thrashing waves. Her surroundings tipped and swayed, the light—so hurtful—turning the room and everything in it into spectral blurs.

She could just make out the furnishings: a chair covered with deep red velvet and adorned by tasseled damask pillows, wardrobes of intricately carved woods that stood nearly as tall as the ceiling. There was a fire snapping on a hearth where, upon the mantel-shelf there were figurines, their faces of white, smooth china, with tiny eyes and flirtatious smiles.

Upon the floor lay a carpet where sinuous, serpentine motifs of deep burgundy formed patterns upon a background of thick, cream-colored threads.

A gilded mirror filled up the space between two windows. In the mirror she saw a spectral being with hollow, glazed eyes and sunken features that were bloodless and gray, and white hair, shorn nearly short as a man's.

It was dreadful, the pitiful creature. Frightened and wasted. It gaped back at her like a portent of death.

Nearby, a figure stirred. She saw it approach through the spectral light, its face radiating a strange blurry glow. A woman, as beautiful as the figurines on the mantel, with flowing red hair and eyes as cold as Meissen china. She stared, unsmiling, and Maria sensed—as she always did when in the presence of malevolence—a darkness emanating from the very heart of her.

She sank into the bed, withdrawing, forcing the oblivion to return. If she concentrated hard enough . . .

It was there, like evening shadows, and in her mind she reached for it and pulled it over her like a comforting blanket—warm, snug, feeling it slide into her thoughts and body, filling her up in a tide of equanimity that gently caressed her brain. Softer and softer rose the flow, with warm, soothing undulations until, at long last, she disappeared.

I PROPPED THE LITTLE DOLL IN A CHAIR NEAR the window. Its shaggy head drooped sideways, onto its shoulder. Its body—worn, dingy muslin plumped by down feathers— was lumpy and floppy. Bertha had, at some time, dressed it in a pale pink sleeping gown with ruffles around the throat, wrists, and skirt hem. Its round blue eyes stared at me.

"It's appalling," Edwina declared. "First she talks to ghosts, and now demands to play with doll babies that belonged to a dead girl."

"She wasn't dead when she owned it," I pointed out.

"And that's supposed to make it all right?"

I shrugged.

"It's . . . frightening. Look at it. Its face is cracked right up the middle."

I shifted my gaze to Edwina's. "You're starting to annoy me again."

Edwina flopped into a chair. "I'm going mad with all this. As mad as she. This boredom is crucifying."

"Then leave."

Edwina's blue eyes narrowed and she sank more deeply into the chair. "You're not getting rid of me that easily."

"More's the pity."

"Sometimes I hate you, Trey."

I gave her a flat smile.

"I'm hungry."

"Then eat."

"What, pray tell? That dreadful little scullery maid vows there isn't a morsel of meat left to eat in this dreary place, aside from pigeon, of course. If I have to ingest another one of those filthy birds, I'll vomit."

"Again?"

I left my chair and moved across the room toward the doll. Outside the window, the weather was bleak, with swollen dark bellies of rain clouds swaging low over the horizon. It cast a gray, dismal haze through the window-panes.

Gently, I picked up the doll, cradled the fractured head in one hand, and stared down into its eyes.

WITH THE STRIKE OF MIDNIGHT, I SAT AT THE pianoforte, a candle placed upon the ebony case beside the doll—Sarah. The candle glow reflected off the doll's painted eyes and formed a yellow halo upon the keys.

I didn't need the light. I had played the song a thousand times in the dark, a million times in my head. *Maria's Song,* my tribute of love to a woman who had once saved my soul—who now needed saving herself, and I felt helpless to do it.

I lay my hands upon the keys—no longer the hands of the man I once had been. They were hard and scarred, and I wondered if they still contained the ability to wander the keys in so caressing a fashion.

Closing my eyes, I let my fingers drift, each note resonating through the cavernous room, resonating through my heart. But the tune evoked no peace in me, only frustration; en-

couraged my anger, the need to storm into
Maria's room and shake her out of her idiocy.

Damnable patience!

How long could I maintain it? I was a man
who always took what I wanted, when I
wanted it, and to hell with the consequences.

"Sarah," came the whisper, and my hands
froze upon the keys as I turned my head.

She stood like a shadow beyond the light,
vaguely visible in the long red nightgown I
had obtained from Edwina. With her silver
hair, she might have been an angelic illusion.

My heart climbed my throat and I wanted
to jump from the stool and take her in my
arms, clutch her to my chest, and cover her
face with impassioned kisses.

Yet I sat, motionless, breathless, as if in the
company of a bird; unwilling to frighten it, in
hopes it would venture closer so I might revel
in its wild spirit.

Slowly, my hands continued to skim the
keys, the song drawing her closer, to the edge
of the candlelight that reflected from her remarkable eyes. Hope beat inside my chest.
The air burned inside my lungs.

She stared at the doll, tears rising to her
eyes and spilling down her cheeks. Then she
turned those blue orbs, framed by winged
brows and long, pale eyelashes, to mine, and
even as I watched, the cloak of madness

began to crumble, little by little, allowing reality to filter through her confusion.

She gasped and stumbled back, turned one way, then another, her gaze flashing around the room until flying back to me. Her eyes widened. Her lips parted as she drew in a sharp breath, released it in whimper—and she collapsed in a faint to the floor.

I PACED HER BEDROOM THROUGHOUT THE NIGHT, watching her sleep until at last, exhausted, I dropped into a chair, the doll in my lap, and closed my eyes.

My thoughts teemed with the prospect that Maria had made a sort of breakthrough; the image of her awakening playing through my mind as melodiously as the strands of *Maria's Song*.

Surely I had not imagined it. Her eyes, burning into mine those brief seconds before her collapse, had inspired me with hope . . . and something else. Some niggling disturbance I was too frightened to acknowledge. It crawled in my stomach like acid. It seeped through my veins in a hot torrent.

Sarah.

"Where are the children?" Bertha had asked.

The children. The doll.

Sarah.

Dear God, was it possible?

While imprisoned in that hellhole, had Maria given birth to a child? A girl she had named Sarah?

I had refused to acknowledge to myself to what lengths of depravity she had been subjected. But now the thought was there. Maniacs, brute workers who would naturally assuage their bestialities on an innocent such as she.

The horrid images squirmed through my imagination and conscience until a groan worked up my throat and I covered my eyes, filled with a rage that made me shake with a need to commit murder. The anger and hate I had felt for my grandmother before was minuscule to what I experienced now. I ached to rip out her heart.

At last, wearied by my thoughts and my body's physical and emotional war, I drifted to sleep.

Edwina's scream awoke me with a jolt, and I stared up into Maria's maddened eyes briefly before I instinctively ducked, just as she drove an iron poker down into the chair where my head had rested. The chair tipped, spilling me onto the floor; I rolled to my back as she stood over me, her hair a wild spray around her flushed face, her teeth showing in fury.

"Bastard! Give her to me."

She swung the poker again. It trenched

into the floor by my head, and I grabbed it, fought to hold it as she lurched backward, attempting to take it.

"Filthy, dishonorable fiend!" she screamed. "I won't let you take her, do you hear me? I won't let you take her again!"

Removing the doll from under my body, I flung it at her feet.

Dropping the poker, she swept it up, clutched it to her bosom and retreated to the bed, huddled against the headboard and gently kissed the doll's face, stroked its matted hair.

"There, there," she wept softly. "Mama's here, my darling."

Edwina fell beside me, helped me to sit up. We watched Maria as she rocked, tears running down her cheeks as she smiled into the doll's staring eyes.

❧ 13 ❧

AS DAWN EMERGED THROUGH THE SULLEN clouds, I dressed for my journey to Menson.

"You can't leave me here alone with her," Edwina cried. "What am I to do if she lapses into a fit again?"

"Stay away from her. Keep the door locked. Should there be a problem with Maria, Herbert will deal with it."

I tied a cravat around my neck before turning to face her. "She has the doll. That should pacify her."

"If there was—is—a child, darling . . . what I mean is . . . what will you do?"

"Ascertain if it's mine."

"And if it's not?"

"I'll probably murder someone."

Stepping from the house, I found Maynord waiting with my horse, its breaths bursts of vapor from its flaring nostrils. It pranced in place, eager to be off, and tossed its dished head, causing the bit to grind against its teeth. My cape swirling in the gusts of frigid air, I left Edwina standing on the threshold, wringing her hands.

The rutted and pitted road to Menson was covered with the season's first thin ice, slowing my progress. By the time I reached the asylum, dark and looming amid the falling rain and sleet, the hour was well past noon. The intense cold gnawed at my feet and hands and made my bones ache.

Ruskin expressed little surprise when I shoved by his startled assistant and entered his office, a small space as gloomy as the cell in which I had found Maria weeks ago. His toad-like eyes wide in his fleshy face, he stumbled back against the wall as I approached, feeling as insane in that moment as the lunatics howling in the distant rooms.

"What the blazes are you doing here . . . Your Grace?"

"Where is she?" I demanded through my teeth, my anger mounting dangerously.

"Your Grace?" He swallowed and blinked. "Do you mean the woman? You took her—"

"Don't disappoint me further with your

miserable attempts at stupidity, Ruskin. I've ridden hours through the damnable cold and rain, and I'm in no mood to tolerate an imbecile."

"I—I beg your pardon, but I cannot think—"

"The child, you moron. Where is she?"

His eyes glazed and his teeth began to chatter. "The child?"

"Maria's daughter. Sarah. Where is she?"

"Your Grace, surely you must understand—"

"Understand that I don't intend to leave until I get what I came for. What have you done with her?"

"I don't know—"

I kicked the desk. It tumbled over with a crash, spilling papers and a lamp onto the floor. The wick flame set fire to the lamp oil and hot tongues lapped through the scattering of papers, igniting them in bright orange plumes that sent black coils of smoke in the air.

Ruskin shrank against the wall, trembling.

"Answer me," I growled.

"Help!" he croaked. "Someone help!"

I slammed him twice against the wall. "If you don't tell me, you filthy little man, I'll kill you. And there won't be a court in England who will hang me for it, because I'm a duke."

Closing one hand around his throat, I began to squeeze.

He gasped and clutched my hand, his eyes bulging. "The child was taken . . ."

I closed my eyes briefly, the confession driving like a fist into my gut. So there *was* a child. No doubts now. Fear and rage became a tumult in me as I stared into his watering eyes.

"Whose child is it?"

"Please, Your Grace, you must understand: I'll lose my position—"

"Better that than your life."

"Yours," he finally managed in a weak voice. "The child is yours, Your Grace."

I felt shamed by the truth, and took an unsteady breath. "What have you done with her?"

"She took her. Your grandmother."

IT HAD BEEN INEVITABLE THAT I FACE HER. AS I stood before her town house in Mayfair, London's sooty rain beating upon my shoulders, I fought the familiar emotions I always experienced before confronting her.

Fury, yes. Disgust, aye.

Dread.

It washed through me as bitingly as the exhaustion and cold that made my bones feel brittle. Even my desire to wring her decrepit neck felt inconsequential to the consternation I always felt in her presence, like one attempting to stand toe-to-toe with a hydra.

One never knew if one of her many faces would embrace with kindness, or bite.

The butler greeted me with a lift of one eyebrow and the news that the dowager duchess was occupied with friends.

"Not for long," I told him, and strode through the foyer into the room where a collection of chattering peers all fell silent upon my unexpected entrance. They gaped at me as if I were a demon suddenly popped into their midst as I stood in the threshold, rain dropping from me and forming a puddle on the floor.

"Get out," I growled at them, my gaze piercing my grandmother, whose expression went from shock to fury.

There was a clatter of china as they put down their teacups, rose from their chairs, and, with hastened curtsies and a muttering of breathless "Your Grace"s, they hurried from the room, met by frantic maids who hustled to retrieve their wraps.

The butler appeared behind me and eased the sodden cloak from my shoulders, disappearing as quickly as he had appeared, closing the door behind him.

I gave my grandmother a stiff bow, more mocking than it was respectful.

"How dare you," she declared, voice shaking with anger, "come into my home unannounced and terrify my guests. Haven't you disgraced me enough?"

"You haven't an inkling of the extent I intend to go to disgrace you, madam, unless you tell me what, exactly, you've done with my daughter."

Her thin eyebrows raised and she lifted her chin. "Ah, your pitiful little nurse must have come to her senses, at last." She smirked. "What a shame."

"I always thought you a heartless, manipulating bitch, but you continue to surprise me."

Her gaze raked me as her mouth formed a thin smile. "So very much like your father. His taste for tarts superseded his intelligence."

My eyes narrowed. "What the hell are you saying? Father loved my mother very much. He would never have—"

"Silence!"

Grabbing up her cane, she stood, her clawed hands gripping the crook and her weight leaning heavily upon it. Her eyes were like cold flint in her gaunt face.

"I'm too damn old to tolerate this belligerence and stupidity any longer. I've fought for the better part of my life to keep this family from annihilating itself, and what have I to show for it? Years of heartbreak and humiliation, that's what. A reminder every time I looked into your father's eyes—every time I looked at you and

Clayton, a bitter reminder that I was little more than the duke's unwanted responsibility."

"I didn't come here to discuss your miserably failed marriage. I came here to discover where you've hidden my child, and I don't intend to leave until I've wrung the information from you in whatever manner I must to get you to spew up the truth."

She moved toward me, shoulders humped, the cane thumping on the floor. I was struck by her advancing age more than I had ever been.

Clayton and I had often quipped that she would live forever just to spite us. But in that moment, Death appeared to radiate around her like some black, hovering spirit. I felt it in the air. Smelled it, rank and odorous. While age normally mellowed the most hardened soul, it only lent a more cruel disposition to her lined face and glittering eye.

Drawing herself up as much as she was capable, she met my fierce gaze with her own, her expression unnervingly smug. I was jolted by the real possibility that she was about to confess that she had murdered the child.

"So you want the truth," she said. "I wonder if you're man enough to handle it."

I fisted my hands, prepared for the blow, no doubts in my mind that I would surely kill her if she had harmed Sarah.

As if she could read my thoughts, she

smirked. "I blamed myself, of course, and was willing to forgive my husband. At least in the beginning. I understood his disappointment and desperation."

"Madam, *where* is my daughter? If you've harmed her—"

"I had failed to provide him an heir," she continued, watching my eyes narrow as I attempted to make sense of what she was saying. "So when my husband came to me with the news that he had gotten some baron's daughter with child, I was heartbroken, yes. But I was reasonable. And naive. His suggestion that we go abroad for a year, until the child was born, seemed reasonable. No one need know that the child wasn't mine."

As her words began to chip away at my concentration, forcing me to focus on her meaning, I whispered, "Christ, what are you saying?"

"I was grateful, for God's sake. Since he at last had a son, an heir, he would content himself with his home life. He might even be appreciative enough of my sacrifice, and my willingness to keep his filthy little secret, to remain faithful.

"Did you ever wonder, Your Grace"—she sneered the "Your Grace," her gray lips pulled back, showing her long yellow teeth—"why your parents had no more children?"

She chuckled, a mephitic sound to match the hate in her burning eyes. "Because my husband's son enjoyed the company of men."

I blinked, her meaning coiling in the pit of my stomach. I felt caught like a fly in a web, looking into the eyes of a predator intent on devouring me.

Yet I could no more look away than I could flee, despite the dread that made my heart slam painfully against my ribs.

She lifted the cane and slid the crook around my neck, drawing me close, so close I could smell her aged skin, the odor like dust.

"By the time we realized his son's proclivity, I no longer gave a whit about my husband. He had the morals of a tomcat. Therefore, when he announced once again that he had managed to conceive with some young harlot, I had little care. I was content with my own dalliances and comfortable with the rewards of my station.

"I didn't give a damn when he and his son quietly arranged for a marriage between the man who would pass as your and Clayton's father, and the whore. The duke would be assured of his heirs, and the man you believed to be your father could continue with his sordid relationships with those of his own sex.

"So you see, Your Grace, I'm not at all surprised at your appetite for whores and females of inferior blood lines. You are, after all, my husband's son."

As I stood rooted to the floor, the blood draining from my face and sickness churning in my gut, she returned to her chair before the fire and sank into it with a sigh and grunt. The cane fell to the floor, then she reached for her teacup, smiling.

"You do realize what this means, of course." She chuckled. "Since you were conceived out of wedlock, you're no duke at all. Should you continue this idiotic quest to marry your little nurse, I'll expose you and Clayton for what you are.

"While such a revelation will hardly affect your brother—unlike you, he has managed to attain a rather grand fortune on his own—you, thanks to your stupidity, have nothing but your title to keep you afloat. What little respect you still have among the ton will vaporize like mist.

"You'll be a pariah, if you aren't already. You'll be penniless. And you'll be homeless. What will you do with the remainder of your sorry life . . . break your back toiling in another lead mine, barely reaping enough coins to keep your belly fed?"

Slowly I walked to the chair and stared down on her gray head as she continued sipping her tea. "You're a bloody liar." My voice shook.

"Am I?"

I turned away and moved to the window, looked out on the bustle of traffic, the clatter of horses and coaches muted by the veil of constant rain.

The realization that my grandmother—nay, not my grandmother; a cold, heartless crone who was no more bound to me by blood than the passing strangers—was telling the truth paralyzed me.

Flashes of childhood memories bombarded me. Images of my parents—companionable, friendly, but expressing no outward show of marital devotion.

Everything I was—and stood for—had been a lie.

Should I turn my back on her, my title and what few monetary possessions I still held would revert to her.

I turned to find her watching me, a smile on her lips.

"Bitch," I said through my teeth. "Miserable bitch."

❧ 14 ❧

ON THE BLEAK HILLTOP ABOVE THORN ROSE
Manor I sat on my heavily breathing
horse and stared down at my home, with its
grotesque carvings of crumbling griffins and
its rambling paths flanked by wind-twisted
firs.

I was drunk with ale and self-disgust.

Once again, I had allowed the dowager
duchess to manipulate me. I had only fooled
myself since retrieving Maria from Menson,
believing that the Devil Duke was capable of
altruistic ideals.

That true love conquers all.

Blatant rubbish. The foolish idea of a
black-hearted scoundrel who briefly believed
that there was a modicum of goodness
squirming around inside him—and who was

desperate to find it in hopes of saving himself from complete spiritual ruin.

Aye, I had succumbed to the duchess's blackmail—to sacrifice my own flesh and blood, my daughter, and Maria's sanity. What choice did I have?

What twisted fate that I, who had done my best to humiliate Clayton because his goodness had been a constant reminder of my failures, must now spare him the embarrassment of our filthy familial secrets.

News of our sullied lineage would destroy not just Clayton, but his children, as well. I knew too well the snobbery of our peers. A man was only as good as his title and blood line. Despite my own heinous reputation, my title kept the hungry financial wolves from my door.

I rode to the stables and left my lathered horse with Maynord, who was as soused as I. As I made my way to the house, I froze at the sound of dogs' frenzied barking.

"Damn," I said through my teeth as the pair of snarling sheep dogs rounded the house, driving through the flurry and fog straight at me, their tails tucked low in anticipation of the attack.

I knew every bristled hair upon their backs, well acquainted with their hatred of me. My brother's dogs had the uncanny ability to recognize a devil when they saw one, and more than once I had anticipated their total mutilation of my person.

But worse even than their snarling threat was the realization that Clayton was at Thorn Rose. He was the last person on the face of the earth that I desired to see in that moment.

"Down!" came the shout, and I looked toward the door to discover my brother smirking at my discomposure. The dogs immediately fell back, turning from four-footed fiends to tail-wagging darlings that grinned at their master with such adoration, my resentment for Clayton flourished so fiercely I was wont to slug him.

"They won't harm you," Clayton said as I stepped cautiously around the animals, into the house.

"They would rip off my legs at the first opportunity and you know it."

"Animals sense when you don't like them." Clayton fell in beside me as I moved down the hallway, the dogs padding obediently at his side. "I take it you've spent some time at the Black Bull."

"You were always remarkably astute, Clay."

"Astute has nothing to do with it. You're popped."

Herbert appeared, smiling and alert, as he

always was when Clayton visited Thorn Rose. The bloody servant believed my brother hung the moon, the sun, and the stars.

As he reached for my cloak, I looked him in the eye and sneered, "Traitor."

His gray eyebrow shot up, and with a sniff, he yanked the cloak from my hand, turned on his heels, and marched away.

"When did you arrive?" I asked as I turned down the gallery that glowed with lit girandoles and lamps. "I see you've provided me plenty of tapers and oil. As usual."

"Miracle doesn't care for gloom."

I froze at the sound of his wife's name. If Miracle was here, so was—

"Uncle Duke!" The small, feminine creature bounded down the gallery, a child with an exquisite little face, fiery ringlets, the same color as her mother's, bouncing wildly around her flushed cheeks. And her eyes, sparkling green gems full of such glee over seeing me that I felt my body become brittle. I was filled with a desperation that nearly unbalanced me.

Margaret, with ribbons and lace flapping madly, flung her arms around my knees and beamed like sun rays into my eyes. "Uncle Duke, I'm so glad to see you."

I forced a smile and patted her on the head. "Hello, Maggie."

"Did you miss me?"

I glanced at Clayton, whose arms were crossed over his chest, his smile taunting. "Very much," I managed.

"Papa got me a kitten. Would you like to see it?"

"Of course."

"Splendid. She's in the parlor with Mama and Lady Edwina. Hurry!"

She spun on her tiptoes and dashed away, her laughter ringing like little bells.

I followed, feeling suddenly stone-cold sober. Pray God that Edwina had said nothing of my reasons for traveling to Menson. I was an adept liar, but right now, I wasn't certain I could pull it off.

The scene in the parlor was one of cheeriness, the fire casting tremendous warmth and light, as were the dozens of lamps and candles situated on every available space.

Edwina and Miracle stood as I entered, their faces glowing in anticipation. Yet it wasn't their anticipating countenances that I focused on—but Maria. Sitting between the women, looking as heart-stoppingly beautiful as I had ever seen her.

Dressed in one of Miracle's pretty dresses, she cradled the doll wrapped in bunting in one arm as she sipped a cup of tea and gazed serenely into the hearth—far removed from the harridan who had attempted to murder me with a poker a few nights before.

In that moment, I wished with every fiber of my heart that she had managed it. The very image of her with the doll roused a sense of despair and self-disgust so strong, I felt explosive.

Miracle approached me first, her red hair haloed by the firelight, her eyes sparkling like her daughter's. Despite her usual disapproval of my existence, her mien was one of enthusiasm, and I knew even before Miracle spoke that Edwina had spewed out the reason for my absence from Thorn Rose. I fixed the wench with a glower that made her blush and take a cautious retreat to the far side of the room.

"Tell us," Miracle hastened, catching one of my hands and gripping it so excitedly, my fingers throbbed. "Was there a child, sir?"

I refocused on Maria, watched as she smiled down into the doll's big blue eyes.

"Well?" Clayton moved close to my side, drawing my gaze to his. My heart slammed in my ears. Sweat rose to my brow.

"See my kitten, Uncle Duke?" Maggie trilled, forcing me to turn away from Clayton and look down as she smiled and lifted the black and white squirming kitten for my perusal. "I've named her Pepper. Isn't she simply charming?"

I stared into Maggie's innocent face, some emotion I could not fathom in that moment taking hold of my heart. Until that instant I had never appreciated the child's extreme beauty, her vivaciousness, or the reasons why my brother became a sap in her company. The idea that somewhere I had a daughter who was equally as lovely made the air suddenly too hot and heavy to endure.

Shoving aside my brother, I moved to the store of liquor and poured myself a drink, walked to the window and flung back the drapes.

The panes were damp with condensation, and I swiped it away to look out over the barren countryside that was fast being blanketed with snow. I pressed a cold, wet finger to my hot brow and felt a fresh stirring of hate for the dowager duchess, whose gloating face rose in my mind so demonic-like, I felt staggered.

I turned and looked into my brother's eyes, then took a deep quaff of the port. "So tell me . . . how are your sons, Clayton?"

Clayton and Miracle stared at me, their surprise obvious. In all the years of their marriage, I had never asked about the welfare of their children—their three sons all older than Maggie, but equally handsome.

Clayton and his wife exchanged bemused

glances before Miracle replied softly, "They're well, sir. Thank you for asking."

Edwina moved close, her expression curious and concerned. "Are you going to answer us or not, darling? What did you learn at Menson?"

I watched the child sit before the fire and nuzzle the kitten. "The boys are how old, now?" I asked, ignoring Edwina.

Clayton cleared his throat. "Sean is ten. Jason is eight. And Michael is seven."

"Happy and healthy, I assume. Certain to follow in their father's esteemed footsteps, revered and adored by all."

Clayton's eyes narrowed. "Get to the point, Trey. You've never given a damn about my children. What are you about?"

Edwina touched my arm, drawing my gaze to her eyes, which were as sharp as knife blades. With the exception of Clay, she alone recognized my moods and my thoughts before I spoke them.

She smiled encouragingly. "Maria has improved tremendously since you've been gone, darling. As docile as a kitten. She gets on particularly well with Miracle."

"It seems she's always docile as a kitten whenever I'm not around. Perhaps I would do her a tremendous favor in simply disappearing."

I moved toward Maria, the heat from the

hearth and my mounting irritation inviting a rush of fire in my blood. As I stood beside her, staring as she smiled into the doll's lifeless face, I finished my port in one deep drink, then said, "Would that please you, Maria? Would you like me to leave? Get the hell out of your life?"

She rocked the doll and hummed sweetly, stroked its matted hair. I looked down into the doll's eyes that seemed to sear into my own, an accusatory stare that caused every essence of guilt to rouse, and with it a madness as depraved as that which occupied Maria's mind.

With a curse, I snatched the doll from her arms, intent on ridding myself of all reminders that I had sacrificed her sanity, and perhaps our child, for the sake of my own and Clayton's future.

I flung the doll into the flames.

There followed a chorus of astonished cries from Edwina and Miracle, a string of expletives from Clayton. As horror washed over Maria's face, she jumped from the chair and flailed like a blind woman as she screamed for Sarah.

Slammed by my own cruelty, I stumbled back, Maria's pain wrenching me from my momentary insanity as I realized what I had done.

"Oh Christ," I groaned, and dove toward the flames, the heat searing my hands as I attempted to grab the doll that was already incinerating.

Clayton grabbed me and flung me aside, his fists gripping my lapels as he sneered in my face, "Too late, you jackass."

As Miracle hastened to calm Maria, Clayton drove me back, his teeth showing in fury. "You sick son of a bitch, what the hell are you doing? I should thrash you, you idiot. Are you attempting to destroy her completely?"

For the first time in my life I had put Clayton's happiness and welfare before my own. And before Maria's, as well. Yet in his ignorance over my behavior, he now glared at me with such loathing I wanted to kill him.

I drove my fist into his face hard enough to send him spiraling back, the sound of the awful impact turning my stomach. He sprawled on the floor, his mouth bloodied and shock glazing his eyes.

From a distance, I heard his wife cry out, drowned by Maria's continued sobs and Edwina's excited babbling. The dogs leapt to their feet, adding to the racket with their protective snarls and ear-splitting yaps.

Too much!

It all crashed upon me in a cacophony that made my head swim with confusion. I stumbled from the room, knocking aside Herbert and Iris, who were rushing into the parlor, and hurried like one chased by demons from the house, into the driving wind and snow, oblivious to the biting cold that raked at my body with freezing spears.

I ran, attempting to flee my own mania and shame as much as the women's cries of alarm.

Thorny needles of the bent firs scraped my flesh as I hastened along the slippery paths, my shins crashing through stunted brush, the image of the burning doll juxtaposed against the shock in my brother's eyes.

At last I found myself at the edge of a glassy pond, ankle-deep in the peat from the muddy shoal. There I fell upon a bench where Maria and I had once shared stolen moments, enjoying the scent of wildflowers and the serenity of gliding swans. My burned hands throbbed, and I swept up palms full of snow and curled my fingers around it, the cold temporarily easing the pain of my singed flesh.

I bowed my head and closed my eyes, listening to the silence.

Oh, that I could quiet the thoughts in my head, obliterate all but the memories of those precious moments when I had held Maria in my arms, making love to her magnificent mouth, immersing my senses in her taste and smell, the precious warmth of her body as the summer heat beat down on us as fiercely as that which had raged in our loins.

How long I remained there, I know not. Until the snow in my hands had long melted and the pain of my burns had been numbed by cold. Until my clothes and hair had become powdered with snow. Until the chill had penetrated my soul and made me shake uncontrollably.

As I opened my eyes, I looked up to find Edwina sitting beside me, tucked within her hooded cloak. There was no condemnation in her face. There wouldn't be. She was the only person in the world, besides Maria, who had ever understood my lapses into depravity, and forgave me for them.

"Are you all right?" she asked gently.

"I hit my brother," I said. "My brother. As often as I've wanted to smash him, I've never done it, until now. My God, if I ever hoped that I had the smallest inkling of decency left in my soul, I know now that I haven't. What was I thinking, to subject Maria to that cruel display, then to drive my fist into Clayton's face?"

She covered my cold hand with her own. "Something has upset you, darling. What is it?"

I pulled my hand from hers, moved to the water's edge, and stared down at the surface, dark and still beneath the thin coat of ice.

"Tell me, Edwina. Would you love me still—would you have loved me at all—had I been untitled? Had I been nothing more than a blacksmith or a carpenter or a sheep farmer? Or a miner? Would you have found as much pleasure under my body if my hands had been hardened from labor?"

"That's a silly question, Your Grace."

"Of course it is. Despite your own sordid reputation, you wouldn't have given me a nod, had I been less than a duke. Despite the fact that I have made a muck of my finances, my title would open doors and opportunities for you. Correct me if I'm wrong."

"At first," she replied, her voice cautious. "But I've since admitted to you how I feel."

"So you declare, yet I saw your repulsion when I worked the mine. You cringed when I touched you with soiled hands."

"Such menial labor is below you, darling. I was appalled that a man of your rank would stoop to such behavior. It simply isn't normal."

Turning, I looked into her eyes. "And if I now told you that I'm not a duke at all—in fact, if I were to tell you that my entire blue-blooded lineage is a lie, would you hasten back to London in search of another titled bastard to offer your child legitimacy?"

"This conversation is ridiculous. What has it got to do with anything, Trey?"

"Answer me."

She opened and closed her mouth, stared at me through lashes that were dusted with snowflakes. "I—I don't know."

"Just as I thought."

I turned back to the pond, fresh anger igniting in my chest.

Edwina moved to my side. "I fear something has happened to unsettle you. Tell me."

I drew in a deep cold breath, then said, "There is a child. A daughter. Born seven months after Maria's incarceration at Menson. The dowager duchess removed her from the asylum and sent her off. I don't know where."

"Do you intend to find her?" came the tremulous response.

Drawing my shoulders back, I replied, "No."

"FOR OUR ENTIRE ADULT LIVES, I'VE WATCHED you sully our father's good name and reputation. I've tolerated your belligerence and the embarrassment you inflicted on me by your abhorrent behavior. I don't really give a damn that you punched me. Hell, you've wanted to do it for years; get it out of your system if it will make you feel better.

"But now you confess to me that Maria had a child—your own daughter, your flesh and blood—and you have no intention of finding her, even though it may help Maria, a woman you profess to love? I've never felt more sickened to look at you, Trey. Christ, you disgust me."

His mouth swollen and his cheek bruised, Clayton paced as I slouched before the hearth fire in my bedroom, staring into the flames as I imbibed my third glass of port.

"Fine," I said. "Get the hell out. Go home and take your wife and kid and snarling mutts with you. I didn't invite you to Thorn Rose anyway. What the hell are you doing here?"

"I wanted to help in some way."

"Clayton the philanthropist. The do-gooder. Destined for sainthood. You turn up on my doorstep with food and I'm supposed to greet your generosity with great favor and appreciation, when all it does is remind me of my own failures."

"I'm your brother, for God's sake. What do you expect me to do?"

He stopped and glared at me, his expression contemptuous. "I thought when you fell in love with Maria, you had a chance at redemption. I understood from my own experience how the love of the right woman could change a man. I found that with Miracle.

"The night you told our grandmother to go to hell and rode off for Huddersfield to find Maria, I knew in my heart that you could—

would—turn your life around. I understood the anger and grief you experienced when she disappeared and you believed she had married another.

"The following years, when your character went totally to hell, I excused your behavior as belonging to a man whose heart had been totally shattered. But now you have Maria back. Granted, she's ill. But you've just discovered a cure that might save her, and you've chosen to neglect it.

"But more appalling than that—despite Maria—you have a daughter, Trey, and the fact that you don't give a damn is a blatant sin against God. I've a good mind to totally disown you."

"Be my guest."

The door opened and Miracle said, "Both of you come quickly. It's Maria."

As Clayton joined her I looked into his wife's eyes, which regarded me with as much judgment as her husband's—anger and disgust.

Clayton paused at the threshold and said, "Are you coming?"

I remained silent, and the two left the room, Clayton cursing under his breath and his wife attempting to calm him.

I sank more deeply into my chair, allowing the heat of the port to replace the cold that had earlier chilled me, allowing the inebriation to numb the emotions inflicted by my own behavior and Clayton's tirade.

He had every right to feel disgust. But it was no greater than my own.

Aye, out of resentment for my brother I had often acted like an ass.

But despite that, each time I had looked into his face, a mirror of my own, I had known a bond that had been stronger than life itself. Until the moment that I had been confronted by the dowager duchess's spiteful blackmail, I had not known the extent of that bond. I had not recognized the bond for what it truly was.

Love.

What hateful irony that I should recognize it now, when forced to choose between Clayton's happiness and reputation . . . and Maria's. How did a man destroy one love for another? I, a man who once believed himself incapable of loving, now found myself ripped apart by the emotion.

At last I roused and left the room, my steps like those of a man on his way to the gallows. Herbert, who stood outside the salon, turned his face away as I looked at him, his disrespect making my face hot and reviving the anger and frustration roiling in my gut.

Entering the salon, I stopped. Clayton, Miracle, and Edwina appeared frozen, focused on the heart-stopping image of Maria, her expression filled with sublime bliss. My body ached to turn and rush from the room in complete despair.

Precious little Maggie sat on Maria's lap, her head resting on Maria's shoulder. Maggie's tiny hands gripped one of Maria's, and she kissed it gently as she smiled up into Maria's beaming face.

"You mustn't cry anymore," the child crooned. "Promise you won't cry anymore. It makes me very sad."

"I promise," Maria said. "Never again, my darling Sarah."

❧ 15 ❧

DESPAIRING, MIRACLE WRUNG HER HANDS and looked from her husband back to me. "What shall we do? What in heaven shall we do?"

Clayton glanced at me. "Don't even think it. I shan't sell you my daughter."

My eyebrows went up and I leaned one shoulder against the door jamb and crossed my arms. We did have a dilemma.

I had cast the doll into the flames. Should I wrench little Maggie from her arms now, I might destroy Maria forever. The time had come, at long last, to do my best to convey the truth to yon frightened and confused lady.

Ignoring the glower from Maggie's father and mother, I moved cautiously across the room and sank to one knee beside Maria. The child's beaming eyes regarded me with an understanding that set me back on my heels.

Attempting a smile—something I could not normally conjure easily—I took Maggie's little hand in mine, and for the first time realized how smooth and soft and tiny were her fingers. The idea occurred to me that I had never so much as touched a child. Had barely looked at one with little more than a feeling of nuisance.

Maria's bright blue eyes turned to me, and fear replaced the shimmering glow of pleasure and heat upon her cheeks.

"Maria," I said as gently as possible. "Will you take a walk with me?"

"Certainly not," she replied.

"Just for a moment. I promise to hurry you back to Sarah."

"But why would you wish to speak to me?"

Though her eyes were bright and blue as robin's eggs, there was still a haze of confusion about them. Nay, she did not know me. She knew not that I had taken her from Menson.

Whatever wall she had erected in her mind to deal with that hellish madhouse remained yet, and with fresh vigor I wanted all the more to strangle the woman who had used my father's name for her own selfish gain.

"You see yonder friends? Miracle and Clayton? They swear to you upon the lives of their

children that they will not harm your Sarah . . .
or take her from you."

"I don't trust you, sir. In fact, I don't like
you."

I did my best to keep the frustration from
my face.

"Why, Maria? What is there about me that
you find so distasteful?"

"You . . ."—she looked away—"are far too
fierce. And hateful."

"Have I hurt you in some way?"

"Yes."

She nodded and clutched Maggie to her.
The innocence in Maria's face flashed with an
anger that made her smooth brow bead with
sweat.

"I . . . I cannot recall now. But I will and you
shall be all the more sorry for it."

I took her hand in mine. "A short walk. A
gentle talk. I ask for nothing more. 'Tis time
for honesty, Maria."

"Nay." She shook her head. "I fear there is
no honesty in your words. Only lies."

I took a deep breath. "Paul is welcome to
come if you like."

A look of anticipation brightened her face
and she looked swiftly around the room, her
gaze stopping abruptly in the shadows near
the window. A moment of silence passed,
then she nodded, albeit with trepidation.

"Very well, then. But only a short walk."

With tremendous reluctance she handed over the child to Miracle, who released a long breath of relief and hurried back to her husband.

With Herbert's help, we bundled Maria in woolen stockings and thick-soled shoes, then draped her in heavy sweaters and Miracle's cloak, which hung from Maria's narrow shoulders as if she were a child wearing her mother's coat.

I took her small hand in mine and moved toward the door. She resisted, looking back over her shoulder until she appeared certain that her companion spirit joined her.

The snow blew in gusts, and I was pleased when she huddled closer to me, as she had those years ago. We followed the footsteps Edwina and I had earlier imprinted in the white fluff, until we came to the little bench beside the pond.

She appraised it with wrinkled brow and a sharp down-turn of her red lips. Her breathing quickened.

Putting my arm around her, I held her closely, sharing my warmth, fearing she would bolt at any moment.

"Do you recall this place?" I asked her.

"No," she said with an adamant shake of her head, and I felt her tremble against me.

"We came here often."

She closed her eyes.

"I held your hand. I kissed your lips. We made love in yonder meadow."

"Nay. You're lying to me." She shook her head and retreated to the far end of the bench. "I would never lay with you, sir."

"Maria." I swallowed. "I'm Sarah's father."

Her eyes opened wide and her gaze flew across the icy pond. Her breath came in quick vaporous puffs and her hands wrung nervously.

"You lie."

"You came to Thorn Rose as a nurse. To help me. You healed me, Maria, and we fell in love."

Jumping to her feet, she glared at me with her hands curled into trembling little fists. She looked away, toward a stand of bent firs.

"He's lying. Tell me he's lying. Nay! Even you, my own brother, would defend his reasons for bringing me here?"

I slowly stood.

"Nay!" she cried, covering her ears. "He did not love me. He sent me away. She told me so. Sent me away to hide the bastard child he put in me."

"No!" I shouted.

"He chose another. He married another!"

"I chose you, Maria. 'Twas my . . ." The words

tore at my tongue. " 'Twas the dowager duchess who sent you away. I thought you went to Huddersfield. I thought you married another. I had no idea about the child."

She backed away, her world of reality shattering her wall of denial. The memories tumbled in on her, and she spun in desperation in a circle, looking for the spirit of her brother who was no longer there.

She backed away, toward the pond. "Fiend. Devil. You knew about the child. You knew! You locked me away in that dreadful place so no one would know."

"Not I, Maria. I . . . loved you."

"The child yonder, in the house. 'Tis not my own Sarah, is she?"

I swallowed and lowered my gaze. "No." I shook my head. " 'Tis my brother's child, Maria."

A look of heart-rending pain crossed her face, and she tore at her hair with her frail fingers. "What have you done with her?" she screamed. "What have you done with my Sarah?"

Cautious, I moved toward her, no longer feeling the cold bite of the wind and snow. "I vow to you that I have done nothing to your daughter, Maria. Our daughter."

"Then where is she? Give her to me now!"

Guilt pressed down on me like a mammoth weight—as if every bone in my body would snap. Maria had every right to despise me. I had never despised myself so much as I did in that moment.

The cold sliced through me like a knife and stung my eyes. The stark look of agony on Maria's face made me feel hellishly insane. Murderous.

"God damn you!" I shouted, hands clenched. "Listen to what I'm saying. I had nothing to do with this—"

She twirled away and ran onto the iced-over pond, sinking shin-deep into the snow, her cape tangling around her legs.

I called her name frantically, my heart sinking as I first heard the sharp crack of ice, and Maria tried desperately to lunge toward the snow-covered bank.

Too late.

In one horrible moment, she disappeared in the black frigid hole of the thin ice.

I ran. Stumbled. Whipped off my cape and crashed through the ice, feeling its grip upon my legs, then hips, and waist—frigid cold causing my teeth to clamp as I grabbed for Maria.

She slipped through my numbing fingers, disappearing into the dense water. I plunged again, blindly reaching until I found her.

Rising, gasping for air, the brutal bite of the

cold air intensifying the pain of my freezing body, I hauled Maria onto the shore, where we lay amid the blanket of snow, shaking, so cold that even the flakes of snow that drifted upon our faces felt warm.

She remained silent as I kissed her brow, her eyes, her cheeks. "Maria," I whispered. "What shall we do?"

Maria remained silent and limp in my arms. I watched as the snowflakes clung to her long lashes and kissed upon her lips.

There came sounds of footsteps running.

"For the love of God," Clayton called.

He bent over us, whipped up my cape from the ground and, taking Maria from my arms, wrapped it around her snugly. Then he removed his own. As I attempted to stand, he tossed the garment around my shoulders and repeated, "For the love of God. This is insanity." In a lower voice, he looked into my eyes and said, "I fear the both of you should be interred in Menson."

I didn't argue. I feared he was right.

THE HEARTH FIRE DID LITTLE TO ASSUAGE THE cold that made my bones feel achy and brittle. I sat staring into the flames as my brother wedged a snifter of port between my fingers. Herbert stood to one side, staring at me as if I were a lunatic.

Clayton turned to him.

"Are you daft, man? What the devil are you looking at? Get the hell upstairs and fetch my brother dry clothes before he catches his death."

"What have you done with Maria?" I asked, my voice hoarse.

"Edwina and Miracle are seeing to her."

"It's useless. I'm a fiend. A devil. Her ruination. She'll never forgive me. Never."

Clayton sat beside me. "Look at me."

I did so. Reluctantly.

"I want the truth from you. About the child."

Curling my cold lips, I looked him in the eyes. "Trust me, Clayton. For once in your life, trust that I'm doing the right thing."

"Trey, the right thing in your mind is too often skewed. What you perceive as right—"

"You needn't remind me that I'm a fool. I've never been so aware of it before."

"I really don't know why I continue to bother with you."

Lowering my gaze from his, I felt my face flush with heat as I sipped my port. "We're brothers. Twin souls—"

"No." He frowned. "Trey, you have no soul."

The words slammed me like a cruel fist.

Leaving my chair, my body shivering harder as I left the comfort of the fire, I moved to the window and looked out upon the black night. Snow banked upon the mullioned panes and sparkled with the reflection of the hearth fire.

"God, how you must hate me," I said.

No response.

Partially turning, I looked at my brother, his back to me. The ache of rejection bit at me as sharply as Maria's hatred for me. I, who had never given a damn about anyone's opinion but my own.

"I love you," I said.

Clayton slowly turned to stare at me.

"What?" I lifted my snifter and swirled the port round and round in the glass. "Is that so hard to believe?"

Still he said nothing.

"I suppose it is, isn't it? I haven't been the finest example of a brother. Or human being, for that matter. Is it beyond the possibility that a man can change?

"For what it's worth, I have said I love you to only one other person in my life. Maria. Ah, to love . . . and be unloved in return. 'Tis a fair retribution for the havoc I have played with people's lives."

"I don't hate you," Clayton said in a flat tone.

"No?" I smiled. "You don't hate me. You don't love me. You feel nothing. I fear that's more disturbing even than hate."

I finished my port as Herbert returned to the room, dry clothes in his arms. He refused to look at me as he helped me undress and don the dry shirt and pants. Upon collecting the wet garments, he left the room without a single utterance.

Clayton stared into the dancing flames as I returned to the chair beside him. We remained silent for a spell. I listened to the tall case clock in the foyer chime eight times, then heard the murmur of discourse between Miracle and Edwina as they approached.

Edwina entered the room, her face pale as she wrung her hands. "The young woman wishes to see you, darling."

Clayton and I exchanged looks. I cleared my throat.

"Are you certain she's not hiding a knife beneath her sheets?" I asked.

"She appears very calm."

"But is she lucid?"

Edwina lifted one finely arched brow and considered me a long moment. Then she shrugged.

"She's not raving like a banshee, if that's what you mean."

"Has she mentioned Sarah?"

"No."

"Has she mentioned me?"

She nodded. "Briefly."

I glared at her, waiting. "Well? What did she say?"

"Such language is far too blasphemous to be repeated by a lady."

Clayton snorted, causing Edwina's face to flush.

With a flounce of her skirt, she moved to the fire, her narrowed gaze fixed on my brother. "I suppose neither of you have given a thought to what this debacle means to me."

"No," we replied in unison.

She sniffed and turned one shoulder to us. "That I should be forced to watch the man I love fawn and grieve over some nose-wiping nurse—the daughter of a meager vicar; a lunatic. 'Tis insufferable! My future is questionable—"

"Spare us, Edwina. I'm hardly in the mood for your theatrics."

"Or your self-absorption," Clayton added, causing her eyes to widen.

"My self-absorption?" She tossed back her head and pointed at me. "Your brother epitomizes self-absorption. He defines selfishness. I'm expected to behave as if this debacle hasn't affected me? The man I was to marry left me at the altar—"

Clayton shook his head. "It's not as if this sham of a marriage was real. You needed a name for the child you so recklessly conceived with God knows whom, and my brother needed money. You were nothing more to one another than a means to an end."

A spasm of emotion flashed in her eyes. Her mask of contempt began a slow erosion, melting from her countenance like wax before a flame.

As her gaze moved back to mine, I was once again a witness to the feelings she had shielded during our time as lovers, and the sudden fierce blade of realization and recognition slashed at me.

I understood.

Everything.

I knew the sadness glistening upon her damp eye. The painful swelling of her wounded heart.

Leaving my chair, I took her in my arms, felt the trembling in her body that she so desperately attempted to hide.

"I understand," I whispered in her ear as I stroked her hair.

"Do you?" She swallowed. "Of course you do. That's the pity, Your Grace. The damnable pity of it all, isn't it?"

Placing one hand upon my chest, she pushed me away, lifted her chin, and allowed me a faint, brittle smile.

"What irony that we should discover now that we're both as vulnerably human as everyone else. Hearts mangled by Cupid's arrows. It would be hysterical if it weren't so remarkably pitiful."

She moved to the door. "For what it's worth, darling, I suggest that you begin again where the young woman is concerned. Few women can resist you when you're on the scent. Woo her. Praise her. Make her feel as if she's the most important element of your existence. Her happiness, of course, is your ultimate challenge."

She lay a hand upon her rounded belly and quit the room.

❧ 16 ❧

MARIA NO LONGER REGARDED ME WITH madness.

As I stood before her, watching the firelight reflect from her face—from her eyes that were hard and glittering like blue diamonds—I almost yearned for the oblivion of insanity.

"What have you done with my daughter?" she asked.

"Our daughter, Maria."

"Nay." She shook her head and her thin fingers fiercely gripped the chair arms. "The child ceased being yours the moment you chose another over me. The moment you sent me away. How handsomely did your grandmother reward you, Your Grace?"

"I'm a duke. There is little she could provide me that I didn't already have."

Her lips curved and her eyes narrowed. "As I recall, you had a proclivity for whores and gambling. A few hundred pounds would go a long way toward satisfying your debts."

"Maria—"

"And of course there is your upstanding lineage. God forbid that a bastard born of a lowly commoner's daughter would sully the Hawthornes' blue blood."

I gave her a smile as cold as her own, the irony of her words making my teeth clench.

"I assure you I would not be the first titled blue blood to father a child out of wedlock. There are, no doubt, as many illegitimate offspring of my illustrious peers as there are pampered darlings counting the seconds until their fathers stop breathing."

Her gaze followed me as I moved to a chair near her and sat down.

Maria tipped her head to one side as she appraised me, her expression one of smug pleasure.

"The years haven't been kind to you, Your Grace. You're gaunt. Graying. Your brow has been lined by your degenerate life."

She leaned toward me, her fingers digging into the chair arm. "I'm glad."

"Maria. Think rationally—"

"Rationally? Can you not recognize madness when you see it? Hatred for what it is? Your Grace, you expect me to be rational when I have languished in brutality for the last years? When I have known little but starvation and humiliation?

"You expect rationality when I have given birth amid fetid squalor, and watched helplessly as that child was torn from my arms and taken from me? If so, you're more insane that I ever was."

I looked away, my face burning at her contemptuous words. "I'm sorry."

"You're sorry."

For a brief moment the insanity came roaring back, flashing in her eyes. Her body trembled. Her breathing came in short, audible gasps.

"You're sorry. How very laughable. Did you honestly expect that with such a miserable utterance, I would forgive you?"

"No." I shook my head.

"I'll never forgive you. I'll curse your name until the day I die, Your Grace. I live for the moment when I witness the heart being ripped from your body, ravaged by fear, confusion, disillusionment, and grief. I would tear it out with my own hand if I could, and crow with pleasure as it convulses in its final struggling beat within my bloodied fingers."

"Jesus." I stood.

Maria jumped to her feet, her palm connecting with my cheek with such force I was rocked back on my heels.

Again, she struck. And again. Each blow more forceful, the fiery sting of pain more urgent.

I stood there, my feet braced apart, tasting the coppery blood upon my tongue until, exhausted, she dropped into the chair and covered her face with her hands.

"Get out! Get out!" She wept, her body rocking forward and back.

I ached to reach for her. I yearned to prostrate myself at her feet. To beg her to listen to the truth, but most of all forgive me.

'Twas not my own trespasses, but the manipulations of the dowager duchess that had brought us to this pitiful moment.

As I knuckled the thread of blood from my chin, I looked into Maria's eyes, which no longer embraced me with love and compassion. They were bright with fury and hatred.

"Were I to blame for your grotesque fate, why would I have rescued you from that dismal place? Why would I bring you back to

Thorn Rose and minister to your body and soul?"

"Perhaps your conscience gnawed at you, Your Grace."

"Would a man with such a conscience have interred you there in the first place? If I truly be the sort of beast who would subject you to the brutalities of Menson, who would deprive you of our child, you would yet be shrinking from abusive hands and existing in the vacuum of insanity—chatting with the ghost of your brother—"

"Stop!" She covered her ears with her hands; her bloodless lips quivered.

I forced myself to look away.

Conscience.

How dare I even contemplate the possibility? Had I a conscience, I would even now be searching for our daughter.

Yet here I stood, posturing like some guiltless, misunderstood victim, while the woman I loved was being torn apart with grief for her child.

What a despicable fraud I was.

AH, TORTURE. IT WAS ALL TORTURE.

Torment. Refined to some twisted, self-inflicted brutality that kept me pacing throughout the night—shivering still from the cold of the frigid water from which I had rescued Maria.

Chill crawled under my skin. Scraped at my bones. Thickened my blood until my heart became a weight that felt crushing within my chest. Chill filled up every corner of my bedroom, despite the hearth flames licking at the darkness.

My mounting anger ignited a fire of indignation that Maria, even in her sane moments, would think me the kind of man who would subject her to such misery and grief. One word spoken from her lips, one glance from her eyes could so easily slay me without drawing a single drop of blood from my veins.

Useless. Pure folly to even attempt a conciliation with her.

Thanks to the dowager duchess, I had made an eternal enemy of the only woman I had ever loved—would ever love. This I knew to the marrow of my bones.

I coughed and shivered. Despite the chill that crawled through my body, sweat rose in beads upon my forehead. Heat had begun to coil in my chest, its tentacles creeping through my lungs and squeezing gradually harder and harder until, just before dawn's light forced its way through the bleak, snow-heavy clouds, I collapsed on my bed, exhausted by my frantic pacing and the mounting burden of breathing.

The candles had burned low. The hearth fire had diminished until only embers glowed and hissed as they expired. The hours passed. The condensation that had formed on the windowpanes became ice crystals.

Yet I felt afire.

CURSED SANITY.

As the hours passed, the days crawling by in isolation, Maria yearned with desperation for the insanity that had allowed her to escape within her mind. There the gentle caress of oblivion brought her peace. Peace from the fear, the pain, the heartache. And the hatred. Only within that oblivion would Paul come to her.

Paul—what folly! His presence had been nothing more than an aberration born of her madness. Paul—the only human in her life who had ever truly loved her.

Nay, her mother had not loved her—a weak and pitiful creature so fearing of her husband that she would shrink and quiver as he espoused his fire and brimstone declarations on his children.

Nay, her father, the fierce Vicar of Huddersfield, had not loved her. Had not loved his son. They were objects to be loathed and be-rated. Seeds of Satan spawned by his weak-ness for lust.

How desperate she must have been, to be-lieve that a man such as Hawthorne would truly love her. How naive, to believe he would defy the obligations of his title and lineage to commit his life to a mere vicar's daughter.

Ah, but she had loved him. Despite the madness that had once turned him into a beast.

Nay, not madness, but an infirmity brought on by a wound to his head inflicted by high-waymen who had robbed him and left him for dead. The world thought him mad. She had not.

She had loved him even as the dowager duchess's coach bore her away from Thorn Rose, and Salterdon. How often, as she rotted away in her dismal cell, did she recall that night, standing face to face with the ashen-cheeked old woman whose loathing had been palpable enough to cause Maria to tremble in her presence.

"You'll ruin him.

"You'll make him a laughingstock.

"Your children will be ridiculed. Mocked. They'll go through their lives scorned by their peers.

"If you truly love him . . .

"If you honestly desire his happiness . . .

"He doesn't love you. You must know that. This emotion he's experiencing is nothing more than gratitude for your nursing him back to normality. This . . . lust he experiences is simply the carnal cravings of the male beast.

"What will you do when he finally acknowledges these feelings for what they really are? Will you content yourself to languish, loveless, within the isolation of Thorn Rose while he contents himself with his mistresses?"

The old woman had cocked her head to one side and her eyes had glistened with a malevolence that had jolted Maria.

"Perhaps I'm making too much of it all. I doubt that he would marry you anyway. Perhaps he'll plunk you in a Mayfair town house, to crawl between your lovely young legs when he's in London.

"But he'll grow tired of you eventually, as he does all of his pretty little slatterns. He'll cut you off financially, and where will you be?

"How will you survive?

"No decent man will marry another man's whore."

Her thin lips had curled.

"Leave here, young woman. Now. No goodbyes. Vanish. By the time you arrive back at Huddersfield he will have forgotten you, as he has a hundred others.

"Let this be a lesson to you, lest you make the same mistake twice. I know of no man who is capable of love. 'Tis the rutting they crave, and nothing more."

The door opened and Maria ceased her pacing. The woman called Edwina entered the room, a breakfast tray in her hands. She placed it on a table, next to the tray that contained the untouched meal the maid had delivered the night before.

Edwina gave Maria not the briefest glance as she turned to quit the chamber.

"Who are you?" Maria demanded.

The woman froze.

Gradually, Edwina turned to face her, her usual contempt for Maria displaced by a mien of distress. She placed one hand upon her rounded belly, her lips parting slightly as she grimaced.

"Are you Salterdon's wife?" Maria asked.

"Wife?" Her lips quivered. "You dreadful little beast. How dare you feign such ignorance? You know perfectly well who I am. Please spare me your insane theatrics; you're as lucid as I."

"Answer me."

"What difference does it make?"

"I wonder if you're the reason I've spent the last years languishing in Menson."

Maria's gaze shifted again to Edwina's belly,

and a fresh spasm of pain and anger rushed through her. "The child. 'Tis his, isn't it?"

Edwina's eyes narrowed as Maria approached her.

"Mayhap you're only his whore." She laughed. "Mayhap the dowager duchess spoke truthfully that night."

"I don't know what you're talking about. Get away from me." Edwina backed toward the door.

"Where is Salterdon? I want to see him."

"Why? So you can attempt to claw out his eyes again?"

"Fine. I'll find him myself."

"You'll do no such thing."

Edwina planted her feet, blocking the doorway. "Leave him alone. You've caused enough damage. Had it not been for you, we would be married now."

"Ah." Maria smiled. "So you *are* only his whore."

Edwina's enormous, frantic eyes were like a lance to Maria's heart. Her own devotion, the mindless, heart-stopping emotion she had once felt for Salterdon, cut into her heart with such pain that tears roused in her eyes. Edwina saw them—yes, because Maria could not stay their course down her cheeks.

"Stay away from him," Edwina declared

with a trembling voice. "I shan't allow you to harm him any more than you already have."

"I? Harm him?" Maria lifted her chin, refusing to swipe the scalding tears from her cheek. "The idea is ludicrous."

"He's dying."

The words stopped Maria short.

Her hands fisted, tears streaming down her cheeks, Edwina let out a sob. "I fear he cares little if he lives or dies, thanks to you."

In that instant Maria's every nerve felt unstrung, beyond her mastery to control. What did it mean?

"What are you saying, woman? Speak! Nay, you will not speak, because 'tis a lie. 'Tis nothing but his vile manipulations; I don't believe you. Now tell me where he is!"

"He's been ravaged by fever the last three days. We can't control it. We've summoned the physician from Haworth. But Jules Goodbody is a bungling, inebriated idiot who actually suggested we prepare to confine his body to the family mausoleum.

" 'Summon the vicar,' he told us. 'Pray for his soul, for if anyone on this earth cries out for absolution from his sins, 'tis His Grace.' "

Edwina stepped toward Maria until they stood toe to toe, eye to eye.

Maria felt the heat of Edwina's body. Her

trembling hand grasped Maria's, vise-like, her short nails cutting into Maria's palm.

"This must please you. You want him to die. Admit it."

Maria could not respond. Why? Why! Why did the possibility of Salterdon's passing so painfully swell upon her heart?

Nay, it was not grief. She loathed him!

Unfeeling, lying fiend!

Nay, she did not still love him. 'Twas folly to have cared for him before. Folly to have believed his words of adoration. Folly to have melted beneath his touch. Folly to have allowed him to seduce her into believing that he would sacrifice all to marry her.

Her heart felt rent. Some hateful emotion roused within her, filling up her throat so she could not swallow. It settled like fiery embers in her eyes, inviting tears that she fought unsuccessfully to stop.

"He shan't die!" she suddenly cried. "He cannot!"

Surprise widened Edwina's eyes. Some queer desperation made her cover her lips with one hand, her body shaking.

"You love him still," Edwina whispered.

The words stunned Maria. Frantically, she shook her head, causing the tears to spill down her cheeks. Confusion muddled her thoughts.

"Nay, I do not love him still. 'Tis . . ."

She swallowed and smeared the trickles of dampness across her cheeks with a trembling hand.

" 'Tis only . . . He cannot die. Not yet. Not until he's confessed to me the whereabouts of my daughter."

Maria shoved Edwina aside and fled through the open door.

❦ 17 ❧

MOMENTARILY, SHE PAUSED. AS IF SHE had stumbled through a portal into a past that she had long since buried deep within that insanity, unleashed memories came rushing upon her.

'Twas all familiar to her now.

She knew the way to Salterdon's bedroom. The recollections hammered at her skull, the many steps she had taken down the long gallery those years ago, driven by some emotion to heal him. Unafraid of his madness, driven day after day to look upon his face, finding naught but pleasure in his garbled words and fierce temperament.

The world had deemed him a beast.

Yet . . . yet, *then* she had had the capacity for compassion.

Then she had looked beyond the monstrous facade of the man; witnessed his vulnerability, his pain, his anguish; recognized there beat within his bosom a heart that was misunderstood.

Stop! Cease this hateful and unwelcome reminiscence!

She did not love him.

She did not care that he suffered. 'Twas God's punishment for the hell he had put her through.

She would coerce from him the truth about their daughter. Nothing more!

Traversing the hall, she noted the pictures on the walls: long deceased ancestors, grim men and pompous women with powdered hair and lavish jewels, whose stern gazes were as lifeless in life as they were in their crypts.

She passed a great oak clock, enormous in height, whose case was carved and black with time and rubbing. At the very moment of her passing, it knelled.

The deep sound reverberated through the empty hall and seemed to strike with its brass hammer upon her heart. A chilled and vault-like air suddenly pervaded the corridor. The burning girandoles on the walls cast an odd, gyrating light as if they were disturbed by some fleeing, unseen entity.

At last Maria came to his bedroom.

She halted there a moment, her hand upon the knob as the memories burned more brightly, blinding in their brilliance.

She squared her shoulders and entered the room.

The invalid's companions looked at her with pale faces, and their eyes widened as if some spectre had appeared.

Yet no one spoke.

Clayton stood at his brother's bedside, his wife near, while Iris bent over His Grace and cooled his sweating face with a damp cloth.

Cautiously, Maria moved through the shadows, to Trey's bedside.

She was unprepared.

Maria had not imagined that she would tremble in such a way when she saw him.

Yes, she had shaken with anger, and shivered with fear and pain and disgust while in his presence. But this . . . *emotion* felt traitorous and befuddling.

Panic seized her.

A fist of fiery steel grasped her vitals: a hateful warring of sentiment full of struggle. Love and hate gnashed at one another within her breast and her thoughts clamored for reasoning.

Escape! Now!

He is the cause of your misery!

He is the reason your life became an unending nightmare.

She had looked upon death's grim countenance only once in her life—the instant before the soul of her beloved Paul had slipped from its earthly chamber and reached for Heaven.

Clayton and Miracle stepped aside, allowing Maria to move closer.

She looked into Iris's eyes, noted the sparkling tears there before she backed away, clutching the damp cloth to her enormous bosom.

Nay, he had not yet succumbed. His chest rose with shallow breaths, each a sound like iron grating upon iron.

Help him, came the whisper from the shadowed corner of the vast chamber, startling her.

Paul! He was with her yet. Not a spirit contrived by her lunacy. Yet how shocking and frightening it seemed in that moment.

Maria, you must help him. Only you can save him.

Her faculties roused and she turned sharply to point at the pitifully weak flames within the hearth.

"Stoke the fire," she ordered. Then to Iris, "Collect several of your most dense bedcovers and place them over His Grace. And the lot of you, out. Get out."

"Do you think I'll leave my brother with you unattended?" Clayton asked. "Good God, woman, you've attempted to murder him—"

"Would I murder the man without learning the whereabouts of my daughter?"

She narrowed her eyes as she looked from pale face to face. "Unless you know the truth about my daughter. Do you? The devil is in you if you do not answer me truthfully."

She glared at Clayton. "Reply, damn you. What have you to say?"

He set his gray gaze steady and fixed upon hers. "We don't know any more than you, Maria. We only just learned about the child—as did Trey. 'Tis my grandmother who holds the secret. My brother is innocent in all this."

"You're a bloody liar."

Maria turned away. "Of course you would not give me the truth now—else I would leave this room and let him pass. May the lot of your souls go to hell. Now get out. I shan't lay a healing palm upon him until you do."

Clayton's wife gently grasped her husband's arm. "Come away, Clay. Let them alone."

"You're as daft as she is, if you think—"

"Husband, your brother tarries at death's door. She has little choice but to help him now."

Clayton moved up behind Maria. "And then what, lass? Will you sweat the truth from his dying lips, then smother him with yonder pillow?"

He laid a hand upon her shoulder, and she flinched. She would have drawn away, but his grip held her as if by some magical force.

"I knew you when you were innocent and kind, and believed only the good in your fellow man. You saw beyond my brother's calloused shell to the human capable of loving you. You, above all others, exuded Christian benevolence even upon the most lost of souls."

"And where did it get me?" she said. "Interred in wickeddom."

Silence.

At last, he moved away.

Maria listened as the room emptied. Moments later Iris returned with the bedcovers, which she placed upon Salterdon. Herbert followed, stoking the fire until the flames licked like dragon tongues along the stone hearth, until Salterdon's countenance shone with sweat and the room radiated with light red as the womb of Hell.

Maria sat upon a stool at the foot of the duke's bed after the servants left, her hands gripped fiercely together in her lap as the heat made her body wet and her lungs burn.

Then she heard him groan.

She moved to his side.

As she watched, a glow spread across his waxen, hueless face. Sweat saturated his hair and beaded upon his cheeks' contours.

How weak and pitiful he looked!

She spun away and covered her face with her hands. Glad she should be, at his suffering! Yet . . .

What hateful, niggling feelings squirmed in her heart. What unwelcome memories roused with dreaded clarity.

His smiling face . . . his gentle touch . . . his tender kiss.

Help him, came that familiar whisper, closer now, so near that the words felt like a breeze upon her cheek.

Frantic, Maria turned. The room remained empty.

"Show yourself!" she cried.

Silence.

"Why, suddenly, do you hide from me, Paul?"

Silence.

She moved to the window and tossed aside the heavy drapes. The heat caused the ice to melt upon the panes, and beyond, the night lay black and frigid and still.

"Where are you? Show yourself! Prove to me that you exist and have never been a figment of my lunacy!"

Have faith.

"Faith? Brother, I have long since lost faith."

Nay, you've not lost faith, Maria. 'Tis faith alone that has kept you alive.

Maria closed her eyes and rested her forehead against the pane. "You kept me alive, Paul. No other. Yet now you taunt me. You withhold your beautiful, beloved face from me.

"Why will you not help me now? If it's true what they say, that the man dying on yon bed is innocent of abandoning me to that dreaded asylum, why have you not said so? If you do indeed exist, why will you not reveal the truth about my daughter?"

She turned back to the vacant, sweltering room. "I'll tell you why: because you don't exist. Not since you died in my arms those many years ago. You're nothing more than the lingering hallucinations of a maniac."

Silence again.

Her gaze darted around the room, a sense of panic rising within her.

"Paul? Paul! Are you there? I . . . I didn't mean it. Don't leave me. I simply want the truth. I want to understand."

Maria waited, the quiet pressing down on her.

At last, she turned and moved toward the bed, each step hesitant, her body feeling cumbersome and wooden. Her heart felt as chilled and void as the night beyond the window.

Wretched faith! Faith had caused her suffering, filling her endless days and nights spent pacing her filthy stone cell, praying to a God who had abandoned her.

Why? Why? Why? she had uttered in the darkness.

She, who had practiced only goodness and tolerance all of her young life.

She, who had never uttered so much as an unkind word, never lifted an ungentle finger against even the most loathsome of insects.

She, who had practiced patience and understanding at her father's cruelty and domination.

But after an agony so lingering that death ought to have been a welcome blessing, she had at last closed the eyes of that departed, spiritless faith, and with great calm, had embraced madness.

Salterdon rolled his head from side to side, his fever stoked by the sweltering air.

Help him.

Maria covered her ears with her hands, as if the act would somehow vanquish the voice in her mind.

Touch him.

"Nay, I will not! The man is loathsome to me!"

He's lost. Lost. All hope and faith is lost to him—

"Then let him die."

Save him, Maria. Save yourself.

Suddenly Salterdon's eyes sprang open. He fixed her with pupils that were glassy and afire. His lips parted, and he whispered, "Maria."

And she seemed to hear a sound like music.

The tune that had haunted her thoughts for month upon month. It had played over and over in her mind, soothing her and lancing her, inviting fond visions that tore her heart in two.

Maria's Song.

He had composed it those years ago when he, lost of his faculties, unable to communicate, had reached out to her in the only way he could. Each stroke of the ivory key had become a gentle caress upon her soul.

What fiend played it now?

She fled to the door and threw it open, then stepped into the empty hallway.

No music here. It resided only in her mind—yet another wicked trickery of her memory.

Maria returned to the room and took a chair near Salterdon's bedside. His eyes closed again, his body writhed beneath the burden of the heat that bore down on him, and within him. His lungs rattled with every breath.

The distant case clock struck midnight. And time passed.

Later it struck one. Then two.

Upon each hour she roused and stoked the fire, feeling its heat singe her flesh and soak her garment with sweat until she yearned to throw open the window and relieve her own suffering.

Yet another hour stole over her, and she dozed.

Suddenly a chill kissed her cheek and arms and she awoke, uneasy. She rose as if lifted by some unseen force—frigid fingers upon the back of her neck, guiding her to Salterdon's bed.

Silent and still he lay, his eyes wide and staring, his face colorless.

The duke, friend, lover, fiend, was dead!

An eddying darkness seemed to swirl round her, and some emotion roused in her bosom. Fear. Yes! Grief. No, no, not grief. Surely not grief.

Yet she had no strength to deny the traitorous grief. A prayer rushed to her lips.

"Dear Heavenly God, spare him."

She placed a trembling hand upon his brow—warm yet, warm, and closed her eyes.

"Dear Heavenly God, spare him."

Beyond the windowpanes the wind moved through the nearby boughs of trees, groaning like a thousand souls. The terrifying yet beautiful sound filled the room, and Maria cried out again and again, entreating the bodiless angels to save the once-cherished master of her heart.

The windowpanes trembled. Flames within the hearth heaved with fresh vigor, their luminescence splashing upon the walls like nymphs dancing.

What frightening energy besieged her! Fire and wind. The song of souls. It swept through her body and down her arm, and as she flung back her head, a vision radiated above her in a blinding white light.

Paul! His brilliant blue eyes smiled at her. His beloved face—so distinct—was as beautiful as God Himself.

Faith, Maria. 'Tis with you yet. Never doubt Me. I live within you, and you in I. I shall show you miracles yet.

The vision faded, drawn down some spiraling white abyss into an indefinite distance, where it died. *He* was gone. The wind was gone. The singing of souls—all gone.

The man beneath her hand moved. His eyelids quivered.

Salterdon lived.

Gratitude swelled in Maria's heart and she fell to her knees at his bedside, her hands clasped at her breast.

The bedroom door burst open and hurried footsteps approached.

"What the devil is going on in here?" Salterdon's brother demanded.

Miracle swept around Maria and hurried to Trey's bedside. "His fever is broken!"

"Thank God," Clayton declared.

Maria closed her eyes and whispered, "Thank God."

≈ 18 ≈

MARIA REMAINED AT SALTERDON'S BEDSIDE throughout the night as he slept.

Sunday morning dawned bright, glistening from the snow and ice. Maria gazed wearily out on the blanketed landscape as Clayton and Miracle donned their heavy capes and prepared to set off for the church, whose steeple shone like Heaven's beacon on the distant horizon.

"We have a great deal to give thanks for this morning," Miracle said.

"Edwina, are you certain you don't care to join us?" Clayton asked.

Maria turned her head and regarded Edwina's reflection in the mirror on the wall. The woman's pale face appeared as fatigued as her own. And something else. Sadness and despair lined her brow. Her shoulders rose and fell as she took a deep breath to respond.

"I'm certain that should I step upon the threshold, the roof would fall in. I think not, Clayton."

"Suit yourself."

Clayton moved up behind Maria and put a gentle hand on her shoulder. "We shan't be long, lass. Will you be all right?"

She nodded, her gaze fixed again on the distant spire.

I will show you miracles yet.

"Good. We'll see you in a spell. And . . . thank you again, Maria."

" 'Tis God you should be thanking," she replied.

"Of course."

Clayton and Miracle quit the room, and silence filled it up.

Maria watched the coach, drawn by high-prancing white horses, depart the manor to be soon swallowed by the moor.

She opened the window, allowing the brisk air to kiss her cheeks as she turned her face into the sun and closed her eyes.

Now the faint sound of church bells touched upon her ears, as did the cawing of rooks that lined the sunken stone walls surrounding the house. Their glossy black wings sparkled under the sunlight.

"I'm freezing," Edwina snapped.

Maria closed the window, turned away from the picturesque vision, and moved once again to Salterdon's bed.

She stretched one hand out to touch his forehead.

Nay, she would not touch him. Her emotions were too keen and disturbing. The blind hatred that had gnawed at her the last years had vanished, replaced by the unwelcome emotion of remembered fondness.

Fickle heart!

Cursed sanity!

"You love him again, don't you?" Edwina asked.

Maria's gaze shifted to Edwina's eyes—so full of despair—then to her rounded belly. A fresh and sharp pain stroked her heart.

"Of course you do." Edwina approached. Her lips quivered. "He's not an easy man to love in some respects. But love him we do. Yes. Love him and hate him, as well. He's an . . . addiction. Precious poison. There's something about men such as Salterdon, who beg us to tame the beast. We crave the unattainable."

Edwina paused momentarily and placed a hand upon her belly.

"The child moves?" Maria asked.

"Yes."

Edwina joined her at the bedside. Before

she could stop herself, Maria placed her palm upon the woman's rounded womb and, as if in response, the tiny being moved against her fingers.

Edwina gasped and a shiver ran through her, causing her body to jerk.

" 'Tis a boy," Maria whispered.

"How do you know?"

"I feel his heart beat. 'Tis strong and fierce. What month—"

"April."

Maria returned to the window. Emotion closed off her throat momentarily.

"April. Sarah was born in April. 'Tis a fine month for a child to be born."

Silence. Then . . .

"I know about Sarah."

Slowly, Maria turned to face her.

"I know all about her. I've known all along."

Maria stared into Edwina's eyes, her breath trapped within her lungs.

Edwina drew in a deep breath, then slowly released it, her shoulders slumping as she averted her gaze. "The child is dead, Maria."

Wretched pain roused within her—she clutched her bosom; the room spun.

Suddenly Edwina's arms were around her, helping her to a chair. She sank upon it and covered her face with her hands.

"Trey knew, of course. We all knew. We

didn't dare tell you. You were too fragile. He feared the news would completely destroy you."

Edwina sank to her knees beside the chair and took Maria's hand between hers. Tears ran from her eyes as she continued, every word rending Maria's existence. Sarah, dead. Dear Merciful God—

"The child died a few weeks after birth. Despite what you think, she was well taken care of until the end."

"No," Maria sobbed. "Not my precious Sarah."

"I'm sorry. Dreadfully sorry."

Maria jumped from the chair and fled to the window, shoved it open, and took great gulps of cold air.

"We were at the altar when the nurse arrived with the news of your whereabouts— and that Trey's grandmother had known all along that you were in Menson. The dowager duchess had little choice but to confess all. That she had interred you there. That there had been a child conceived, and that she had died."

The rooks rose from the stone wall in a great black cloud of popping wings. The church bells no longer knelled.

"Of course he was obliged to free you from that horrible madhouse. He had loved you very much, once. But eventually, he moved on. We fell in love. I fully understand how you must feel."

"No. No, you could never understand how I feel."

"Of course I do. Am I not now in the same situation? Bearing the child of the man I love? Unmarried? Lost for want of his affections? Your presence here has confused him. He feels responsible for your hysteria."

Edwina moved up behind her. "I beg you. Be gone from Thorn Rose, Maria. Let him go and allow him to love again. I ask it for our child. Our . . . son. You're yet a young woman, while I—"

"Stop!"

Maria turned on her, her fists clenched and shaking.

Her desperate eyes overflowing with tears, Edwina wept, "I'm sorry. So sorry."

"Where is she buried? Tell me! Where is my daughter buried?"

"I—I don't know. What does it matter? She's with God now. With Paul."

"Paul?" Maria narrowed her eyes, and Edwina backed away.

As suddenly as the despair had risen in her heart, an odd numbness filled her. She no longer cared to look into Edwina's beseeching eyes. No longer cared to look upon the countenance of her old friend, lover, father of her sweet, departed Sarah.

Maria quit the room, barely feeling the coldness of the long hallway as she moved woodenly to her own chamber, shoulders squared and chin level. The drapes in her room were closed. The hearth, black and empty.

Shivering with cold, she stood in the center of the room and clutched herself, the monster of delirium and delusion once again yawning in her mind, beckoning with skeletal finger.

Come with me, Maria. 'Tis safe here. Warm. Dark. No more pain. No more memories.

Have faith, Maria!

"Paul, Paul, why didn't you tell me?"

Maria, come. No more heartbreak. No more lies. I will show you miracles yet.

"Hateful miracles!" She wept as she fell onto the bed and closed her eyes.

"Miss? Miss Ashton?"

Maria opened her eyes; blinked sleepily. No darkness. No warmth. She rolled to her back and looked into Iris's wide eyes.

The round little maid wrung her hands as she stood near a window, the drapes now open, and regarded Maria from a distance. "I hate to disturb ye, lass. But someone 'as come for ye."

Maria frowned and sat up. Her head throbbed

and her eyes felt abraded. How long had she slept? Not long. The morning sun still spilled with golden radiance through the east window-panes.

"Someone to see me?"

The servant nodded. "Aye. Says it's right important."

"Who is it?"

"Wouldn't say, miss. Just that it be a matter of life and death."

Who would come for her here?

Why?

Suspicion roused as Maria slid from the bed.

" 'Ere now." Iris reached for the woolen shawl tossed over a chair back. "Best ye bundle in this. 'Tis dreadful cold. Let me put this round yer shoulders, miss; yer shiverin' some-thin' terrible. Can't have ye gettin' ill again. 'Is Grace would skin me alive for allowin' it."

The shawl felt heavy and warm and wel-come as Iris wrapped it around her. "How is His Grace?"

"Sleepin' deeply, still. Lady Edwina be with 'im, o'course."

With some reluctance, Maria followed the maid from the room, down the long corridor, descending the staircase, her gaze locking on the man bundled in cloak and hat, shuffling his muddy boots on the marble foyer floor.

Iris made a quick exit as Maria hesitated on the bottom step.

The man peered at her from the shadow of his hat.

"Who are you?" Maria asked.

"I be here to speak to Miss Ashton. Maria Ashton."

"What do you want with her?"

He moved closer. "I'll speak with Miss Ashton if ye don't mind."

Maria drew her shoulders back and stepped from the stair. "I am Maria Ashton."

She felt the discomfiting impact of his perusal as he regarded her at length.

"Nay, ye ain't Maria Ashton of Huddersfield," he finally said. "I know the lass. Ye ain't her."

Maria moved closer, eyes narrowing as she attempted to regard his face, lined and weathered like old leather. "I am Maria Ashton. From Huddersfield."

"Daughter of the vicar?"

"Aye." She nodded.

He stepped nearer still, until she could clearly see the stubble of his gray beard and smell his aroma of ale and tobacco.

"Demn me, 'tis you," he said. "I wouldna known ye, lass. Wot the divil have ye come to?"

"Who are you? And why are you here?"

"Name is Ralf. Ralf Joiner, lass. D'ya not recognize me?"

"No."

"I keep the church grounds fer yer da. The Vicar of Huddersfield."

Her father.

Nay, she did not recognize the man. His name tickled no familiarity in her mind. Suspicion roused within her and she cast a look toward the door through which Iris had disappeared.

He clamped one hard, scarred hand upon her wrist, and she gasped, attempted to back away, yet he held her with desperation.

"I've a message from yer father," he said in little more than a whisper.

She attempted to yank her arm away and fear made her heart beat fast. "I don't believe you. Let me go."

"Miss, he's askin' fer ya. Yer father—"

"Let me go or I'll scream!"

"He's dyin', lass."

Maria stilled.

"Aye, lass. He's bad ill. The entire village be ill, it seems."

He looked past Maria, up the stairs.

She turned and saw Edwina there, her fingers clutching her velvet skirt and her face wan.

"This is some trick, isn't it?" Maria demanded.

"I don't know what you're talking about," Edwina replied.

" 'Tis true, lass."

She looked again at the man, and he removed his hat. "Don't ya recognize me, Miss Ashton? I tend the church's gardens, and me and me sons dig the graves at cemetery. Ralf, lass. Yer brother Paul called me Digger."

A sense of desperation rising in her, Maria searched his old face. Yes. Yes, it was coming back to her now. How he had aged, the last years! Once strong of body, he now appeared almost frail, his shoulders bent.

"How did my father know that I'm here?" she asked.

"Don't know, lass. He just called me to his bedside and cried to make haste to Haworth, and Thorn Rose. Said ya would be here. Said he must see ya afore he passes."

He shuffled his feet and twisted the hat in his hands. "I've brought his conveyance, Miss. If we hurry, we might make it afore nightfall."

Her father dying. How strangely the words affected her. She had despised him, cursed him. Blamed him for her pitiful mother's suffering. Yet . . . some odd emotion gripped her heart as she thought of him failing.

Slowly, she turned to look at Edwina.

What of Salterdon?

Pray, what did it matter?

All they had once shared, was dead.

Dead!

Sarah. Her blessed, beautiful Sarah, gone.

Everything was gone. Before her, dressed in emerald velvet, her belly swollen with Salterdon's child, stood a woman whose eyes showed the suffering of circumstance.

She turned to the old man. "Very well. Let's be off."

MARIA'S GRIEF AT HER MOTHER'S PASSING HAD been eased by ghostly Paul, who assured her that the dear lady had taken her place among the sainted souls of Heaven. Indeed, she must have found great relief and peace there—away from her husband's tyrannical behavior.

Mary Ashton had not been a happy woman. Few times had Maria and her brother witnessed a smile upon her lips. Yet her stern mien had not so much frightened them, as saddened them. She had been as much a prisoner of the vicar's fire and brimstone rants as her children. She had deserved so much more.

These thoughts drifted through Maria's mind as the coach in which she and Ralf rode bumped along the well-traveled road.

The canals curved through the Southern Pennines like the black, slick back of a serpent. Along the deep rich hillocks, the sheep grazed contentedly, snuffing through the snow for bits of coarse weed and gorse for nourishment. Come spring, their lush wool would be shorn to be spun in the mills of

Huddersfield, and sold throughout all England as the finest wool money could purchase.

Why had she returned here? She had fled Huddersfield to rid her life of her father's constant torment. She should care little if he lived or died.

How had he known that she resided at Thorn Rose?

Had he known, all the years of her confinement at Menson, that she languished there with criminal lunatics?

Why appease him now on his deathbed, when he had caused her family nothing but grief and fear? Why now should she forgive him his trespasses?

Darkness fell heavily upon them, as did the teeth-chattering cold. At long last, the conveyance stopped at the gate of what once had been Maria's meager home, little more than a cottage, roof covered over by ivy and the barren, twisted arms of trees. Its bleak, blackening facade and dark windows reflected the metal welkin, and upon the weathered door had been painted a yellow cross.

She knew the symbol; the same cross had been branded upon their door during the illness that had swept through Huddersfield those many years ago—taking the life of her precious, suffering Paul.

She quickly looked around at the cottages

surrounding her father's house. Dark, too, were their homes, with little light shimmering beyond their windows. And there as well glowed the yellow crosses upon the doors, symbolizing advancing death.

Resistance roused inside her. She had hoped to never set eyes upon the vicar again. He had branded her a harlot long before she understood the term. She, as pure as a child could want to be, was branded a harlot simply because she had been born female.

Had he brought her here for one last soul-lashing sermon? Would he curse her soul to Hell with his dying breath?

Hell could not possibly be any more frightening or painful than Menson.

With a deep breath she ventured forth, her boots crunching into the snow as she moved to the old gate that swung and creaked with each biting gust of wind.

Along the eroding gray stone wall surrounding the cottage, the ravens lined up like black-suited soldiers, feathers fluffed against the freeze until a sudden billowing of her cloak made them take to the sky in a great cloud of cawing and thumping wings.

She watched as they circled the house, round and round, and the unpleasant realization shimmered up her spine that they were waiting . . . waiting for the Vicar of Huddersfield to die.

Waiting to escort his soul to perdition.

She did not knock, but shoved open the door and entered the room where a single lamp was lit upon a table, a meager flickering that did little to warm the air.

The cottage was just as she remembered it: a little room with whitewashed walls and a partially carpeted floor, several simple but comfortable chairs, two of which faced the fire, and two at the table where they had eaten their meals in total silence. Against the north wall stood a case clock, the hands indicating a few minutes past seven o'clock. Nearby was a cupboard, exhibiting the simple dishes that had been her mother's most prized possessions—delicate white china that had been given to her by her mother upon her passing.

To the right of the little room in which Maria stood frozen motionless, more by dread than by cold, was a narrow staircase. The banisters had been removed once the vicar discovered that his children found pleasure in sliding down them. Up the stairs were three cramped, windowless chambers for sleep, each with a bedstead and chest of drawers.

The stench of death assaulted her, the odor of dust and decay. She quickly covered her nose with one hand and focused on the bed that had been moved close to the hearth.

Hateful emotions rose in her at the sight of

her father, his pale, wasted body and hands so frail they appeared skeletal. And his eyes—pits of fear and despair—fixed upon her face with such emotion, she wanted to flee the cottage.

No true man of faith would appear so frightened of death!

With a wheezing breath, he clamped one cold hand around her wrist, and whispered, "Forgive me."

❦ 19 ❧

THE DOOR CLOSED BEHIND HER, AND SHE WAS alone with the man whom she had so loathed and feared for most of her life.

"Maria, you came," he said, struggling for his next breath. "I prayed that you would."

She twisted her arm free and backed away, clutching her cloak closely to her body, chilled by the cold and the apparition of death she could sense hovering near his emaciated body.

One gnarled hand lifted toward her, and she shrank away. He had never lifted a hand in kindness toward her, her mother, or Paul, and she felt overwhelmed by his hypocrisy. Her hands curled into fists and she fought the overwhelming need to turn and leave the house, to allow him to die alone in his misery.

"Closer, girl. You have no need to fear me

any longer. Can you not see that I'm wasted?" He coughed and blood bubbled through his lips. "Closer. Near me. Stand near me. I haven't long . . ."

"Why now?" she demanded, refusing to move nearer. "Why have you not given a moment's thought of me the last years? Did you not realize that I—"

"Forgive me. 'Tis all I ask."

He blinked at her, limp, wheezing, a bloodless cadaver with slack mouth and eyes grown dim of life.

"Forgive you?" She shook her head. "You cry out to me to come to you, knowing you would place my own life in jeopardy?"

"I could not die alone."

"Where are your parishioners now?" she demanded. "Did they finally see you for the cruel bastard that you are?"

His eyes narrowed briefly, and he turned his head away from her. "Cruel child."

"Child? I'm no longer a child, sir. Far from it." Despite her resolve, she neared the bed. "Look at me."

"Nay, I won't. The hate in your eyes pains me. I ask for your forgiveness only. To die with a clear conscience."

"A clear conscience? Have you prostrated your pitiful body upon the graves of your son and wife and begged their forgiveness? Have you ever given them a moment's thought, offered a prayer since you lay their poor bodies in the ground? Have you recited even a solitary monody for their passing?"

"Cruel, cruel girl."

"Aye." Maria nodded as she stood over him. "I am cruel, sir. If I tell you of my own living hell the last years, would you shake your fist at me and declare my torment God's judgment for my childhood disobedience? For placing my own young body between you and my mother to protect her from your beatings?"

She took his gaunt face in her trembling hand and forced it around so she could look into his eyes.

"Tell me, vicar. How did you come to know that I was at Thorn Rose?"

Silence, then . . .

" 'Twas from where you last wrote your mother, girl."

Salterdon's words revived in her brain—that he had come to Huddersfield to search for her after she'd left the manor.

Lies? All lies?

She turned away and sank into the little ladder-back chair near the bed. Exhaustion and despair lay like lead weight upon her shoulders.

The memory of the Lady Edwina, swollen

with His Grace's child, rose before her mind's eye, causing her throat to tighten.

Somewhere, she might never know where, the body of her own child lay buried with nary a single tear shed for her wee soul.

The minutes turned to hours. The cold intensified and the embers within the hearth grew gray with ash.

She listened to the terrible wheezing of her father's lungs, cringed at his spasms each time he coughed.

At last, she wearily roused and moved to the bed.

How shrunken and pitiful he looked, and the anger that had gripped her so fiercely began to melt from her heart. She touched his hand, and did not shiver as his fingers curled around hers.

Closing her eyes, she reached out to Paul in her mind. Yet . . . there was nothing. No whisper of a response. No heralding of angels, as there had been for Salterdon's soul.

"Maria?"

Opening her eyes, she turned to look into the familiar face of John Rees.

"Dear Merciful God in Heaven!" he exclaimed, his face white with shock.

John Rees—the man with whom she had once been infatuated. Adored with the naive purity of a virgin who wept into her pillow at night, knowing that his dedication to God and church would forever override his love for a mortal woman.

Once she would have done anything to win him away from his obsessive devotion to God, so she should have been overjoyed when he unexpectedly turned up at Thorn Rose, prostrating himself upon love's altar, pleading with her to leave the manor to join him in matrimony, even though he knew her soul had been tainted by lust for His Grace. John Rees had loved her enough to forgive her transgressions, yet she had turned him away.

She had known then that the emotion she'd once believed was love for John Rees had not held the depth of passion that a woman feels for a man with whom she yearns to spend the remainder of her life.

Maria forced a smile and lifted her chin. "Aye, John. 'Tis I."

He fell back heavily against the closed door, his eyes wide as he covered his mouth with one hand and murmured, "Oh my God. My dear God. I thought . . . where have you come from, lass?"

"Thorn Rose."

His gaze raked her, and he shook his head. "Nay, I think not. 'Tis Maria's ghost whom I see, come to spirit her father away. Yes? Yes!"

He fell to his knees and clasped his hands

together, muttering rapid prayers as tears poured forth.

She rushed to him, dropped to her knees before him, and gently cupped her hands around his. "Hush now, John. Hush. I'm no ghost. Flesh and blood I am; I vow it!"

Again, he looked into her eyes, his body trembling. "It isn't possible. I shan't believe it. Yet . . ."

His fingers touched her face, traced the line of her cheek. She knew his thoughts; he needn't speak them.

No longer was she the rosy-cheeked innocent whom he had once proclaimed the most beautiful woman to grace God's earth. Aye, he must surely think her a wraith, gaunt and shorn as she was.

No longer a beauty.

No longer an innocent.

No longer the woman worthy of his adoration.

Her own tears rose at the gentleness of his touch. How long had it been since someone had so kindly stroked her? She pressed her cheek against his palm and savored its warmth, which rushed like fire to her heart.

"I cannot believe it," he whispered. "I don't understand—"

"I'll tell you all, John. 'Tis a sordid and sorry tale, and I fear you shall despise me even more when I'm finished."

"Despise you?" John swallowed and clutched her hands in his. "Maria, there is no sin you might have committed that I and God would not forgive."

"Very well, then. Come near while I see to my father."

AS HER FATHER SLEPT, SHE CONFESSED ALL TO John, once her father's prized curate—a young man with kindness and dreams of saving the soul of every poor, sinful wretch in England. As he had all of their lives, he regarded her with compassion and love. And desire.

Aye, it was there yet in his brown eyes. A lingering demon that he had fought to vanquish since he'd grown old enough to experience the sensation of lust and desire. Alas, her father had skewed his mind regarding the love between a man and woman.

Too often she had heard the vicar's terms of deprivation and sins of the flesh echoed in John's comments, and she had shivered at the thought of ending up like her mother. Mary Ashton had once been a vibrant, beautiful lass, full of love and desire for a husband who had ultimately crucified her—deemed her a harlot, and their own children seeds of the demon lust.

They huddled close to the meager fire as Maria finished her confession—all of it.

How she had surrendered so immorally to His Grace.

How the dowager duchess had entombed her in the asylum.

How she had given birth to Sarah and lapsed into total madness when the child was taken from her—and ultimately died.

He listened without speaking, the tears as she informed him that her precious child had died striking him like a blow. He shuddered, groaned, and buried his handsome face in his hands.

"My God, my God," he repeated, his body shaking with the sobs he tried desperately to contain. "My darling Maria. How you've suffered. I would give up my own life to remove the horror you've suffered from your mind and heart."

She cradled his head upon her shoulder and stroked his hair. " 'Tis done, John. Aye, I suffered, but 'twas nothing more than I deserved, succumbing as I did to His Grace."

"I should have tried harder to make you love me."

"Sweet, gentle John. It would never have worked between us. I am what I am, and you—"

"Stop. Stop! I won't allow you to berate yourself. Not before me or before God. And not in your father's house."

He stood abruptly and paced around the room like one caged, thrusting his hands through his hair one moment, then fisting them at his sides as he moved to her father's bed and looked down into the wasted man's still face.

"Don't dare give the son of a bitch that satisfaction," he said through his teeth as he turned his dark gaze back on Maria.

She did not know John Rees in that moment. Nay, she did not recognize him, the gentle and Godly man whose face was now flushed, his mouth a sneer.

For an instant, a mere instant, she saw a flash of madness in his eyes. Tumult and turmoil.

Jumping to her feet, she cried, "Please! I've forgiven him, John. And so must you."

"Forgiveness? Ha!" He spun away. "There have been times over the last years, Maria, that I aspired to kill him myself."

"John!"

"God forgive me."

He stared at the ceiling, tears coursing down his cheeks. "I have prostrated myself at His altar more times than I care to recall, begging Him to forgive the horrible thoughts regarding your father that have gnawed away at my brain and conscience.

"Aye, I cursed him.

"I cursed him for ruining me as a man, and driving you into the arms of His Grace.

"I cursed him for the torment he heaped upon your pitiful mother, even as she took her last breath.

"I cursed him for his hypocrisy.

"I cursed him for his cruelty toward his flock, who believed his twisted opinions of God meant condemnation of their souls."

His voice was a tremulous whisper as he slowly approached her.

"Aye, I even questioned my beliefs, my calling. In my misery, I questioned my decision to remain in the ministry. Had I been a different man, with the thoughts and emotions of normal men, mayhap I would never have lost you. Mayhap you would have loved me, had I been a man who burned with ambition for something other than God. A farmer, perhaps. A soldier. A merchant. A man you would have respected."

He shuddered, and his eyes became dark. "But I realized . . . aye, I realized that a farmer, soldier, or merchant could never fulfill your desires and expectations. Not any longer.

The lass who once prized the most humble possessions would crave the opulence of the aristocracy."

Maria glanced around the simple room, then back to John's face. " 'Tisn't so, John."

John pointed toward her father.

"He told me you were dead, Maria. Aye. He did. 'Dead,' he said, and uttered a curse upon your soul."

She winced and turned back to the fire.

John moved up behind her, his body brushing hers as he laid one hand upon her shoulder.

"I searched for you, you know. After Salterdon came to Huddersfield looking for you."

Maria closed her eyes, shaken by the truth, and relief, that Salterdon *had* searched for her.

"I searched for months, Maria. Everywhere, even to London. At last I gave up. I'm sorry. What could I do? My parishioners needed me and I . . . I had to move on with my life. Had I known—"

"You couldn't know, John. 'Twas good that you moved on."

He picked up the poker and stared at the fire, nudged the embers away from the betty before saying, "I married, Maria."

"Married?"

The firelight reflected the tear trails on his cheeks, and his mien had a sadness that robbed her of breath.

She reached for him, his hand trembling at her touch. She tried to rally enthusiasm, though her body felt tense.

She smiled. "Married, John? To whom? Do I know her?"

"Nay, you wouldn't know her. Jane Myles. From Edgerton, where I had taken post as vicar for a while. A kind lass. Simple. Not pretty . . . like you."

He took a breath and slowly released it. "She loved me at first sight, I think, and I was so heart-shaken over you . . .

"I cared for her very much, although I wasn't in love with her. But she was good and sweet, a wonderful companion—"

"A perfect vicar's wife?"

"Aye." He nodded and tugged at his clergy collar as if it were suddenly too tight.

"Where is she? I would love to—"

"She's dead."

He turned away.

"Dead. Oh, John, I'm so sorry."

John moved to a window and stared out at the night, one hand pressed upon the gray windowpane. "When your father told me you were dead, I was . . . shattered. Jane and I had only been married a few months. I had already told her about you, of course; I was honest with her from the beginning. Honest, if nothing else.

"Sweet, kindhearted Jane. I lost her then. Yes, 'twas then she began to die a little more every day."

"I don't understand."

At last, he moved away from the window and walked to the bed where her father lay as gray as ash upon the white sheets. For a long moment John neither moved nor spoke, the only sound in the room the quiet crackling of the fire and her father's rattling breaths.

John appeared as pale as the dying invalid, almost as lifeless.

"He told me you were dead," he repeated. "Do you know how violently I contemplated murdering Salterdon? I had never hated a human being in my life. I had never experienced even a twinge of fury. Naive fool that I was, I had always believed that I could forgive and save the soul of Satan himself, so sanctimonious were my convictions."

He slowly raised his gaze to Maria's, his eyes red-rimmed and swollen. "Tell me, Maria. Truthfully. Do you still love him?"

She blinked and swallowed, despair rousing in her breast.

Aye, despair.

Despair that she should be forced to acknowledge her lingering feelings for Salterdon; despair that she should be forced to acknowledge them to a man who regarded her with so much love, she felt her heart break.

"Right." He cleared his throat and forced a semblance of a smile to his lips. "Of course you do. Please, no apologies. 'Tis nothing more than what I deserve, after what I put Jane through. Those years of her adoring me, quiet sobs into her pillow while I dreamed of you. But I had to know."

"I'm sorry. Had he truly turned his back on me, as I first believed—"

"Stop." He lifted a folded blanket from the foot of the bed and approached her. "You look cold, darling. Here, this should warm you."

She smiled into his eyes as he gently wrapped the blanket around her shoulders, then nudged aside a tendril of hair on her brow.

"I don't deserve you. There isn't a man on the face of this earth who deserves Maria Ashton's love and devotion. Salterdon is an extremely lucky man."

" 'Tis done with him. You must know that, John. He's moved on with his life. Soon he'll have a wife and a child to cherish. Aye . . . he is an extremely lucky man, and I wish him well."

John laughed softly as he sat in a chair be-

fore the fire, clasped hands in his lap and his
gaze downcast.

"You would have made the perfect vicar's
wife: forgiving to a fault. You deserve to wear
this collar more than I. You and I—together—
might have worked miracles."

She moved up beside him and laid a hand
on his shoulder. Silent, they watched the
flames dance among the wood, her thoughts
returning again to Trey; the memories of his
face, the gentleness of his touch that had
once made her heart and body sing with pleasure.

John placed his hand upon hers, and
looked up into her eyes, holding her gaze with
his, emotions moving across his countenance
like strange shadows.

"Do you think he loves her?" he asked.
"The Lady Edwina?"

"I don't know, John."

"If it weren't for the coming child . . . would
you have remained at Thorn Rose and fought
for him?"

"I—"

"Does he still love you? *Does* he?"

"What does it matter? I shan't stand between him and the woman who loves him
and is carrying his child."

"Aye, he loves you. Had he not, he wouldn't
have rescued you from that hellish place. He

wouldn't have fought those long weeks to re-
vive you. I recall his look of anguish when he
showed up at Huddersfield and discovered
you weren't here. The times through the next
few months when he returned and returned
yet again, frantic to find you. A man who
loves that deeply doesn't give up that easily.

"Besides, if he loved that woman, he would
have married her by now, wouldn't he? He
was waiting for you."

Frowning, Maria shook her head. "It doesn't
matter now."

His hand closed more fiercely around hers,
and he stared again into the fire. Moments
ticked by until he said, "I have a confession to
make. I should have told you already, when I
first mentioned Jane."

She waited in silence.

"I didn't want to upset you, considering . . ."

"What is it, John?"

He took a ragged breath. "I have a child,
lass."

"A child." Maria swallowed and her hands
clasped fiercely together.

"Aye." He nodded.

She sank into the chair beside him.

"A daughter," he admitted softly.

The tears rose. She couldn't stop them.
The admission awakened the pain she had
experienced since losing Sarah, the sadness

she felt when Lady Edwina had told her that the child was dead.

A sob escaped her and she looked away, doing her best to swallow back the emotion that filled her throat. She swept away the tears on her cheeks and forced a smile for his sake.

"That's wonderful," she finally managed. "So wonderful, John. I'm so very happy for you. What is her name?"

He looked into her eyes. "Maria," he said.

∽ 20 ∾

I AWAKENED FROM A FOG.

Those years I had desperately struggled to forget, memories of that time when I had been little more than a mental cripple, rushed back at me as I lay there in the dark, warm womb of my comfortable chamber. Those nightmarish times when I had lain twisted in my bedsheets, incapable of speech and movement, my thoughts locked like prisoners inside my brain.

Maria had come to save me.

Maria, with her angelic face, her halo of pale hair, her voice like the music of angels, had spirited me out of my madness, infused me with the fight to recover from my injuries.

I needed her now as I had needed her then.

I garnered my strength and whispered, "Maria?"

"Trey?"

A form moved toward me through the shadows. I focused hard on my brother's face, which regarded me with such solemnity, I felt my heart climb into my throat.

Then he reached out and took my hand in his; a smile touched his mouth. "You're fine now. Over the worst of it. Iris has brought you a tray of food. A slice of manchet and some jam."

"I'm not an idiot again?" I asked.

"Well." Clayton grinned. "I suppose that's debatable."

He helped me sit up and plumped my pillows. "It's a sour night, to be sure. The storm is vicious. Are you cold? I'll have Henry bring more—"

"Where is Maria?"

Clay turned away as the door opened and Edwina floated in, her face aglow from the lamps placed around the chamber.

"Smashing!" she cried upon seeing me. "You look marvelous, darling!"

She positioned herself next to me on the bed. Her eyes twinkled as she took my hand and placed it on her rounded belly.

I continued to watch my brother as he sat in a chair near the hearth and crossed his legs. He reached for his drink and centered his gaze on Edwina. There was something in his sobriety that unnerved me.

"The child moves, Trey. Do you feel it?"

Still, I regarded my brother. "Where is Maria?"

Edwina sighed. "Maria, Maria, Maria. Must every conversation we have begin with Maria?"

"Where is she? I want to see her."

Clayton sipped from his snifter and remained silent.

At last, I looked up at Edwina. Her smile appeared forced, and her eyes had become sharp as flint.

"You must focus now on recovery, darling. You've been very ill. You're weak and need to eat."

"I'm not eating a bloody thing until I see Maria."

She reached for a slice of manchet and lifted it to my lips.

"Stuff it," I told her, and knocked it away.

I proceeded to kick away the covers and roll from the bed. The room spun, and suddenly Clayton was there, doing his best to force me down on the mattress.

"You'll not be doing yourself any favors—"

"Get the hell away from me."

I shoved him aside and stumbled to my feet, then grabbed the bedpost for support while the chamber made a slow undulation in my brain.

"Something's wrong. I feel it."

Twisting my hand in Clayton's shirt, I pulled him close as I glared into his eyes. "What have you done with her? Spit it out, man."

"I haven't done a damned thing with her. What do you think I am?"

"Then let me see her. Bring her to me."

"She's gone," came Edwina's voice, cold as the howling wind outside the house.

Gone.

Unsteadily, I turned.

Edwina, having left the bed, backed toward the hearth, wringing her hands. "She's gone, Trey. Left."

"Explain."

"A man came. From Huddersfield. Her father is dying. It seems he desired to make peace with her before he passed."

I looked at my brother.

" 'Tis true," Clayton said. "She was gone yesterday when we returned from church. Iris herself heard the exchange between them."

"You left Maria here alone with that bitch?" I thrust one finger toward Edwina.

"How dare you!" she cried.

"Shut up!" I then asked Clayton, "Who was he, the man? How the hell would you not believe this is our grandmother's doing—again?"

Clayton forced my hand from his shirt, and stepped back.

"You don't," I said through my teeth, anger wild within me.

"I doubt that Grandmother would be that stupid."

"Stupid?" I laughed, a maniacal sound that caused Edwina to gasp and Clayton to pale.

"Our grandmother isn't stupid, Clay. She's evil personified. She's a goddamn lunatic, yet you march off to church and leave Maria here alone and vulnerable? That wasted old bitch probably had someone waiting for the first opportunity—"

"I'm sorry."

Clayton once more attempted to push me back on the bed.

"You're sorry?"

With all the strength I could muster, I shoved him away. He backed into the night table with enough impact to send it toppling to the floor.

Exhausted, I sank onto the bed, still gripping the bedpost, against which I rested my brow and closed my eyes. My illness and fever had left me weak, my breathing labored.

"I should have murdered the old bitch when I had the chance."

The door flew open and Miracle rushed in, Maggie clinging to her mother's skirts and her eyes enormous.

"What's going on in here?" She ran toward Clay.

"Get out," I growled, so threateningly Miracle froze in her tracks and tucked the child protectively against her. "And get that child out of my sight. Now!"

Clayton nodded and Miracle, scooping Maggie up in her arms, hurried from the room. Then he turned on me.

"Speak to my wife and daughter like that again, and I'll leave you here to rot in the morass of your own misery, you son of a bitch."

"Fine. Good. Get the hell out of here. I'm fed up with your sanctimonious babble as it is. And take that bitch with you when you go." I motioned toward Edwina.

"Very well. If you want me out of your life, Trey, so be it."

Clayton turned on his heel and stormed from the room, leaving Edwina cringing in the shadows. Slowly, I shifted my gaze to hers.

"You heard me. Get out. I've tolerated your company long enough."

"But darling—"

"Shut up," I sneered, and managed enough strength to stand. Step by cautious step, I approached her, positioning myself between her and the door as I did so.

"You don't frighten me, Salterdon." She lifted her chin. "Your tantrums never have."

"Idiotic woman. Tantrum doesn't come close to describing what I'm about to unleash on you."

"You wouldn't dare strike me. I'm with child."

"What do you care? You've never cared for another human being your entire life, Edwina."

She took a step back, her eyes growing wider. "You're a fine one to talk."

As I stared into her flushed face, saw the nervous trembling of her body, an ember of suspicion began to flicker in my brain.

Surely I could not have been so daft.

As the possibility began to flourish, the memories of the last months bombarded me—how Edwina had turned up again and again at my usual haunts, befriending me and seducing me, using my own vulnerabilities to manipulate me.

Why hadn't I recognized it for what it was?

Edwina would have had no qualms whatsoever in birthing her child and pandering it off to the lowliest beggar in London or Paris. Why, suddenly, had she become so desperate to find a father to legitimize her baby?

"I wonder . . ." Tipping my head to one side, I continued to advance. "Were you in on this subterfuge with my grandmother the entire time?"

"I don't know what you mean, Trey."

"Was I daft enough to believe our entire relationship was anything other than my grandmother's manipulation—to get me married off so I would get over this obsession I had for Maria?"

"Obviously your fever has deranged you—again."

"I doubt it."

She could retreat no further, and when she made a move to dash to one side, I grabbed her arm with one hand. The other I wrapped around her slender throat, tipping back her head so she was forced to look into my eyes.

"Be very, very careful, Edwina. I'm not so weakened that I couldn't snap your beautiful neck like a rotten twig. Now tell me the truth. All of it."

"I—I can't breathe!"

Releasing my grip slightly, I pulled her closer. "All of it."

Her eyes pooled with tears that ran down her cheeks. She nodded. "Yes. I'll tell you everything. Just let me go. Please."

I continued to hold her, my teeth clenched, my anger mounting as I realized that I, who had spent the majority of my life manipulating humankind, had been so insidiously gulled.

I released her and she grabbed her throat, the pale flesh gone red with the imprint of my fingertips. She coughed. Gasped. Then backed toward the wall as she said in a husky whisper, "You're going to need a drink for this, I think. Shall I call Herbert?"

I nodded and sank into a chair, gazing blindly at the fire dancing within the hearth. I felt utterly, bone-chillingly cold, and began to shiver.

Edwina rang for Herbert, then eased down into an accompanying chair. Her sapphire-blue skirts flowed in folds over her knees to the floor. The rich color made her hair look as fiery as the flames gyrating amid the embers.

We waited in silence until the door opened and Herbert appeared, bleary-eyed, his white hair standing in wild tufts upon his head.

"His Grace desires a drink. And make it generous," Edwina ordered the sleepy servant. With a bow, he quit the room.

Was I prepared for the truth? The entire truth? Was I mentally strong enough to refrain from killing Edwina with my bare hands?

I doubted it.

The vague tickling of a memory returned and grew, sweeping me back to those tortuous days of my mania, when Maria had first arrived at Thorn Rose.

She appeared to me, draped in soft, flowing white cotton, a guttering candle held aloft in one hand. She floated toward me like a vision, moonlit hair shimmering in the candlelight.

"Do you sleep, Your Grace?" came her whispered words, and she bent over me, regarded my face and eyes, her own reflecting the bright flame in her hand. Her smell washed over me, sweet and clean and feminine. I felt dizzy and desperate, but when the familiar anger roused inside me, something about her child-like look enraptured me, and I lay still, barely breathing, like one in the company of a fawn. Should I so much as blink, she might flee . . .

She looked so frightened. So tentative. Of what, I wondered.

Me, of course. I was the monster.

Yet the angel smoothed the counterpane over my chest, then lightly touched her fingers to my hair on the pillow.

"I'm certain you don't mean to be cruel, Your Grace. 'Tis the anger and the belief that God and mankind have deserted you. Trust, sir, that they have not . . .

"Until tomorrow, goodnight, Your Grace," she said softly, and drew her hand down over my lids, closing them. I did not open them again until she had quit the room, taking the light with her.

Lying in the dark, I thought:

Don't go. Please . . . don't go.

"Your Grace?"

I blinked away the memory and found Herbert at my side, snifter in hand.

"Will that be all, Your Grace?" he asked.

Taking the drink, I nodded, and waited until he had closed the door before refocusing on Edwina.

Her face as pale as the china tiles around the hearth, she stared at me without blinking. She began.

"Your grandmother learned of my pregnancy from Lord Rutherford. He is the father of my child, Trey. I've known it all along. But what was I to do?"

"Rutherford is married."

She nodded. "Presumably happily so . . . or so his naive young wife believes. Your grandmother was well aware of our friendship—yours and mine—and she suspected that eventually you'd learn the truth about Maria—where she was, I mean. She simply wanted you matrimonially bound, should that time arise. So she came to me and offered to financially reward me if I could dupe you into marriage. It wasn't an unpleasant prospect. I needed a husband—"

"Get on with it."

She swallowed and nodded. "That's it. I needed a husband. You needed money . . . I—we all—were arrogant enough to believe that once you married, you would put her behind you, would get over this gnawing love/hate obsession you continue to carry for her. As

I've confessed, I eventually came to be in love with you."

"Where is my daughter?"

There was silence as Edwina shifted, discomposed, in her chair.

"Where is *Maria?* What has my grandmother done with her?"

"Truthfully, to my knowledge, she left here for Huddersfield. If your grandmother had anything whatsoever to do with her disappearance, I don't know it. How could I? I haven't left your side since we came to Thorn Rose. You know that, Trey. You *know* it."

"Why didn't you stop her, Edwina?"

"Why?" She laughed, a sharp bark of disbelief. "Why should I? I was thrilled to see the back of her."

I finished my port and placed the snifter on the floor, my gaze never leaving hers. "Where is Sarah?"

"Trey—"

"Answer me, dammit!"

"She's dead."

Dead.

I sank back in my chair as I watched Edwina cover her face with her hands, as if doing her best to shield herself from me.

"You're lying," I said.

She shook her head. "I'm so sorry, darling."

My eyes narrowed as I said through my

teeth, "If that were the case, why didn't you stop me before I bothered to go to London to confront my grandmother?"

"You wouldn't have believed me, Trey. You'd vow that it was only another manipulation—"

"Most importantly . . ." I leaned toward her, and with a threatening tone that made her sink back in the chair, said, "Why wouldn't my grandmother have confessed to Sarah's death?"

"I . . . don't know. Perhaps . . ." She struggled with her thoughts, rubbed her temple with a trembling hand. "I don't know. I haven't a clue about what transpired between you and your grandmother, darling. How could I?"

I felt my strength drain from me and I fell back in the chair. Why? It made no sense. The dowager duchess would have gloated over my daughter's death. Would have expounded on how fortunate it was for us all that she had died, saving our lineage from scandal and humiliation.

As I continued to glare into Edwina's frightened eyes, a realization slammed me. As if she knew it, she sank more deeply into her chair, her fingers digging into the chair arms in preparation of what was to come.

"You told her."

Edwina swallowed.

"You told Maria the child was dead. Didn't you, Edwina? That would explain why she left. Maria never would have fled Thorn Rose if she believed I could help her find Sarah. Despise me she must, but she never would have turned her back on the hope that I would somehow produce our daughter. You bitch. You heartless, manipulating bitch. You're no better than my grandmother. A cruel, heartless, scheming slut."

"What will you do now?" she demanded, a whisper of panic in her voice.

"I'm going to Huddersfield. And if Maria truly is there, I intend to bring her home."

"You're going nowhere in your condition. You'd be dead in a fortnight, if not sooner." She tilted her chin in a spiteful angle. "And what good will crawling on your belly to her do? She loathes you, Salterdon. She told me so."

Her eyes narrowed and she leaned toward me.

"If a man loved a woman as obsessively as you do Maria, why wouldn't you have moved heaven and earth to find your own daughter—when you believed her to be alive? You're hiding something. I know it. We all know it.

"Why else would you ride out of Thorn Rose like some bat out of hell to discover if there was a child, then return with no ambition whatsoever to locate her? Just what kind of man would keep that information from a woman mourning her lost child?"

I sank back in the chair and closed my eyes. "Get out. I don't ever want to see you again, Edwina. Have Iris help you pack. I want you out of here with my brother and his family first thing in the morning."

"Fine."

She stood and moved to the door, where she paused and looked back.

"What if you were to go to Huddersfield and find her? You'll never convince her to love you again. Not only does she despise you, believing you were involved in condemning her to Menson, but now she loathes you for Sarah's death. She blames you as much as your grandmother for that."

"Get out!"

"Go to hell!" she cried, and slammed the door.

❧ 21 ❧

Six months later

AT LONG LAST, I WAS TO BE ALONE. COM-
pletely alone.

As I reposed in the wild, unkempt garden that spring morning, I watched Herbert approach, his eyes downcast and his shoulders slumped. Beyond him waited a conveyance that would remove him from Thorn Rose, taking him away to his new employer, Warwick of Braithwaite.

"Your Grace." He greeted me with a slight bow and forced a smile. "Is there anything I might do for you before I take leave? Anything at all?"

"Yes." I nodded and motioned toward an accompanying chair. "Sit for a moment. Just a moment."

He sat, his spine stiff, his expression

pained as a warm breeze fluffed his white hair.

I regarded him fondly, and with a curl of my lips. "You needn't feel so remorseful, Herbert."

" 'Tisn't right, Your Grace. Leaving you here unattended. A man of your—"

I held up my hand to silence him.

"No point in both of us starving. You've been a good man to me these last years."

"I do greatly appreciate your recommendation to Warwick, Your Grace."

"Earl Warwick's a good man and from a fine family—a respected lineage back to the War of the Roses, I believe. Remain awake and sober, and you'll do him proud, I'm sure."

Herbert nodded and smoothed back his hair as he allowed his gaze to roam the garden and the swells and vales beyond. "I'll miss Thorn Rose, Your Grace. 'Twas always beautiful this time of year."

"Aye, it is that."

There was silence for a moment, then, "Sir, now that I'm no longer an employee . . . May I have the liberty of speaking freely?"

I nodded.

He did not look at me, but focused on the nearby clumps of yew and holly and the scattering of small brown birds flitting among the privets.

"Your Grace," he began gently. "What are you to do now? Do you intend to remain here, wasting away? Alone? Would you not at least entertain the idea of going to your brother—for help, I mean."

"No."

Herbert sighed. "Very well, then." He cleared his throat. "What about the woman? Miss Ashton."

A trembling grief stole through me. I made a brief sound that vibrated with emotion, then stopped and cleared my throat.

"Hopeless, I'm afraid. She's taken up with that vicar—what's his name—John Rees."

"Married, Your Grace?"

"Only a matter of time, I suspect."

I looked up at the sky, brilliant blue streaked by clouds as wispy as cobwebs. "Besides, she's apparently content enough, helping Rees do God's work in Huddersfield."

"If you would only speak to her directly—"

"What point is there? Why should I? She's made it clear that she wants nothing to do with me, Herbert. How can I blame her? I can't. Not in the least, considering . . .

"Besides, the young lady has been through enough, thanks to me. My calling on her now would only open old wounds, and although I would like nothing more than to see her again, I don't think I could handle looking into those eyes and seeing how much she must truly despise me."

Herbert's face flushed as he shifted in his chair and finally turned his gaze on me.

"Poppycock."

"I beg your pardon?"

"Poppycock and balderdash, Your Grace."

I raised one eyebrow, surprised by his forceful tone.

" 'Tis a preposterous assumption, Your Grace. You haven't spoken to the young woman yourself. How can you know what she's thinking, and, more importantly, what she's feeling?"

"It's more than apparent, I think. She didn't return to Thorn Rose after the death of her father. Why should she? She loathes me."

I sighed and watched a flurry of birds lift into the sky. "Perhaps if the child hadn't died . . ."

" 'Tis true, Your Grace, that the child might have helped to mend the wound of her hurt and anger toward you. But that doesn't explain why, knowing how you continue to love her, you haven't approached her and attempted to plead your devotion and woo her back."

Pursing his lips, he glared at me. "Hardly the behavior of a man who so frantically combed this country for months attempting to find her."

He pointed one finger at me and said, " 'Tis easier for you this way, isn't it?"

"Meaning?"

He tapped his temple as his eyes narrowed.

"I haven't quite figured it out yet. But something transpired between you and your grandmother when you went to London to confront her about the child. You left Thorn Rose burning with hope that you would discover a way to help Miss Ashton, and returned a closed and bitter enigma who was willing to sacrifice Maria's sanity, not to mention your own happiness, by refusing to locate your daughter.

"You've cut off all relationship with your own brother. While the two of you have had misunderstandings, there was never one so bad as to bring about this prolonged a breach.

"Could it be, Your Grace, a case of 'out of sight, out of mind'?"

I remained silent.

"Yes," he said. "I do believe so. Your brother is somehow related to whatever discourse you had with the dowager duchess. 'Twould explain why you returned from London with such fury and frustration toward him."

"You think too much," I told him sharply, the truth of his words turning the warm air cold upon my flesh.

He leaned toward me, faded eyes round,

tufts of white hair peaked on each of his temples, giving him the appearance of a hoot owl.

"You have defied your grandmother all of your life. Fought her control over you tooth and nail. You so loved a woman named Maria Ashton that you were willing to blow your heritage to hell in order to marry her.

"Yet you continue to sequester yourself in this place, refusing to face her again. The whole thing smells foul as kippers, if you ask me."

"I didn't ask you," I snapped.

His gray eyebrows drew together as he continued to glare at me. Finally, he gave a quick nod and stood, smoothed his hands down over his coat, then said, "Very well. Then we're finished."

He offered his hand to me, and I grasped it, shook it.

"Good luck to you, Herbert."

"And to you, Your Grace."

I did not watch Herbert depart but sank deeper into the chair, my legs outstretched, gazing at the distant wild swell splashed with vibrant heath-bells and bracken.

My home loomed behind me, Goliath in height and width, empty of a solitary human. Servants all gone. Only me left, to ramble along the dreary corridors, plink away at piano keys, and drink away my guilt until I became oblivious to my loneliness and continuing ache for Maria.

Herbert had been correct, of course. Fresh old bastard—too smart for his own good. Smarter than I, apparently.

I reached for the note on the small table by my chair, the missive having arrived yesterday morning from Paris—a solitary line that had unleashed a sort of mourning in me, a profound sense of loss that had made me sleepless throughout the night.

The babe is born. I have a son.

What bitter irony that Edwina, who cared not a whit for such a gift, would be blessed with a son, while Maria . . .

Christ, when had I become such a coward?

Herbert was right. For the first time in my life, I had allowed the dowager duchess to manipulate me.

Out of sight, out of mind.

Correct there, as well.

Yet here I sat, my head pounding from another night of drinking myself into oblivion in an attempt to numb myself from the pain gnawing at my black heart.

Aye, I deserved this sorry life. Destitution. Misery. Humiliation. It would do myself, my brother, my lineage, a favor if I put a bullet in my head.

I turned my face toward the sun.

The damnable memories were always there, lurking, forcing their way before my mind's eye.

I had sat in this very place with Maria, mesmerized by her image—her wide blue eyes so innocent and vulnerable, her lips the color of ripe plums. Her smile was not the sort a man, even a man as jaded as I, could easily ignore, or forget.

Sweet, beautiful angel. Savior of my soul.

Without her, I was lost.

A sudden and too familiar sense of desperation roused inside me. I jumped from the chair and strode with fierce determination along the cobbled footpath, until I reached the stables.

Maynord had taken leave of Thorn Rose the day before—skulked away in the dead of night with most of my tack. There was no one but myself left to feed the swine, milk the damned cow, and see to Noblesse.

The horse regarded me with suspicious eyes as I grabbed up a brush and began to groom him, my strokes growing harder as my frustration mounted.

"I'm done with, old boy. Just the two of us now."

Stroke. Stroke.

"It's nothing more than I deserve. I've been a blight on humankind all of my life. Dammit!"

Noblesse snorted and shifted away.

"They'll find us nothing more than a lot of moldering bones in a few months, and who the hell will care? Not one damned soul, that's who. Not that I blame them. My brother will think 'good riddance.' "

I threw the brush against the stable wall, causing the stallion to flinch and sidle away from me.

Dropping into the sweet-smelling straw, I leaned against the stall wall and let out a sigh. Noblesse nuzzled my shoulder, then sniffed at my hair, his warm breath scented with oats and hay.

"Why the blazes should I care how our illegitimacy affects Clay? He's a wealthy man. He built up Basingstoke's coffers with his own blood, sweat, and tears. It's me I'm worried about. Daft, misguided bastard that I am.

"If I had a grain of conscience and intelligence, I would mount you right now and return to Huddersfield, go to bended knee, and beg her to marry me—before she marries that pompous, sanctimonious young vicar and breaks my heart completely.

"But what then?" I scratched between the horse's ears.

I looked through the stable door, at the manor with its high-pitched gables silhouetted against the blue sky—all that I had left, all other properties sold to satisfy my gambling debts. It was only a matter of time—months, weeks, perhaps—before I would be forced to sell my home.

I glanced around the stables, once sparkling, each stall once filled with the finest horseflesh in all of England.

Even here, the memories of Maria roused in my mind's eye: Maria nestled in sweet straw while a newborn filly nuzzled her hand.

Cursing, I stumbled to my feet and saddled the horse.

I RODE WITH NO PARTICULAR DESTINATION IN mind, simply allowed the animal his head while I tried to avoid the clash of thoughts in my mind. As we meandered along the pebbly bridle paths disappearing beneath the wild growth of spring thatch, my eye feasted upon each swell and sweep, more beautiful than I had ever seen them.

Why had I never noticed before the wild, colorful sprinkling of turf by heath-bell and bracken, the moss-covered crags and the aged firs twisted and bent by the winds?

My thighs hugged Noblesse as he descended the declivity and splashed across the gill that bounced and bubbled around his fetlocks until we reached the fern bank on the other side. Then up, laboring along the incline of the mossy swell, up, up, the stallion's sides warming beneath me. Reaching the summit, he paused, lifting his nostrils into the breeze as if detecting some threat.

I stared down on the remains of the mine.

More memories I was not prepared to embrace.

I tried to rein Noblesse around, but he snorted and pranced, his dancing hooves stirring up dust. He fought the bit, teeth grinding upon the metal as he half reared and tossed his head. No encouragement of spur or crop would convince him down the slope toward home—as if he was somehow being obstructed from moving.

With no warning, he collected himself and tossed back his head so forcefully that a rein snapped. I grabbed hold of his mane as he descended the swell toward the mine, his hooves scrambling and scraping amid the loose stone until, at last, we stood upon the deserted road leading toward the mine.

I dismounted, breathing heavily, sweating from the heat of the afternoon and the efforts of fighting the oddly belligerent animal. No sooner had my boots touched the ground when Noblesse bolted up the incline, disappearing over the summit with a thundering of feet.

Damn, damn, damn.

I reluctantly looked around me, first at the collapsed entrance of the mine, then at the lines of stone houses blackened with soot, their windows void as dead eyes and roof timbers jutting up against the fair sky like incindered bones.

The silence of death settled like a shroud upon me, and I shuddered.

I envisioned the long line of stoop-shouldered miners shuffling from the pit, their faces smeared by thick dust and sweat, chests heaving with wracking coughs as their wives left their homes to greet them.

There, beneath the tree, Maria had reclined on a patch-work quilt and allowed sunlight to bathe her face.

There, upon the boulders lining the road, I sat with a dozen men and imbibed ale as I listened to their conversations.

I had worked alongside them. Sweated and cursed and bled beside them. Dreamed of becoming the man I knew I could be. Wanted to be.

Worthy of Maria.

Worthy of self-respect.

Wearily, I dropped onto a boulder, and with elbows on my knees, closed my eyes.

Minutes stretched into hours, and the shadows of the cottage shells elongated toward me. The air cooled and came in sharp gusts.

I would eventually acknowledge the whispery voice for what it was—years later, when I became a more spiritual man—a voice of unspeakable strangeness that touched my ear and sparked the first inkling of an epiphany in my thoughts.

I heard it, and questioned whence it came as I stood and looked around me. No doubt some trick of the wind, now moaning through the collapsed stone and timbers. Perhaps a shuddering of the branches over my head, a trembling of colliding leaves?

What delusions flashed through my brain!

I saw clearly the miners, familiar friends, with shovels and picks shouldered, marching like troops into the mine. The homes were rebuilt. I smelled the fresh lumber and heard the boisterous conversations of men.

And there, among them, stood another: a stranger, tall and slender, with pale hair and eyes as blue as a summer sky.

He stared directly at me, a kind smile on his face. Then he cupped his hands around his mouth, and shouted, "Hurry! You haven't much time!"

Then he was gone.

The miners were gone.

I was alone again.

The wondrous shock of awareness came like an earthquake; it sprang trembling and quaking through my heart and spirit.

I would buy the mine and rebuild it!

I would find some way to do it—mortgage Thorn Rose, if I must.

But I *would* rebuild it. For myself.

And Maria.

❧ 22 ❧

BY THE TIME I REACHED HUDDERSFIELD, THE day was nigh over and dusk painted the eastern sky a somnolent purple. The April breeze cooled my flesh and smelled of tender grass, and wildflowers covered the black earth in sprays of blue and yellow.

Cursed, I was, that every living thing around me encouraged memories of Maria: the smallest bird, the tiniest flower, the warm sun upon my shoulders.

Even in that moment, as my horse shifted beneath me, her words came back to me, and the vision:

Maria sitting at my feet with book in hand, her silvery flowing hair reflecting the firelight like a mirror.

"Do you recall, Your Grace, how, when we were

children, each new season was the prelude to new experiences? Spring brought birds and flowers, summer the long, warm days of sunshine and fragrant heather. Autumn was a time for harvest and color, of gold and red falling leaves in which we frolicked and daydreamed of winter snow. Winter was roaring fires and snuggling deeply beneath good down comforters, and listening to the howl of wind and sleet scratching at our windowpanes. It was a time to share secrets and to dream of the coming spring.

"I wonder, Your Grace, when, exactly, did the seasons become so monotonous and something to be dreaded? When did the summers become too intolerably hot and long, and the winters too cold? Why did the autumn leaves become a drudgery to be raked and burned? Why did the springs become far too dismally wet and chilly?

"When, exactly, did our every aspiration, dream, and hope become simply another anticipated disappointment?"

I had made this journey a dozen times since the day I awakened to discover Maria had left me. A dozen times of wandering the paths along the Huddersfield canals, finding myself standing outside her little cottage and hoping against hope to catch a glimpse of her.

How strangely I had been appraised by the townfolk as I asked them about her.

"Is she well?

"Is she happy?

"Has she married?" I held my breath in anticipation that she had.

I had watched her walk to the church, where John Rees waited to greet her, his expression one of such delight that I felt murderous. That he should now become the beneficiary of her kindness, her sweet smiles and gentle touches, knifed at my soul.

The pain was there still.

Although I had had no intention of returning to Huddersfield on my way to London, here I was again, unforgivable thoughts plaguing my mind.

I would confront her.

Confess my feelings on bent knee.

She had loved me once.

I would make her love me again.

To the devil with John Rees.

I stabled my horse and rented a room for the night. Then I made my way to the church, where I sat on a bench beneath a twisted old rowan and listened to the chorus of voices sounding like angels from heaven. The sky was starless, the air cool enough to make me shiver.

At long last, the singing ended. The church doors opened and there stood John Rees in cloak and collar . . . and at his side, Maria.

Not the Maria whose face had been gaunt

from fear and sadness. Not the lass whose emaciated body had been as light as goose down. She stood at Rees's side offering each of his congregation a gentle touch and the smile that had once radiated through my darkness to heal my spirit.

How lovely!

Her hair was no longer the sheared and shaggy mess from her days in Menson. What a rare and beautiful shade it was, rolling in silken waves over her brows and framing her eyes, the flaxen strands reflecting the candle glow from within the nave.

And those eyes—smiling once again with such depth of compassion, it seemed that each man, woman, and child she looked upon must feel the blissful touch of God Himself.

I remained within the shadow of the rowan for what felt like an eternity, each smile and touch she bestowed on the young vicar aggravating the impatience that had taken a painful hold on my chest.

I shook as the air grew colder, the night darker, the fog obscuring all but the haze of light illuminating the church entry—and the couple who remained there even after the last of the congregation had made their way home.

If he kissed her, I would kill him.

Ah, but John Rees did so want to kiss her.

'Twas in his eyes, his smile, in the way he lightly touched one timid finger upon her cheek to nudge aside an errant lock of hair.

The child appeared then, a girl with long, curling dark locks and a cherubic face, cheeks blooming as pink as little rosebuds. Maria scooped her up in her arms and planted a kiss on her forehead.

Rees closed the doors, gently took Maria's elbow, and escorted her and the child down the steps and along the pathway. They passed within feet of me, and I heard Maria speak.

"I shall call on Mave Smythe first thing in the morning," she said to John. "Poor dear. She's grieving so desperately over the loss of her husband."

"She'll welcome your company," he replied. "You've been a Godsend to my parish. And to me, of course. And my daughter. You know how I feel."

"You needn't speak of your gratitude, John."

I followed them through the dark.

" 'Tisn't gratitude I wish to discuss, Maria. You know that."

"I know. And we *shall* discuss our future . . . someday."

"When?"

"When I'm ready."

"Six months have passed since you returned to Huddersfield. Six months you've worked at my side, mothered my daughter. Yet you continue to shield your heart from me. Why?"

She stopped short and turned to face him, yet she said nothing.

"Why?" he repeated. "You loved me once, Maria. I can make you love me again."

"I do love you, John."

"But you refuse to marry me. I deserve to know why."

As I remained in the shadows, unable to breathe as I awaited her response, I saw in her face a despair as she looked at the child in her arms. Aye, despair. Sadness. Emptiness. Those radiant smiles she had bestowed upon the parishioners had been little more than a facade to hide her own pain.

I felt, in that instant, a shock of grief that rocked me back on my heels. The vision of Maria and the child robbed me of breath and I sank against a nearby tree. Heartrending sadness sluiced through my body as I stared at the image, woman and child. Loss. Irrevocable death. All that I might have cherished stood within my reach.

Maria hugged the child closely as they continued walking toward her cottage. I could no longer hear them. The fog swirled between us, occasionally obliterating my view of them.

I realized with brilliant clarity that she deserved better than some destitute duke, tainted of reputation and of lineage. She had found what she had lost: a home. A child. A decent, God-loving man who would cherish her.

I knew that I could not rob her of that.

Yet I remained, a prisoner of conscience as I watched her move farther and farther from me, watched the gentle sway of her hips, the adoring way in which she cradled the child.

I opened my mouth to call her name, yet remained voiceless.

She paused and turned.

For a moment—a brief moment—I felt as if our gazes touched. She seemed to look directly at me, yet through me. I would never forget her beautiful face, the gentle curve of her brow, the lushness of her lips. The sorrow that I had inadvertently caused her welled upon her countenance like spring water. The memory of those haunted eyes would lance me for the remainder of my life.

THE CHILD'S ARMS AROUND MARIA'S NECK MADE her heart ache. Her sweet breath upon Maria's cheek caused her to smile, despite the impatient frown on John's face.

As he stepped around her to open the cottage door, she looked back through the fog.

Not for the first time, a tickling of anticipation touched her.

What or whom did she expect to see there?

Hope to see there?

John obviously noted her look as well, and the patience and compassion of his countenance turned hard and almost forbidding.

He took the child from her. " 'Tis because of your father, isn't it? Your reason for not allowing yourself to trust me."

Maria stepped away and pulled her shawl more tightly around her. She wanted no reminders of her past.

"I shan't speak ill of the dead, John."

He watched as she strode to the hearth and sat on a chair.

"I'm not your father, Maria! He believed that God's way of dealing with the corrupted soul is to hail painful retribution upon the sinner. Have I ever raised an unkind word or hand against you?"

Maria swung round to stare at him. "Are you saying, John Rees, that I'm deserving of such? Do you accuse my soul of being corrupted?" She nodded. "I think you do."

"Don't be daft, Maria."

"Have I not sinned?"

"Aye. You have."

"You said once, the evening I returned to

Huddersfield, that I had committed no sin that God, and yourself, could not forgive. Yet at each opportunity, you remind me of my past. You pound your fist upon the pulpit and rail on about the sins of the flesh and the demon of lust, without looking from me for so much as a second.

"I refuse to become like my mother, God rest her soul. Shamed by her husband for desiring his touch. Already you demand that I dress the drab. That I speak in whispers. That I not look directly into the eyes of a man, for doing so invites unmentionable attentions. Nay, John Rees, I could never be the wife you expect me to be."

"You're still in love with him, Maria. Why won't you admit it?"

Her heart surged and her breathing quickened. She turned her back to him and stared into the embers.

Those dreaded thoughts and emotions continued to haunt her every waking and sleeping hour: memories of Salterdon.

John moved up beside her as his daughter skipped over to the bed and grabbed up a doll, which she hugged as fiercely as her little arms would allow.

Ah, Sarah. Sweet, beloved angel of Maria's memories and heart. She could not look upon John's daughter without thinking of the child who was lost to her. Imagining that Sarah's hair would be the same color, would fall in luxurious coils and waves around her face—curls she would have inherited from her father. And her eyes—large, silvery gray orbs that sparkled with mischief. Had Sarah survived, she would have been the same age as John's daughter.

John took Maria's hand in his as he bent to one knee. How soulful were his eyes, how searching. She turned her face away, unable to meet them.

"It doesn't matter, darling," he murmured. "You'll eventually come to love me like you once did."

"I'm no longer a child, John. I'm no longer naive or innocent. You might take me as a wife, but there wouldn't be a moment of our lives that you wouldn't look at me and think—"

"Hush." He placed one finger upon her lips. "Don't speak of it."

She ducked her head. "There are a dozen women in this parish who would make you a perfect wife and mother for Maria. You'd be scorned by your congregation, John. You know that. I'm a branded woman. The wife of a vicar should be of irreproachable moral character. I am not."

"All will be forgiven if you marry me."

"I doubt it."

Maria sighed as she watched the child curl up upon her bed, nestling the doll closely to her little body. "You really should be off, John. The child is weary."

"Contemplate it, I beg you. Marry me, Maria. I swear to God that you won't regret it."

"Very well." She gave him a smile that she did not feel in her heart. "I'll contemplate it, John."

His face brightened and he stood, swept the child up in his arms, and quit the cottage.

How silent it was then. And cold. Empty.

She remained for long minutes occasionally glancing toward the staircase that led up to her small bed, dreading the moment she would be forced to climb between the covers and cradle her pillow against her bosom.

During the last long months she had transformed the little cottage, replacing the drab, heavy window curtains with a filmy robin's-egg-blue material that allowed sunlight to spill upon the walls with golden color. In each previously gloomy nook and cranny reposed clumps of sweetly scented flowers—splashes of vibrant yellow, white, and pink.

God had provided her with a comfortable abode, and thanks to John Rees, she wanted for nothing—neither nourishment for her body nor for her soul.

Yet . . .

As she looked around the empty room, she felt shamed by a need that could not be filled by food or biblical verse.

She was fast becoming as yearning as her lonely mother for a man's touch.

'Twas then the memories poured forth. The terrible yearnings to see Salterdon again. He would be married by now, of course. His and Edwina's child might even have been born. This very instant he may be curled up against his wife, sleeping soundly, or . . .

Nay, she would not think it!

Maria stood and furiously flung the chair aside, and at that moment the door, bludgeoned by a gust of wind, flew open.

What odd sensations gripped her!

The fog swirled into a ghostly formation—a man, beyond the hedge wall and gate.

And music, like the tinkling of chimes. *Maria's Song!*

"Trey?"

She ran from the house, into the blast of wind that whipped at her skirts and tumbled her hair. Her eyes teared, her breath became ragged.

And still she ran, across the cobbled street and upon the green—running, chasing the ghostly chimes and the vision of the man who continued to haunt her, who would forever haunt her.

At last she reached the canal, deep and wide and black. And there she fell, covering her face with her hands as she wept.

MARIA STOOD OUTSIDE JOHN'S HOUSE.

No more tears. No more hoping that Salterdon would show up on her doorstep and sweep her away into a fantasy that was only that . . . a fantasy. He was as dead to her as their daughter.

Aye, she was lonely, and lost. A shamed woman scorned by the folk who had once patted her on the head and called her an angel.

She should never have returned to Huddersfield. Why had her father even summoned her? He had died as he lived, gurgling harsh beratings of the sins of the flesh. He had gripped her arm so fiercely, his ragged nails had cut into her flesh. He had stared at her with such fright, it seemed he had looked beyond the gates of death and discovered there was naught but Hell's fire awaiting his soul.

She blinked and looked up at the sky.

Even Paul had deserted her. Why?

Because she had lost hope, and faith?

I will show you miracles yet.

"Then show me, damn you," she said through her teeth.

Only the moan of the wind and rustling of the trees replied.

Maria took a steadying breath, and moved to John's door, beat upon it with her fist. She knew what she must do; what choice did she have? The images of her life winged ever wider before her with each passing day: a spinster, childless, abandoning frivolous dreams of loving and being loved in return. Dying of heartbreak and loneliness like her mother.

Yet, there was a difference. She had been too much in love with Hawthorne to acknowledge the reality. John loved her. Devotedly. Perhaps, in time, she would come to love him too. Not as a friend, but as a husband. She would cherish his child as much as her own sweet Sarah.

At last the door opened. John, brown hair tumbled over his brow and his nightdress stuffed into his breeches, looked at her sleepily, then with alarm.

"Maria? Merciful God, what's happened to you?"

He took her by her arm and escorted her in, directed her toward the lit lantern on a table near the hearth, and sat her in a chair. Then he fell to his knees before her.

"For the love of . . . you're damp through. Your face is scratched. What's happened, darling?"

She forced a smile. "I was chasing ghosts."

He rose to his feet and hurried to the windows, where he yanked the patterned curtains closed. God forbid that some voyeur pass by and see him alone with a woman at such an hour.

Then he slowly turned to face her.

How rigid he looked. And stern. And suspicious.

Maria rose from the chair and moved to a bedroom door. She nudged it open.

The child slept.

How beautiful she was! As delicate as a violet. A simple smile from her cherubic lips thawed the cold numbness of Maria's soul. The child's tickling whisper caused her heart to thump with such delight she was wont to crush her small, precious body to her and bask in the sublimity of the girl's love.

She closed the door and moved toward John, whose brow was furrowed, his hands fisted.

Maria slowly dropped to her knees and ducked her head. Her eyes pooled with tears.

"Cleanse me of sin, John Rees, in the name of our Father, the Son, and the Holy Ghost."

"A moment," he whispered, and hurried from the room, returning with a vessel of holy water.

He prayed for her soul, and doused her

head with water. It ran down her brow and dripped from her chin, onto her breasts.

When done, she lifted her head and stared into his eyes. "Now I'm worthy of being your wife, John. I will marry you."

⮬ 23 ⮭

BARRISTER DOUGLAS M. JACOBSON, ESQ., WAS A son of a bitch, a pragmatical, bloated, officious, flippant coxcomb, with the *tout-ensemble* of a waiter. He had lorded over the Salterdon business and estates for forty years. He had been the dowager duchess's legal and financial protector since the old duke had kicked up his heels.

As I paced the room, waiting for his tardy appearance, the door opened and Ernest Woodruff walked in. A small man with tired eyes that peered at me through wire-rimmed spectacles, he looked surprised as he smiled and bowed.

"Your Grace. What a pleasant surprise."

I liked Woodruff. He reminded me of a

sorely abused old lapdog. And he had a con-science—something I had never truly appreci-ated until that moment.

"Hello, Woodruff." I smiled and offered my hand. "How are you?"

He seemed shocked by my proffered hand-shake, and beamed a tremendous smile as he shook my hand. "Very well, Your Grace. Thank you for asking."

"And the wife? Is she well?"

"Oh, yes." His head bobbed so hard the spectacles slid to the end of his nose. "Quite well, she is. Very well. I'll tell her you asked about her. She'll be chuffed for sure."

He placed a stack of papers on Jacobson's desk and regarded me with a strangely sym-pathetic expression.

"Is something wrong?" I asked.

"I . . ." He cleared his throat and averted his gaze. "We just expected to see you long before this, is all. Your grandmother had informed Jacobson last autumn to expect you."

"Did she." I frowned.

The door opened and Jacobson entered. His face beet red and perspiring profusely, he waved Woodruff away as he dropped his ro-tund frame into the chair behind his desk and glared at me.

Woodruff offered me a slight bow and ex-ited the office.

"Right, Salterdon. Sit down and let's get on with it."

I raised one eyebrow and looked down my nose at him. "You forget yourself, sir."

His face turned a deeper red and his jowls quivered. "I do beg your pardon. *Your Grace*, please make yourself comfortable."

I sat and crossed my legs.

He cleared his throat. "I have a clear conception of the reason for this visit."

"Do you? Then by all means, enlighten me."

"Your grandmother informed me that you would no doubt come demanding proof that you and your brother are, in fact, illegitimate holders of title."

I stared at him and clenched my teeth.

"You want proof, of course. So be it. It is your right."

He shuffled through files and finally thrust two papers to the edge of the desk. "The one here . . ." He pointed to one. "This is the original certificate of your birth. Your birth father, the duke himself. The duchess's station was secured by this record, which was kept by this office since that time. Your mother was one Isabelle Pinter. She was a house servant. Dead now."

Jacobson cleared his throat and shifted in his chair in a manner that roused my suspicion. Knowing what I now knew about my sordid birthright, I would not have been in the least surprised if the dowager duchess was at the root of Miss Isabelle Pinter's demise.

He then pointed to the accompanying paper. "This other is the *official* certificate proclaiming you and Basingstoke to be the offspring of the man who was to, and indeed did, pass as your father."

A moment passed before I could contain my anger enough to speak. As Jacobson settled back in his chair, his expression smug, I felt my face burn with humiliation.

"You do realize," he said, "that should you desire to go public with this information—"

"I understand perfectly the ramifications of such actions, Jacobson. Bastard I may be, but I'm not an idiot."

"And you understand perfectly the ramifications that should transpire regarding your daughter."

I stood from my chair and leaned upon the desk, my body shaking with anger and hate.

"You son of a bitch. I'm fully aware that my daughter is deceased."

He blinked and sucked in his breath.

"You have my permission to tell the bitch to go straight to hell. I'm on to her, Jacobson. Completely."

He blustered and shoved his chair back against the wall with such force the windows rattled.

The door was flung open behind me and Woodruff rushed in, frantically wringing his hands.

"Is there a problem?" he asked.

"No problem," I told him, took a deep breath, and settled back in the chair. "I was just about to discuss my reasons for coming to London with this . . . gentleman."

I looked over my shoulder at Woodruff and gave him a flat smile. "Truly. All's well. I have no intention of snapping your employer's fat neck, unless he intends to provoke me further."

The little man looked at Jacobson, then me, his lips parting as if he would speak, but then thought better of it.

"Get out," Jacobson snapped.

"Yes, sir. Of course."

Woodruff scuttled from the room, not quite closing the door behind him.

"Now down to business," I said, my gaze boring into Jacobson, who continued to quake as if in the presence of the devil himself. "I intend to purchase the Warwick mine adjacent to Thorn Rose."

He swallowed and adjusted his suit coat. "I'm aware of the mine, of course. I handle the Warwick—"

"Shut up and listen. I take it Warwick has no intentions of opening the shaft again, since he hasn't already."

"Correct." He nodded. "The company had intended to sell off the property before the catastrophe. The profits were such that it was hardly worth the bother—"

"I intend to buy it."

"In risk of irritating you further, Your Grace . . ." he shifted his hulk in the chair before adding, "just how in blazes do you intend to pay for it?"

"I'll mortgage Thorn Rose."

His jaw dropped. "I beg your pardon?"

"You heard me correctly, Jacobson. I expect you to take care of the necessary legalities and locate an appropriate source of funding."

"Are you insane, man? You would risk your last holding on a collapsed lead mine that is unlikely to produce a pittance of what Thorn Rose is worth?"

"I was always a gambling man, Jacobson. I'm willing to wager Thorn Rose on the chance that the mine will ultimately make me a very wealthy man . . . again."

"And look where your gambling has gotten you."

"We all eventually are dealt a winning hand, Jacobson."

"Your grandmother would never approve."

My eyes narrowed and my lips curved. "Do you think I give a damn?"

He swiped the sweat from his brow, then

nodded. "Very well. I'll contact Warwick immediately. I believe he's in the city at the present, and I'll call on him this afternoon. If he agrees to sell the property, I'll draw up the necessary papers and see what I can arrange financially."

He looked into my eyes and smirked. "I doubt it will be hard to find a financier. Any man of intelligence would realize that you won't last six months."

I left the office, closing the door soundly behind me. I sank against it, my eyes closed and my stomach churning.

"Your Grace," came Woodruff's gentle voice.

Wearily, I lifted my head and found him near.

"I wish you luck, Your Grace."

"Are you a religious man, Woodruff?"

"Yes, Your Grace. I am."

"Then say a prayer for me, will you?"

"Of course." He smiled.

As I turned to exit the office, he said, "Your Grace?"

"Yes?"

"I . . . couldn't help overhearing your conversation. All of it. Regarding your daughter." He glanced toward Jacobson's closed door. "I . . ." He averted his gaze. "Never mind. I'm sorry. Dreadfully sorry for all of it."

I exited the building. Outside, the stench

and noise of the city bore down on me, as did the miserable humidity of an impending storm. I stepped into an alley and vomited.

BY HALF PAST EIGHT IN THE EVENING, I HAD been turned away from three clubs. Politely as possible, of course; monies owed and all that balderdash.

I arrived at Brookes's at Sixty St. James Street with little hope that I would be allowed entrance. I stood in the rain for a long moment, staring at the entrance before knocking.

Again, the attendant regarded me first with complete discomposure and a stuttering of garbled apologies. Then a voice—recognizable and sending fresh pain through my gut—spoke up behind me.

"He's my guest tonight."

I looked around into my brother's face.

"No thank you," I told him.

"Don't be an ass. It's cold and raining, and we both need a drink."

He took hold of my arm and ushered me into the club. I inhaled the welcome aroma of tobacco and liquor. The boisterous conversation of gamblers roused my constant hunger for Hazard and Faro, and I felt like an alcoholic too long without a drink.

"Do you have a private room available?" Clayton asked the attendant.

"Of course, m'lord. Will you be dining tonight?"

"Yes. My brother looks like he could use a decent meal."

"Pheasant preferred?"

"Pheasant is pleasant."

Clay grinned and we followed the man into a small, plush room where a fire roared in the hearth. I removed my sodden cloak and dropped onto a high-backed chair, my teeth clenched from chill and the aggravation that, once again, my brother had come to my rescue. We had hardly settled before a waiter appeared with our normal snifters of port and brandy.

I closed my eyes with pleasure as the port warmed my insides.

"Fancy meeting you here." Clayton slouched slightly in his chair without looking at me.

"What the hell brings you to London?"

"This and that. A quick visit with Grandmother. Business."

"How is the old bitch?"

"Do you really care?"

"No. I don't."

"Then why ask?"

"Simply hoping you would tell me she is on death's door."

We drank in silence for several minutes. Then Clay put down his empty glass and looked at me at last.

"I spoke with Jacobson this afternoon."

I froze and stared at him over the lip of my glass.

"You'll be happy to know that he spoke with Warwick, and he's willing to sell the mine at a reasonable price. Far less than Thorn Rose is worth."

I felt wooden as I placed the snifter aside and left my chair.

"Sit down," Clayton demanded in a cold voice.

"I think not. I don't intend to listen to you harp on about my stupidity . . . again."

"Quite the contrary. I'm happy to see you finally motivated by ambition."

I barked a laugh and leaned over his shoulder. "What? The saintly and all-knowing samaritan refrains from reminding me what a loser I've been all my life? No lecture that my sudden ambition is the final straw, and that I'm certain to fail and lose the estate that's belonged to the Salterdons for six generations?"

"No."

I moved around the chair, my gaze locked on his. I braced my hands upon the chair arms and sneered, "Why?"

He locked his jaw and glared back at me.

The sick and dreaded realization hit me like a brick.

"You son of a bitch."

"It was the rational thing to do, Trey. If you think for a moment that I would allow you to gamble away our family's last estate—"

"Damn you!" I twisted my hands in his coat, hauled him from the chair, and flung him against the wall with such force he groaned and winced. "If I wanted your bloody money I would have asked for it!"

"No, you wouldn't. You're too goddamn proud for your own good."

"Damn you!"

I flung him away. We circled one another like fighting cocks.

"I won't do it," I said through my teeth.

"You have no choice."

"The hell you say."

"Warwick is a friend of mine. A very good friend. I spoke to him this afternoon, with Jacobson. Unless you allow me to finance this deal, Warwick will refuse to sell you the mine."

I swung at him.

He ducked, grabbed me by my collar, and drilled me into the wall, one arm braced across my throat, cutting off my breath.

"Why do you hate me so, Trey? Why, dammit, when I've sacrificed so much to help you?"

I closed my eyes and tried to shove him away, but I was too damn tired.

"You, sacrifice? A pence here and there to

satisfy my gambling debts, followed by your humiliating chastising? You arrogant bastard, you don't know what sacrifice is. I lost the only woman I will ever love because of god-damn sacrifice."

"What the hell are you saying?"

"I wished to God I hated you, Clayton. I thought I did, for most of my life. Perhaps I did. I don't know any longer."

"Explain yourself. Just what the devil sort of sacrifice have you ever made for me?"

I turned my face away, the truth a barb on my tongue. I longed to confess the sordid details about our parentage, but what the devil difference would it make?

"You're right," I finally said. "I've done nothing remotely benevolent my entire life. Not for you, or anyone. Never have. Most likely I never will."

I shoved him away and straightened my coat.

"Enjoy your pheasant," I told him.

I DIDN'T BOTHER HAILING A CAB TO THE SALTER-don town house in Mayfair. The old man, my father, had first purchased the abode for his wife: a gift, he said, though everyone knew it was actually a place to park her relatives—all of whom he despised—when they came to visit in London. I had often heard him grumble that he couldn't abide sleeping under the same roof with her parents.

Eventually, after his wife's parents had died, he had utilized the house for his own pleasures—afternoon dalliances with the mistress of the moment, or lovely little strumpets like Isabelle Pinter.

I had entertained my own share of those lovely little strumpets there, as had my brother, before he met Miracle.

I walked, head bent against the rain, while rancor ate at my insides and I constantly waged war in my mind, wondering if I should tell my brother to go to hell and forget all hopes of reopening the mine.

But the memory of Thomas Whitefield's words kept gnawing at me.

"The vein is there. A big one. Enough to keep these men secure for the rest of their miserable lives."

I couldn't shake the haunting image of Thomas in my mind—his eyes bright with the burning fires of the smelt; the hope—nay, confidence—that had vibrated in his voice as he whispered of the mine's potential.

I had never been a dreamer, yet now a dream pounded within me, harder with each beat of my heart.

Approaching the apartment, I cast only a momentary glance at the street, where a cab was parked next to the curb beneath a gaslight. As I mounted the steps, fumbling in my cloak pocket for the key, a voice stopped me in my tracks.

"Your Grace?"

Turning, I looked through the downpour.

Ernest Woodruff stood outside the cab, rain running in runnels off his hat.

"What the blazes, Woodruff?" I said.

"Your Grace." He gave me a quick bow and stepped closer. The nearby gaslamp caused his damp face to shimmer like molten gold. "A word with you?"

Frowning, I gave him a quick nod, and unlocked the door, stepping aside to allow him entrance into the apartment.

"Bloody wicked night, Your Grace."

"It is." I shrugged off my cloak, and reached for his, motioning with my head toward the near salon.

He entered the room with hesitant steps, wringing his hands as I poured us each a drink.

"You look damn frozen, Woodruff. How long have you been waiting?"

"Doesn't matter. I'm fine." He quaffed the drink surprisingly fast. His hands were trembling.

"Sit down, man, before you fall down." I escorted him to a chair. "What the devil is this about?"

He swiped his face with one hand, his gaze shifting back to the decanter of port. "Would you mind?" He handed me his snifter.

I refilled it, took a chair beside him, and waited.

Woodruff stared into his glass a long moment, then took a deep breath. "First, let me say that my decision to come here wasn't an easy one, Your Grace. I've worked for Jacobson for twenty years. Twenty damnable, miserable years. I don't like him; have never liked him. But the financial compensation has been worth the verbal abuse he frequently unleashes on me."

Leaning back against the chair, he met my gaze directly. "But there comes a time in a man's life when he must stand for a cause. A worthy cause. I haven't been particularly proud of myself over the years—bowing to Jacobson's questionable morals and business practices. But 'tis the nature of the beast, the practice of law, is it not?"

"Yes," I said. "I suppose it is."

He cleared his throat. "Your Grace, I couldn't help but overhear your conversation with Jacobson this afternoon. And I couldn't help but notice your demeanor when you left his office—a man struggling with his pride, somewhat fearful, yet determined to risk his all for a last chance to achieve that which will restore his dignity, and reward him with hope that a brighter future lies in store for him."

I grinned. "I'm sure you didn't come here in this miserable weather and wait hours outside this apartment just to pat me on the back for tightening the noose around my own neck."

"No," he replied in a gentle, hesitant voice. "I simply wish you to understand that in that moment, when I looked into your eyes, I came to a realization myself. A man is not a man without his dignity. I have been too long without my dignity, Your Grace."

He reached into his suit pocket and withdrew two papers, which were folded in half. For a long moment he regarded them, the papers trembling in his shaking hand. Then he handed them to me, his gaze holding mine.

I opened them, and regarded the certificates of my and Clayton's births for a frozen moment before slowly looking into his eyes.

Woodruff swallowed and motioned toward the papers. "They are the only proof of your and Basingstoke's illegitimate birth, Your Grace. The only reason they still exist is because the dowager duchess used them to manipulate your father. She kept them after his death, of course, in case an issue ever arose regarding yourself or your brother.

"For your information, Your Grace, Isabelle

Pinter went to her grave with her secret. The only other persons who know of this unfortunate issue are myself and Jacobson. Should those papers disappear, there would not be a scrap of evidence to attest to the truth of your birthright . . . or lack thereof."

I looked at the yellowed paper in my hand, thoughts scrambling through my brain. Without this document I would be a free man once again, liberated from the dowager's manipulations. Aye, she could declare me a fraud; she could disparage my father's—and her husband's—reputations and my own and Clayton's. But . . .

Only then did I lift my head to note that Woodruff had moved toward the door, paused, and looked back at me.

"I have tendered my resignation at Jacobson's. I think it is high time that I venture out on my own, Your Grace. Make my own future instead of waiting for someone to do it for me." A smile touched his lips. "Good luck to you, Your Grace."

I remained in the chair, the papers open on my lap. I glanced toward the fire, my fingers lingering upon the documents. Aye, I could destroy them. As they burned into ashes, I could make haste to Huddersfield and try one last time to make Maria love me again, with the dowager's threats no longer looming over my head.

"Your Grace."

Woodruff again stood in the doorway, clutching his hat in his white-knuckled fists. How odd were his eyes, shimmering glassily with tears.

"The child," he said in so soft a whisper I was forced to strain to hear him. "Your daughter . . ."

My heart seemed to freeze in my chest, and I held my breath.

"Your daughter, Your Grace, is not dead."

~ 24 ~

I ARRIVED AT THE DOWAGER'S TOWN HOUSE just short of eleven that same evening. The windows were dark. The old duchess would have been abed hours ago.

I banged on the door for several minutes before a sleepy servant opened the door a crack and peered out at me. I shoved the door open and strode to the staircase and ascended, the papers that Woodruff has presented me tucked safely within my cloak pocket.

A sense of inebriation thumped at my temples. Not a drunkenness from spirits, but from a dizzying exuberance that, for the second time that day, I was about to make a life-altering decision. I was about to take control of my life.

I would toss the damning documents into the fire, right before the dowager's eyes, and tell her to piss off.

The bedroom door was open, and I paused at the threshold, looking toward the tester bed. She was not there, and I looked toward the high-backed chair before the dying fire.

She was there, roosting like an old crow before the hearth.

Quietly, slowly, I moved across the room and stood beside her, removing the documents from my pocket.

Her head had fallen forward in sleep.

I had never seen her this way, her silver hair loose and falling in thin wispy threads around her. The shawl wrapped around her shoulders emphasized the frailness of her form, and her white nightdress appeared little more than something to hold her brittle old bones together.

I sank into a chair beside her, staring into her sunken, wrinkled face.

She stirred as if sensing my presence, lifted her head, and looked into my eyes.

"Ah," she said, and in an uncustomary fashion nervously nudged back the strands of hair from her face, as if she were embarrassed to have been found so disheveled. She clutched the shawl tightly around herself and shrank more deeply into the chair.

"It seems the rules of polite conventions have completely escaped you, Trey. One does not drop in at this hour unannounced or uninvited." She tipped up her chin and lifted one sparse eyebrow. "I do hope there is a rational excuse for your disturbing me in this fashion."

"Quite rational," I replied, fingering the papers in my lap. "Possibly the most rational act in my entire life."

Her gaze drifted down to the papers and remained there for a long moment. At last, she gave a heavy sigh, and said, "Very well. Get on with it then."

"These are the documents of my and Clay's birth by Isabelle Pinter."

"I see."

"I want you to see me destroy them. Upon doing so, I intend to walk out that door and never see you again."

She pursed her lips and rested her head back against the chair. There was an odd glint of amusement in her eyes.

"Very well," she said. "Proceed. Get it over with and then get the hell out of my house."

I stood and moved to the hearth, the papers between my fingers. Staring down into the low flames, I said, "I also know where my daughter is, and that she is alive and well. I fully intend to claim her and deliver her to Maria. At that point, I hope with all my heart that I can convince Maria to love me again, to forgive your beastly cruelties, and to marry me."

"And if she doesn't?"

"At least she'll have her daughter back."

She continued to fix me with her faded eyes, her mouth twisted in a taunting smile.

I looked at the papers. At her. The papers again. The fire. Her eyes.

A staggering and sickening realization began to sour my stomach. I suddenly knew *why* she was smiling in so knowing and vicious a manner. She thought me a coward. A man desperate enough to destroy the proof of my lineage. I had been, once. Before Maria.

Holding her gaze, I tossed the papers into her lap.

Her expression froze, and the smugness appeared to melt from her mien.

Going to one knee before her, I looked into her stunned, sunken eyes. "I don't need the Salterdon lineage to define my manhood. Salterdon and all his worthless titles have nothing whatsoever to do with the man, the husband, the father that I intend to become. You can go to hell."

I stood and moved toward the door.

"Trey."

Turning, I looked at her face, and what I saw left me breathless.

For an instant, just an instant, the firelight erased the lines from her face. In a breath of a moment she was a young woman again, her eyes filled with tears that flowed down her cheeks in silver trails.

"All I ever wanted was for him to love me," she said softly. "To love me with the passion and obsession with which I loved him. I was willing to do anything to keep him. Anything. Ignore his affairs, go along with his lies, accept his children by other women, wishing every moment of my life that they had been a part of me."

I swallowed and briefly closed my eyes as the anger that had burdened me my entire life fell away. I pitied the innocent young woman who had married for love, and who had remained unloved for all of her life.

"Cherish her," she whispered, her chin quivering, then she tossed the papers into the flames.

I DID NOT ARRIVE IN HUDDERSFIELD UNTIL NOON of the next day. The earth sparkled beneath a spring sun as I dismounted my weary horse and strode, nay, ran, to Maria's door, and beat upon it with my fist.

There was no response. Frantic, breathing hard, I looked up and down the cobbled street, and struck off running again, my lungs aching, sweat rising so I was forced to remove my cloak, dropping it to the ground and running until John Rees's little cottage came into view.

I fell against the cottage door and struggled for a breath, then banged upon it with my fist.

It opened immediately.

I stared down into a woman's startled eyes before I sidestepped around her and demanded, "Maria Ashton. Is she here?"

"Who the blazes do ya think ya are—" she began.

"Dammit, is she here or not?" My gaze flashed around the small, tidy parlor. "Where the hell is she? Is she with Rees?"

There came a sound, and I quickly turned.

A child stood upon the threshold of her bedroom, her dark hair framing her cherubic little cheeks, her eyes a reflection of my own.

I moved toward her, slowly.

"Here now, I'll not have ya . . ."

Her words faded from my consciousness as I focused on my daughter's face. I eased down onto my knees, absorbing every nuance of her features: Maria's sweet mouth. My dark hair. My gray eyes . . .

"Sarah," I whispered, shaking.

Then through my blissful haze came the words:

". . . Rees and Miss Ashton are bein' married this very minute . . ."

My head snapped around and I stared at her. "Married."

"Aye. If they ain't already . . ."

Burying my hands in my hair and closing my eyes, I whispered, "Jesus. Oh God. Please. *Please*, don't do this to me."

I stood cautiously, so as not to frighten my daughter. Gently as possible, I scooped her up in my arms, pressed a kiss upon her smooth brow, and murmured into her little ear, "We're going to go to the church."

"To see my papa?" she said, her sparkling eyes looking into mine.

My heart turned over in my chest. "Aye." I forced a smile and nodded. "To see your papa."

Much to the distress of the child's keeper, I exited the cottage, each swift step closer to the chapel causing my heart to slam harder while the words kept repeating in my mind: "Please. Please. God, please don't let me be too late."

Nearly running, I mounted the steps and threw open the door.

And nearly staggered with gratitude as I heard the somber words that drifted through the quiet chamber: "Should anyone know of any reason these two people should not be married, speak now or forever hold your peace."

"I do," I whispered, the words caught in my throat. "*I do*," I repeated loudly.

Maria turned, her wide eyes locking with mine. Ah, merciful God, those eyes. Those lips. That sweet face that had haunted me from the first moment I had looked upon it.

"Don't," I said. "Maria . . . I beg you."

John Rees groaned and covered his face with his hands. Stumbling to a pew, he sank onto it, his countenance twisted in despair. He reached for Maria's hand, his grip forcing her to fix her stunned gaze upon his.

She loved me still. I knew it. I saw it in her trembling body, the war that raged inside her that she tried desperately to contain.

Frantic, she returned her gaze to mine, then to the child in my arms, realization forming on her face even as John Rees spoke.

"Your father told me you were dead. He asked that Jane and I take the child . . . I couldn't tell you. I knew you loved him still. I couldn't lose you both . . ."

I saw the tears rise to her blue eyes as the flowers in her hand spilled to the floor. And as I extended my hand to her, she ran down the church aisle toward me . . . and our daughter.

ᴄᴏ 25 ᴅᴏ

"I ALWAYS SUSPECTED YOU WERE A LUNATIC, Trey. Now I'm quite certain of it. You needn't put yourself through this, you know."

I glanced at Clay, who sat upon his horse looking splendid in his pristine hacking suit. Around us, the sounds of the working mine felt nearly as intolerable as the dust and sweat felt covering my face.

"Why don't you make yourself useful, get off that damned horse, and grab a pick. This mine is partly yours, you know—in manner of speaking."

"This perdition is all yours," he replied. "I'm simply curious why you and your men continue to bother. You've been hacking away at that dirt and rock for most of a year, and what has it gotten you? Bloodied hands and an aching back."

I watched the ponies struggle along the metal tracks, dragging their carts behind them. After nearly a year of toil and struggle, my hopes still hinged on the words of a man who had died poor as a church mouse.

Could Thomas Whitefield have been wrong? Was there no more lead, no rich vein that was going to make my paltry coffers full again?

"Your Grace," came a cry, and I turned to see my stablehand rein his frothing animal to a stop. " 'Tis time, Your Grace. The babe is on its way!"

I mounted my horse, and the three of us rode toward Thorn Rose as if all the hounds from hell were following.

Miracle met us at the door, a determined look on her face. "Everything is well. There is no need to panic."

I tried to move around her but she blocked my way.

"You'll not step a foot into that room until you wash."

I turned to Clay. "Do something about her, or I will."

He grinned. "Be my guest. I dare you to try."

"Papa!"

Sarah Maria dashed from the salon, followed by my niece, Maggie. I fell to one knee and opened my arms to greet my daughter.

She skidded to a stop, wrinkled her little nose in displeasure, and shook her head. "Wash first," she said. "Then a hug."

A cry erupted from upstairs, and I felt the blood rush from my face.

Miracle barked an order to the nanny, who gently took the children and escorted them back to the parlor. Glaring at me, she demanded, "Wash." Then, lifting her skirts, she hurried up the stairs.

Clay clapped a hand on my shoulder. "Drink first. Wash later."

I nodded and followed him, sinking down into a chair near the French doors overlooking the grounds surrounding my home. Clayton pressed a snifter into my hand and laughed.

"Get used to it. I did. Women may appear fragile as glass, but they aren't."

"Right." I quaffed the port and extended my glass for more.

I DID NOT WASH. I DRANK. I PACED. I WANDERED through the gardens and picked great bunches of anemones, and tied them together with Sarah's hair ribbons.

I sat on the floor outside our bedroom, my

back against the wall, my eyes closed tightly each time I heard Maria cry out.

And the hours ploughed on, until nightfall had filled up the house with shadows and the nanny had tucked the children into bed.

I examined Miracle's face each time she left the room; noted that she spoke quietly to my brother, keeping her face as expressionless as possible.

At the stroke of midnight, Clayton wearily descended the staircase to fetch us each another drink. Sitting beneath the halo of light from the sconce on the wall, I stared down at the wilted anemones in my hand.

"Something's wrong," I said softly. "I know it."

Have faith, came the soft whisper.

I looked around, expecting to find that my brother had returned. Nay, he was not there. I was alone and obviously hallucinating from too much port and worry.

I will show you miracles yet.

Looking off into the dark, crushing the anemones in my hand, I said, "Then show me, damn you."

There came a racket of excited voices from the lower floor. Jumping to my feet, I moved to the top of the stairs and looked down at my foreman's soot- and sweat-streaked face.

The memory of that dreadful day when the mine had exploded nearly two years ago rushed over me, and I sank against the balustrade, gripping it as I said, "Christ, Mr. Stubbs. What the hell has happened?"

"Happened?" His dark face broke into a wide smile. "We've just struck a vein, Your Grace. Aye, a right good one, by the looks of it."

Clayton moved beside the man and gazed up at me with a grin as he lifted one snifter in a toast. "By God, you did it, you son of a bitch."

Yet the news brought me no pleasure, no relief. It would all mean nothing without Maria.

"Trey?"

I quickly turned and found Miracle standing in the open doorway of our bedroom. I swallowed, searching her eyes.

She smiled, and I felt my knees go weak.

"Would you like to see your wife now, Your Grace?"

I followed Miracle into the room.

Maria lay with her eyes closed, her face damp with sweat, her hair like strands of gold as it reflected the lamplights. How fragile she looked! So weary, so pale. I felt my heart climb into my throat.

Then her lashes fluttered open; she found me with her wide blue eyes, and smiled.

"There you are," she said.

I moved to the bed, unable to take my gaze from her treasured face.

"What have you there?" She weakly pointed to my hand.

"Anemones." I laid them upon the pillow by her head. "I'm afraid they're dead."

She turned her head and nuzzled them with her nose. "Nay, not dead, love. Just a little wilted. Like me."

I pressed my lips to hers, and murmured,

> "Coy anemone that ne'er uncloses
> Her lips until they're blown on by the wind."

Maria smiled into my eyes. "Would you care to meet your sons now, Your Grace?"

"A son!" I laughed and touched her cheek. "Maria, you've given me a son."

She shook her head. "You misunderstood, sir. I have given you *sons*."

Slowly, I straightened.

Maria pointed beyond me, and I turned to see Miracle with a babe cradled in each arm. As she moved into the lamplight I looked down on their tiny pink faces, the whispery voice returning to me yet again.

I will show you miracles yet.

I sank onto the bed beside my wife. Her arms opened to me and I lay my head upon her sweet breasts and closed my eyes, savoring the touch of her fingers upon my cheeks.

"Husband," she whispered. "All is well. Why do you weep?"

"Because I love you," I said. "And I will love you forever."

Pocket Books proudly presents *USA TODAY* bestselling author Katherine Sutcliffe's steamy historical romance...

FEVER
0-7434-1197-8

In the bayous of the American South, penniless orphan Juliette Broussard is plucked from an isolated French convent by Max, her godfather, who betroths her to his shiftless son Tyler. Juliette wants nothing to do with marriage—until she comes face-to-face with a handsome, blue-eyed stranger. Juliette and Chantz Boudreaux, Max's bastard son, are swept into a passionate liaison the moment he saves her from drowning in the Mississippi River.

Now available from Pocket Books
www.simonsayslove.com

09479

Don't miss these passionate historical romances from *USA TODAY* bestselling author Melanie George

THE ART OF SEDUCTION
0-7434-4272-5

A sparkling, sensual romance about a duke who finds that the girl he once adored is now the woman he desires.

THE PLEASURE SEEKERS
0-7434-4273-3

A sexy novel of dangerous delight, where England's most independent woman meets her match in the ton's most seductive gentleman.

Now available from Pocket Books
www.simonsayslove.com

09474

Don't miss this sizzling trilogy by *USA TODAY* bestselling author Susan Mallery

For the Marcelli sisters of California wine country, the season is ripe for romance!

CONSTANCE ASHLEY

KATHERINE SUTCLIFFE

is the *USA Today* bestselling author of twenty-two
novels, including the *Romantic Times* KISS award-
winning *Fever*. She has won numerous other awards,
including the *Affaire de Coeur* Silver Pen for Favorite
Author of the Year, and a *Romantic Times* Reviewer's
Choice Award, and she has been a Romance Writers of
America RITA Awards finalist several times.

Sutcliffe has also worked as consultant head writer for
the daytime dramas *Another World* and *As the World Turns*,
on which she appeared as herself. When not writing, she
enjoys spending time with her children, as well as with
her Arabian horses, pygmy goats, and house rabbit. She
is married to an English-born geologist, and invites
readers to visit her website at
www.katherinesutcliffe.net.

USA Today bestselling author Katherine Sutcliffe sweeps
fans away to the passionate affair she began in *Devotion*, as
one man's search for his lost love leads him to the heights of

OBSESSION

Trey Hawthorne, the Duke of Salterdon, once had a reputation
that would humble the Marquis de Sade. Then he found his
heart's desire in gentle, innocent Maria Ashton, whose healing
touch ignited a forbidden passion between the noble duke and
the lowborn vicar's daughter. Defying his family, Hawthorne
intended to wed Maria—but she mysteriously vanished before
he could take her as his bride. After tirelessly searching for her
for months, Trey gave up hope and reverted to his former
wicked ways.

Now, chance has led Trey to his beloved at last—but the
devastating truth behind her disappearance might prove more
than he can bear. As he fights to rescue his beautiful Maria from
a life of torment, Trey wonders if in saving her, he will also
finally save himself—or if the fight will cost him everything....

"Katherine Sutcliffe writes romantic, exciting stories filled
with memorable characters and delightful surprises."
—Linda Lael Miller, *New York Times*
bestselling author of *Shotgun Bride*

Visit us online at www.simonsayslove.com

$6.99 U.S./$10.50 Can.

ISBN 0-7434-1198-6

41198>

0 76714 00699 7

UPC

S

PRINTED IN U.S.A.